"David Nash writes with a blade. *Van Gogh's Ear* is the kind of novel which is instantly engrossing and disturbing, and it leaves us in awe. Ross is devil and angel in a dark, high octane cosmos, and I could not look away as he spun out his revenge. This is fierce and fine writing, and Mr. Nash shows us again the potency of fiction."—Ron Carlson, author of *The Signal*

"What a dark, flame-lit, searing cauldron of love and desire David Nash has illuminated here. *Van Gogh's Ear* astounds in its emotional ferocity, its wide-eyed look at the nature of torment, the emotional hell we each create for ourselves and those we love: and always, at hand, the possibility for redemption. Love, that which would save us all, each to each. This is biblical literature at its most contemporary: Venice, California; sand and the board-walk and beach; the dark side of the music scene and those who so populate — written in a prose, line by line, that aches to be received, its cadences melodically fit and thundering within the dark well of these lives where the heart so insistently drums. Only David Nash could write this novel. Like a friend, a chance intersection in the dark night of a soul, this book will change your life. Leonard Cohen writes, 'Forget your perfect offering / There is a crack, a crack in everything / That's how the light gets in.' *Van Gogh's Ear* is that light."
                    —T. M. McNally, author of *Low Flying Aircraft*

From the mountains of Utah to the seaside underbelly of Venice, California come two brothers on a voyage of holy revenge and realization. Ross hunts the rapist of his one true love, Lizzy. His younger brother, Brentwood, is unknowingly along for the ride.

Culminating with three murders committed on Christmas Eve, this is a dark, contemporary story of a young man who destroys what he loves most. *Van Gogh's Ear* is the soul-rending account of love between two brothers. It is the narrative of their last few months together in a world where love tears apart and the lessons of the mind are rarely those of the heart.

Van Gogh's Ear

STAR CLOUD PRESS
Scottsdale, Arizona

Van Gogh's Ear

DAVID NASH

Published by

~ STAR CLOUD PRESS® ~

6137 East Mescal Street
Scottsdale, Arizona 85254-5418

www.StarCloudPress.com

ISBN: 978-1-932842-02-9 — cloth — $ 34.95
ISBN: 978-1-932842-03-6 — soft cover — $ 19.95
ISBN: 978-1-932842-41-8 — e-book— $ 9.95

Library of Congress Control Number: 2008939841

Printed in the United States of America

for Jay Boyer,
as I was one of those
getting out of that van.

IN GRATEFUL ACKNOWLEDGMENT
to Jennifer Waters and Kristen Little
for their excellent and tireless editing skills,
a general *gracias* to Brian Stewart, for he is Sparky,
and heartfelt thanks to Paul Howe,
that inimitable Platypus in New Jersey.

Ah, God! what trances of torments does that man endure who is consumed with one unachieved revengeful desire. He sleeps with clenched hands; and wakes with his own bloody nails in his palms.

God help thee, old man, thy thoughts have created a creature in thee; and he whose intense thinking thus makes him a Prometheus; a vulture feeds upon that heart for ever; that vulture the very creature he creates.

I

I killed my brother.

I killed him the morning after.

Why, you can even call me *The Christmas Eve Killer.*

Perhaps you know me already. Have heard of me. Read about me. And then, perhaps not.

But indeed, and in either case, you may call me that. That's what everyone else does now. In this place where I am. And of course there are other names. The newspapers had a jolly good time of it. Came up with all kinds of nifties. From all over the country, I am told. And even all over the world. Why you can call me *The Silent Night Slayer.* Or I could be the *Little Drummer Boy Butcher. The Jingle Bells Jackal. Mistle Toy Murderer. Satan's Little Helper. Santa's Little HELLper. Kris Kringkill.*

Among other bang-up headlines: *Slay Bells Ring. Hell's Elves.* Oh, and *Come All Ye Slayful. Seasons Bleatings.* Or just plain good, old, *Jingle Hell.* (You know, if any of them had bothered to call me: *Decollate The Halls!* — now that's proper punning).

And so on and so forth.

Yes. All of this and I'll tell you what. I don't know if I'm a killer at all. Did I kill? Did I murder? I think not. Did I take life? Maybe. In some sort of way. But Killer? Murderer? Well, I just don't know if I'm rightly on board with that sort of negative

1

connotation type of phrasing for that little Christmas day jackpot I suddenly there found myself in.

But yes, *The Christmas Eve Killer* is what I'm heretofore generally speaking known as by all in my new home. That's what I'm called now. Ever since that bloody bright night with all the lights and decorations and gifts for everyone that was good that year and if you were bad you still got something too. That's what they call me now for wrapping my brother in a string of lights red, white, and green — some even blinking, and then hanging him off the side of the house like an ornament on a tree. But it was he, really, who did all the wrapping. I must say.

He hung and I stood there over him on the roof. Almost like I was lording (could I not have rather been just an angel?). Lording it all up there above it all. All trickled in blood and strickled with tears. Black jackboots. Red hat. With seasonal cheer blaring into the street from the red star-strung window below ("Blue Christmas," the old Mills Brothers version which was always Ross's favorite because that was Mom's favorite as well).

And when they finally rushed up to get me. Came a-crashing and a-dashing to the top of the roof to the top of it all, to get me, well . . . on their way up they found a few unpleasantries nestled nicely down below: There was Lizzy lovely in one room. Seminude white and as pure as a holy ghost pear. My dove plant doll. Although yes and alright, she was bespotted too. We all had the marks of life on us. Life was everywhere. Making a mess of all the death.

And in the anteroom, Sinboni. All nice and pretty and Christmas paper-wrapped. He even had a bow below his red nose. I believe it was blue, you know, as blue bleeds to black. Yet

2

he hadn't a clue; he never knew for he was rather stumped by that point of the evening.

And like I said, me on top of it all. (Twinkle-twinkle! Now isn't that rich?)

And so now here I sit all wretched and wrung and accused and convicted of it all. Goddamnit. Judged to be responsible. Accountable. For the death both inside and without. Yes, even of the darkest one of all. The one of little ol' black bag of bones, Soda. Rolled right up underneath the tree in his big-wheeled chair. His head dangled off to one side like a giant chocolate-swirled lollipop soggy bent at the neck from too much sucking and licking.

And good old Jesús (as in, "Hey-*Zeus!*"— not like the stuff we saltine-minded gauche gringos adorn our crackers with, please) Plástico was there too, just left lying on the roof. He had been there for all of it. In fact, played a rather large part. Providing much counsel when called upon. Yes, indeed, just so long as his head stayed screwed on for not too awful long. It was Soda who found him originally. Underneath the trash. In an alley. Ross's last tug on him was a gentle one.

So there were three dead, you see. But I can only be allowed to lay claim to one. One killing. One Murder? I think not, for I did nothing wickedly. Nothing with barbar. In a vein inhumane.

However, on the one particular count of my brother, to that I do confess. I believe so. For I did afflict and debilitate him. Eventually. I did disable him. Disadvantage, immobilize, and impair him. Made certain his incapacitation, infirmation, and deactivation. I handi-capped him. Abbreviated him. I in-formed him.

3

I dislegged him. More accurately: disarmed him. Just put him away and confined him to my thoughts where he now only lives and watches like a caged beast through the frail and fragile bars of my deliberation as I run run run the race to learn how I saved him from his demons by killing him — or letting him be killed — and sent him away from me, only to inherit my own little cagey perch. And with those demons learn what he must have already known, perhaps even been so begrudgingly birthrighted with: the fact that love tears apart, and that the lessons of the mind are rarely those of the heart.

For Ross had finally gone to war the only fucking sure-fire way he knew how to make certain that victory would be his. Except his war was with his life and his world and its creators — all the way up the genealogical vine to the last one in line who was God Himself.

And Ross had been playing chicken for a while now until he just finally took out a screwdriver and took off his steering wheel and tossed it out his window for all on the other side to see, and smiled and clucked his very parched tongue and laid his heavy, green peril bottle all the way down on the gas — out to prove that if there was a God, God would be a bigger chicken than he.

Or maybe it was just revenge. On himself. On the way he behaved. The thorns and years of ingrown guilt and shameful self-inflicted burden. It's just all so hard to sort out.

So I put him back in his own star-dappled, eventide sky. Where he wanted to be. Seated on a roof shaped like a chair with big bright, shiny-spoked wheels (the kind without baseball cards, because now it's not important that anyone know he's coming)

4

for the rest of his next life — and solidified his insanity in a place it can exist. Because there, right and wrong do not exist.

Isn't that even worse than killing?

But he wanted me to kill him. He asked me to. Yes, yes, well, he never really *asked* me to. He just led me to it, over a period of time, a nice long time with much forethought. So I had to.

I had to push him off the roof (for I did not pull him back) because he loved me. He fucking loved me and would have done the same for me except that would have never happened because I never did have the same capacities that Ross had. The same burdens and such. But I still kind of hated him for it.

So I didn't kill him.

But he's gone anyway.

I miss him. He's all I had. He used to change my urine-stained sheets in the morning when it was still dark, before Father got up. Save me a beating.

That was one of the things he used to do.

He would comb my hair. He did that too.

It's confusing when acts of love and allegiance become selfish and so final. Even more confusing now, as someone himself confined, than it ever was before.

On that last day — our last day together, his last day for this life — all his words finally made sense, and then sucked the meaning right out of me.

We had only been back from Malibu an hour or so. Done with the Sin. All the bones of sin. A sin bone. A Sin-Bone now made sense.

It was a pack-and-penny day. A day for bargains all gone into night. Ross was up there on the rooftop again, just like the old song says to do when this old world starts dragging you down.

He was up there caterwauling and catcalling, hectoring ghosts and then getting real quiet like he just figured something out or finally found another zephyr of a friend. And then he'd start it all up again. He was up there by himself for the first time, his two best friends now gone for good. And one forever.

I lay just underneath him. Wrestling away with blood and blight in the dankness of a winter midnight on the Venice Beach of California.

The red and blue section of Venice (now blotted and sparkling stained with all the jeerful colors of the season). Just a few blocks from the beach and the boardwalk. The only two white guys in the neighborhood, safely tuckered away in our apartment — the upper room of the second floor on top of a local drug-den. A small, concrete grey-like mono-block, knitted tightly into the rows of the little homes that all had gates with locks in a locale still old enough to have the wasted space of back alleys to hide the garbage trucks on trash day.

The roof — flat and unfettered save the water tank, a couple of rusty metal folding chairs, and an old wooden barstool with a spinning, squeaking seat that Ross had borrowed (without asking) from the first bar we played in L.A. — was probably an unfinished afterthought for a third floor. It was a roof corralled by a one-foot hedge of concrete.

This was Ross' little patio and personal fête champêtre portal to his Walpurgisnacht Nights — an escape from his Walter Mitigating days (during which he slept most of the time anyway).

It was small, some five hundred square feet, the same dimension as our upper room below. But as a miniature Tower of Babel, where he could live out his fable, its purpose was properly served. Ross was hanging upside down from the hedge still very much alive tapping on my bedroom window just beneath.

"Hey, Wood. Brentwood, man. What's happening? What's doing? Come on up here and share a moment with me would you now?"

This was another one of those times when Ross again had managed to drink so much that he'd drunk himself sober. He rapped and tapped on my window, and out of fear I feigned sleep. But his voice was suddenly new, like I had never heard it before. It was still and small and so oddly calm that for the first time I sensed fear in it. I turned over in my egg-shell foam mattress on the floor to face the window. He was hanging there on his rope. He hung there upside down, glassy and hushed, blacked and silhouetted, his long, raven-strawed hair reaching for the earth — all of him playing with gravity. He looked like a doll that was finally losing its stuffing, blacker than the black that hung behind him on the last night that I would see him alive.

He was blackness wrapped in color. A darkness enclosed by shimmers of fitful light. A god-shaped hole trapped in electric.

He had his one front tooth out as well. The one he'd always told me had been knocked out playing football early on in high school. The one Father always used as a reference point when promising to remove the other one "as well." *"Mind your goddamn business or I'll knock out the other one as well,"* as if to take credit for the first (which I do believe now should very well be granted).

7

In any case, it was a clean extraction. A false one was glued right back in by some man who, while he did go to dental school for a real long time, still had not figured out how to manage his "fucking halitosis all up in my face" (such was the way Ross would say it). After Father did his own death and we buried all the health insurance inside the coffin with him (material goods do go on to the next world — don't ever let any lying preacher-man, or any other waxing philosophical man of straw tell you different), Ross culled the nervous no good habit cum obsession of toying, playing, yanking, and knocking it around all by himself. All on his lonesome. He then took it upon himself to just putting it right back in and wearing it at his leisure.

He had figured out a good cheap way (shoplifting SuperGlue) that was just as effective as any old bad-breathed, dorbel dentist. And although when he started to neglect it, sometime after Lizzy's last long distance call — when it kind of made the higher-ups of his gums a little grey and scaly — it stuck all the same. (He never smiled much anyway, unless he was without his tooth.) It would stick just as good until he got nervous again. Which was often. But nobody ever knew except for me. (He could toy with his tooth without even a soul noticing, and, as in all other manner of gesticu-genuflection, be as cool as dead men's shoes.)

It soon just became part of his wardrobe, something he'd wear when the occasion was fitting. And there were occasions when he felt it most fitting to be without. Like a tie and wingtips on Saturday, not Sunday. Or wearing running shoes to a funeral (Ross liked to jog around the cemetery a little bit right before one and a long time afterwards). There's a time and a place for everything.

I wondered if he had bothered to change the gold, silk robe with the purple and black embroidered hyena he had been wearing that night. Or at least tried to wash the blood off it. Or even wash some of it off his hands and face.

And then he dropped right side-up.

"Hey, man. Hey, Wood. I just have a question for you. A question for you and that only you can answer so come on up here for a minute and I believe you been saving a question for me I believe going on five years now that maybe I suppose I can answer. That question about me and fatal, holy reinvention. Or was it just simple and plain — me and trying to reinvent myself? No matter. So come on up. Ask it. Come on. You've come with me this far now. Just come join me for nightlight conversation. You know, like we used to. With the nightlight."

"I'm coming, Ross."

And then, quick as the not-so-now drunken Helix the Cat that he was, he shimmied like a simian up his rope and was gone. And I was surprised at how suddenly my room got light, was reminded of how many stars were actually in the night, and that the world outside wasn't that black after all.

I was strangely indifferent, entirely disassociated after witnessing what I had earlier that night, even though I was as much a part of him and what had happened as he was. Or at least so I thought at the time.

II

The only safe access to the roof was over the stove and through the window at the back of the only other room in our apartment. It led to a kind of fire-escape ladder that ran the full height of the house.

As I made my way up the top twelve rungs of the ladder I could hear him singing. Singing one of his favorite songs, "I Don't Know Enough About You" by The Mills Brothers. Singing was the one thing that he could always do at any time despite the circumstances, and the one thing that he could always do very well. I got to the top and heaved myself over the little one-foot wall. The wall that might keep someone from falling.

And he was all lit up too. From deep within him it seemed. Like a glow worm dipped in crimson and then covered in new wool.

Not only was he still in the gold robe, but the ruby, satin slippers as well. He even had the gold around his neck and the gold-plated director's sunglasses wrapped around his eyes. (Sin the director was dead — he'd finally lost his head). He was dancing very slowly. Like an old, tired, remembering-man whom everyone had forgotten; stowed in a home for the missed and misbegotten. Not at all like his usual self. He was doing his little two-step soft-shoe that old Tablet had taught him, clicking his slippered heels occasionally, as he so loved to do, and had done so many times with both Tablet and Soda while they pretended and rehearsed to one day replace his Brothers Mills.

He had his back to me, center of the roof, front of his stage, occasionally turning to wink at me, like I was someone watching from the wings offstage. A couple of times turning and facing me to sing certain lines like "Jack of all trades," or "Oh what a spin I'm in." But I knew he wasn't singing to me. And I knew just whom he was singing to.

It was the song he'd always have playing over the speakers just before our band took the stage. Slow and harmonic — a nice pre-rock 'n roll sit-down-and-snap-your-fingers kind of melody — with that careful and courteously restrained snare-brushed, salad-mixing beat. Quite the opposite of what would ensue once we took the stage at one of the local bars or clubs back in Utah or down in ol' May-hee-co. "Puts me in the mood, Brentwood. Lets the crowd know I'm coming. Gots to let them know you're coming, Wood. Gots to let them know."

I know a little bit,
about a lot of things,
but I don't know enough about you,
just when I think you're mine,
you tried a different line,
and baby what can I do,

I read the latest news,
no buttons on my shoes,
but baby I'm confused about you,
you've got me in a spin,

11

oh what a spin I'm in,
'cause I don't know enough about you,

Jack of all trades, master of none,
and isn't it a shame,
I'm so sure that you'd be good for me,
if you'd only play my game,
you know I went to school and I'm nobody's fool,
that is to say until I met you,
I know a little bit about a lot of things,
but I don't know enough about you

He shuffled in the borrowed ruby satin slippers. His toes hanging about an inch over their edge, the unbeknownst borrowee not quite as large as Ross's size thirteens. He spun during the chorus, the robe (also, but not like his heart, two sizes too small) rising and filling with air like a happy skirt in some nice and trite old-fashioned movie. He was still naked underneath, his groin and thighs still speckled and sprayed red. He had let it all dry, even smeared some of it across his mouth. He was either very proud, or not at all aware. Regardless, prideful or oblivious (or just a lordly ignoramus), the long-suffering cur had made it to the cusp — where his own immutable existence sought only to mute itself — his réchauffe finally coupling with his recherché.

He cocked his arms out and limped his wrists, finally giving in to his best Bobby Darin as he sang the last line, and then he turned quietly and faced me, his face so without expression that its blankness, in and of itself, was stupefying. It looked like deafness.

He sat on the small wall.

He looked at his toes. I could hear the soberness crawling back into his throat.

"It's all here now, Brentwood. It's all here now." He rose and picked up the barstool and carried it back to the wall on the edge of the roof, all the time dragging the electric cord behind him. He took his seat. He traded glances with the tiny, concrete front-yard below and the black, blotched sky that sagged above, and I knew he was asking himself which one might be colder.

He propped his feet on the wall and pushed off, spinning himself on his whirling chair one way for a while, then stopping, and spinning himself the other. The images of the countless times we had tried to get dizzy together all steeped suddenly in my mind. Ross named it "The Dizzy Game." We would both stand and spin with our arms out like a couple of crazy tea-cupped crosses until one of us fell down; playing it from the very beginnings of the earliest of my memories on top of the one big bed that we shared as young toddler brothers to just two months ago when we first landed on the beach of Venice.

I watched Ross as he slowly and so thoughtfully rotated himself there on the edge of the roof on his stolen seat from the bar. I could tell he wasn't trying to get dizzy anymore.

"What's the question, Ross?" I tried to sound impatient.

"Brentwood. Wood, is God a dead man who won't wake up?"

"Jesus, maybe. Anyway, you said that, Ross . . ."

13

"Or is he just asleep? Sleeping like me all pissed off at the fact that his father left him on the altar. If he's sleeping then maybe I got some kind of chance. Some kind of chance somewhere else. Maybe there is some kind of somewhere else where guys like me and him are better off. Where we can sleep. Sleep and dream and be innocent. When you dream you're always innocent. And just leave everything and everyone we did alone. Alone like they want to be and lonely like I should be." He licked his thumb and rubbed it on his cheek. He saw the stain on his thumb. He wet both his thumbs and began to rub the blood off his face, cleaning himself like our mother always would when we made a mess of ourselves at the dinner table, fluttering his thumbs on his fretful whetstone tongue.

He continued to muse. "I used to end up with innocent, hot, white wax on my face. Remember that? From blowing out all those goddamn candles on the stage in Tijuana? Then spend the rest of the night stroking my face with a stick of cream butter. Now look at me. But I done good tonight, Brentwood. Tonight I made good God proud. Tonight I was a worldshaker. The Worldshaker. Not him, dead or asleep or wherever the fuck he is. At least I know I gave him something nice and fine and of good report to dream about."

I stood still in my place in front of him. I heard the helicopters in the distance. The L.A. cops that routinely buzzed neighborhoods like ours. Their eager-eye spotlights probing the streets and polka-dotting the houses, at times making the whole city look like a big carnival curtain-call for an audience we could never see. One of the lights hit our roof. I stared at it in the sky. Ross licked and clucked on his very own cucking-stool and kept

to cleaning his face. Licking and pawing, licking and pawing —
in one blink looking like a shadow-boxing Cassius gearing up for
the first-round bell of his last fight right before he changed his
name, before *he* met God, and in another looking like Cassidy,
our old childhood cat that ended up in three pieces while sleeping
and keeping warm next to the radiator fan in the not-for-long
parked Chevy Malibu in our driveway, bathing its face in the
most favorite and expensive chair on the property — and in
either case, looking as glib and graceful as a goodnight ghost.

The helicopter flew on by and disappeared quicker than it
came.

"Mormons, Brentwood. So many of them there in Utah.
Utah Mormons. How the hell did so many fucked-up and nice,
god-fearing and gullible, white, rich and pasty people . . . a whole
rotten bunch of silly, snide truth-hoarding shitty Scooby-Doos,
all wanting to be the Pied Piper when they're all really just a
bunch of nasty, fucking incestuous rats . . . how did they all get
to ganging up together in one fucking place?"

"That was us too, Ross."

"Oh, yes."

"Yeah?"

"What do you mean *was,* Wood?"

"I thought you didn't, or decided that . . ."

"Maybe now more than ever,."

"Ross, if that's true. And I know you don't believe it is. But,
if it is . . . then we're in for a heap full of shit."

"At least we didn't end up like goddamn Father. Kneeling
down, dying with a pen and a blank piece of paper in his hands
. . . shit, at least I wrote something . . . all hooked up to a

doorknob in the basement closet by his very own belt. Strapped good and real tight around his white collared shirt and tie."

"Don't you bring up Mom now, Ross. Goddamn you."

"Snow angels."

"That's enough, Ross."

"Fuck you, Wood. I was the one that found her too."

"You promised you never would."

He was still talking in that new, little voice. Deep and resonant per its usual, but somehow growing more fainthearted by the moment, or maybe more respectful. My own self never knowing how to distinguish between the two.

"I'm sorry, Brentwood. I am sorry. I will not. But the snow angels are sacred and fair to you and me. They can be for talking, if it's nightlight."

"I know."

"You know damn well that without those visits to her in Pleasant Grove amongst all those stones in the winter time, which was the only time that I could allow myself to go, that I would have never prospered. Would have never made the angels in the snow on her grave and taught you how to do the same, so that we could live and love one another. *Families are Forever.* Remember that, Wood? It hung above our fireplace in every house we ever lived in. The great old Mormon maxim that Mom and Father preached so ever incessantly about, breathing it into us and plastering it on every goddamn wall in the house, it was even above the toilet next to where Father used to hang his belts. Man, how many times did we high-tail it from those. Too bad Mom wasn't as quick. And then one of them ends up around the old man's neck. Justice sure is a funny fucker sometimes. But I liked what it meant, or at least tried to mean — *Families are Forever*, even if it was with only that one bastard understanding of our relationship with her in this fucking, god-forsaken life.

"But the snow angels, that was the only time when you and I would hold hands, there on the ground, catching snow flakes on our tongues, if we were lucky, and it was snowing. And we needed that. That's how we survived . . . that's how we made it out . . . that's how I forbade my nightmare from sneaking up on my . . ."

"Ross, why did you ask me up here?" I cut him off. I had never done that before. Never in my life. I had never seen Ross sober and at the same time speaking in tongues of nostalgia and sentimentality. It must have been that combination that pricked my ears with his voice. My impatience was a knee-jerk. An instinctual defense mechanism toward this new addition to all the languages that he spoke. I walked to the back of the roof and looked down into the alley behind the fence in the backyard. The Ford Fairmont was gone. My heart bristled. "Ross. The car is gone. Where did you put the car?"

"Tabby moved it to the front. It's in the street."

The whole world then clanked right through my soul and to the very bottom of my ass. Without even closing my eyes I went blind, all my nails suddenly bitten down to the quick of my heart and I saw myself in my mind standing alone in a blithe and shimmering torrent.

My ears opened wide and felt like two huge holes in my head as I heard the helicopters again and picked out the sirens in the street tracing closer to where we were. I found myself walking toward him with both arms stretched out, trying to throw my

17

arms around the world, like a jack-legged Jesus, and trying like hell to convince myself that these were still the sounds that we heard every night as we fell asleep. But he stopped his stool and raised his right arm to the square before pointing it at me and winking his fingers as he always did when his mind got caught whirring too fast for his thoughts.

He raised his voice as if to bring out the dead. "And without those snow angels I would have never learned how to run and run and run run run. To run and run and drink my vodka right from the *Evian* bottle every day and never miss my ten mile jaunts in the park. I never would have learned how to fall in love with a paper doll that I could call my own. Fall in love until my wheels came off, and love my little Spring-seasoned, cottontailed-girl, Lizzy. And *the rape, the rape, what a very important date, I'm late I'm late I'm late I'm late, for a very important rape.* But it was never really late, it was the first thing that I ever took care of on time."

He got off the stool and stood on the wall. He did not face me, but continued to raise his voice so that I would hear. "Or graduated to the green in the wheelchair with sweet, sweet, black Soda. Oh how we loved our audit ale! Who's dead now too — a dead, happy sleeping man, a snow angel who someone else forgot to go back and keep making.

"All those times on the angels in the most important of any snow taught me the guitar and gave me how to sing and taught me to love the world, and give up those fucking football scholarships to that one white *why* in the sky that I could see on mountain tops during those certain kinds of homecomings. Without them there is no garage sale charade prancing on top of the Fairmont to get us through to Vegas; there is no cleanliness in the desert, and there is no me and you. There is no you. Those angels on top of Mom let me love you.

"I would not be here. And neither would you. And most important of all. I would not have done what I did just a little bit ago. Just a wee couple of hours ago. That which you should not have seen. But you did. And now you know. And you witnessed me having my meaning in life. So don't take it away. Please do not take it away, Brentwood. Not on this night."

I now stood directly behind him. Close enough to touch him. To save him. To grab him. To push him. To kill him. Was there any difference? To touch him. Whoever "him" was, now. Whoever it was that I loved so much. Too much.

"Some things I cannot do alone, Wood. I just cannot."

And I touched him. And he went down. And whoever it is that rules on such things, ruled him a murder, and me the Murderer. And others who have no power to rule, my most unlikely publicly appointed defenders, ruled him a suicide and me a lousy spectator. And I just ruled myself reluctant. And until now most righteously reticent. And yet still others had us both as killers (at least part of that is true) for that is how they had found us on the roof that night in the first place.

Whether gluttonous savior or unwilling executioner my heart was not in it, either way.

For my heart was in him. And yet, somehow, he still orchestrated to leave it with me. Liberated it and left it out there hanging, as he went down, leaving it out there for me to sack — which I did, and finally and once and for all struggle with it alone, and everything that "it" had heretofore held locked inside.

19

My buoyant, frightful brother who learned to frighten so many others (even me), whom I loved so much and who was so heavy to the touch. And even in his awful absence; yes, even as a dead, parished brother, had become even heavier to carry. That fucking smart, selfish bastard.

And yet, Ross, who had lived most of his life in a swirl of bitter, saltwater taffy-pole feelings, had still managed to leave a sweet taste in my mouth.

And I never did get an answer to my five year-old question. But I never did ask it again, as he had requested.

Until now.

III

*P*erhaps none of this would have happened had we not been in a rock band. Or at least not started a band while living in Pleasant Grove, Utah. Or at least just not intended the band for Los Angeles. Moved to L.A.

But that's a lie. Of course it would have happened. Anyway. Being in a band had as little and as much to do with it as listening to the Mills Bros. while committing murder. Making Sin's bones into snow bones.

I'd still be putting pen to paper with the same stripes around my shoulders and shadow bars across my face, drinking the same penitentiary highball (with no mother's milk as any antidote) while pretending to be listening to the same *Orange Blossom Special*, no matter what. The point was, is, and always fucking will be: *I* was, am, and always fucking will be: Ross's brother. *I* was with him. I mean I was *with* him.

Our new home was just three blocks from the beach and boardwalk of Venice. The famous "Venice Beach," as I would soon find out.

Our plan was thus:

In six short weeks we would go from being the unheard mendicants of warm-up band status at has-been holes and dives known as *The Tortilla Factory* (which it actually was until 8pm every night), *The Red Snapper Lounge* (seafood and strip club), and *Attica's Finches* (bird supply and book store); from playing acoustic sets with just one guitar for little, loose change into the pee small hours in the closed-down enclaves on the Third-Street Promenade in Santa Monica and the holy boardwalk itself on Venice Beach: right there smacked and dabbed and crammed in with the chain-saw jugglers, stand-up comedians, fortune tellers, jesus sellers, cumberground chalk-palette screevers, grubstreet amateur acrobats doing flips over tourists standing on cardboard boxes, a hundred middle-aged disco skaters (the ones with the real wheels) dancing like superstars in their stadium of sand, and a genius who sculpted perfect, naked women rising out of the beach and clamoring onto the sidewalk like giant, siren, pornographic, rhythm-crabs moving with the silent, desert tide (all of whom were very nice and some became our best barbecue friends); from even playing a few silent sets, sets in mime, when the cops would come down and shut us down because of a new city law against performing live music in public, and Ross had us pretend to play our instruments while he just mouthed the lyrics, until he tried to beat up a couple of wise-ass frat boys from Westwood for throwing invisible money into our guitar case and we cut that idea out.

And right up to the jewels at the top of the crown we would rise: *The Roxy. The Whiskey. The Troubadour.* Our name, *The Hinge,* hanging high, bright, and proudly in the dark Sunset Blvd. air, a millennium from the pizza parlors and taco stands on the other side of the eastern beach that led to the other salt water. And soon thereafter branching and infusing the other mighty bars and star-clobbered clubs scattered in and around Los Angeles,

California, where only the famous came to see who was next and were able to say they saw them "when."

Ross would have never been much without us. And he knew it. But none of us came close to having coattails as long and strong as the ones he let us grab onto and hold onto for our dear, dear lives. And you better believe we goddamn well knew that.

And right then and right there.

Our plan was to have then made it into the spotlight (no cops behind this one), into a position to take the next step. It was in there, in those places, where all those damn invidious and insidious discoveries would be made that we'd always heard and read about and refused to believe because we knew we would never get there and yet there we would be — if only in my blind-baggage mind.

And it would have only been a matter of time. A simple matter-of-fact matter-of-time before maybe, just maybe, we would have finally accomplished something. Then there would be something underneath our fingernails other than the condemned dirt of a whole lot of wasted time as we would set out to only then scratch the surface of our dream and success.

Then Ross might have been worth it. The sacrifice worthy of the prize. The means possibly even justifying the end.

But Ross had different plans. And a whole different end. And it would all be mean. And just as fast and furious as we flew in on his tails, some of us not even making it out the other side of the Utah Valley, we would all slide down his slippery slippery slope on the wrong side of the mountain. But we had all gone willingly. Knew what we were dealing with. Except for him.

Ironically enough, he was the only one who never had much of a say in his own end. And yet he dictated it the whole way along.

Ross and I lived in the upper room, on top of a house, that was a crackhouse. The price was right: $400 a month for the five of us — now just the two of us — and it was still right. Because of our great garage sale, planned and effected in the days just proceeding our last little religious exodus, we had enough for two months without even having to get jobs. Plus, it was at the eye of the needle for most of the action as far as clubs, possible gigs, and getaways to and from Malibu were concerned. Now all we had to do was find a camel that knew how to kneel. If not, Ross had a bit of experience in the humbling business, humiliating as it would be eventually for me.

It was on the west side of Venice. Just on the invisible and unspoken dividing line between tourists gravitating toward the boardwalk, local innocent incubates who knew better, and the actual dwellers and denizens who perceived their place well and guarded it with a most specific and tactical malaise.

It was a black neighborhood. But Ross and I — just a few of the bright, white kernels that stood out on this sparsely, speckled cob of dusky corn — didn't mind at all being the salients in this salad. Which now, quite honestly, strikes me quite strangely. We had spent our lives as the only two scared white boys growing up in a white neighborhood. The change, a combination of my ignorance and Ross's amazing powers of assimilation, was actually quite soothing. And our landlord — with forearms like oatmeal cans, duckpin bowling balls for biceps, and a weedy little waist — was a black (and I guess I shouldn't just call them all black because as I very soon learned there in the Venice, California being black isn't like being alive or dead or pregnant or Mormon; there are many variations and gradations of black and he was blacker than any other black Black guy I had ever seen; but if black is the darkest it can get then he truly was black and I don't know what everyone else is but they sure are not black if he's black, and he very much was black. I'm speaking of the Blacks now, when I say everyone. Sometimes I'd wish I was that black, if I was going to be black, which wish I more than once did have, especially back in Utah as you got treated real special, like royalty, back in the Utah Valley, if you were black. Mormons loved you if were black; that drippy faux-show (fo'-sho'!) shame kind of love if I can be just so precise) man with happy-go-lookey eyes and a gently tilted, kinglike old smile who assured us there wouldn't be any problems.

He lived downstairs and went by the name of Tablet. Or Tabby, I mean.

When I first met the heroic Tabby it was as he appeared at the top of the stairs of what was to be our brand new last dwelling. He was waiting there just straightening some things at the top in the dark, as I knocked upon and then opened the door at the bottom. All I could see at first was the white that he wore and the white of his teeth and dark-yolked fried egg eyes.

He was dressed pristine clean all in white save for a black belt and shiny black shoes. Other than that, like I said, it was a white Tee and white pants and those supernal choppers and windows to the soul. And they floated down to me with a bit of a jitter one way and then a zig-zag and be-bop to the other.

For Tabby was a tapper. As a matter of fact every time I yelled his name he'd say, "I be dar in just a flinch, son. Yes, suh."

And then come soft-shoeing out of whatever room he was in, right down the hall toward me and then out the door and down the front porch steps outside, just waving me to follow without even turning around to see where I was and singing, whispering, talking the whole time.

> *They say Casey Jones is a railroad man*
> *Jumped on his train with his dick in his hand*
> *Any you whores want to be screwed?*
> *At the word he had one hundred ninety two*
>
> *So he lines them up against the wall*
> *Bets the fireman five dollars he can fuck them all*
> *Got a hundred and ninety and his balls turned blue*
> *Took a shot of corn and fucked the other two . . .*

"Um, excuse me there Mr. Tablet, sir."

"Yuh call me Tabby dar, son. Dat's how ma friends say ma name. An den dey follow me like dis'." He did a Soft Shoe Slide Left. And then a Tippity Tap Right. "Now Ah'm goin' to show yuh." And then he just tapped his ass away. Singing, talking, whispering, and dancing all at the same time.

He seemed crazy but you couldn't help liking him. He was a man of much substantial advancement in years but still had all his hair, which was a mighty and undivided grey and which he kept short and always real "Navy" neat and clean ("De best haircuts dat Ah ever got fo' sho was on board dose ol' gotdamned ships — yes, suh an' Ah bin trying to git me one like dat ever since den"). And his voice was fat and rich. A more than beaming baritone which often did sputter when he spoke (but no way when he sang) like some powerful, old railroad locomotive just on the brink of firing up, and champing at the bit for that right amount of steam. Everyone was his "son." Sometimes they were his "boy." Either that or he just called you "suh." The first man to ever refer to me as such.

He continued to soft-shoe down the narrow space between the house and the chainlink toward the backyard, backdoor, and stairs which led up to our new place.

> *Then Casey died and went to hell,*
> *He fucked the devil's wife and fucked her well.*
>
> *Two little devils started running through the halls*
> *Said, "Papa, catch him 'fore he fuck us all"*
>
> *Now there set old Satan high on the shelf*
> *"You better run Motherfucker, I'm trying to save myself. . ."*

"Now lookey here, son. Dis a crack-house now, son. Yes, suh. Yuh remember now, Ah told yuh dat when yuh first come over visitin' de very first time."

And then he got in a boxing pose and started shadow boxing. Except the shadow was me. "See dat lef' jab! Is yo' scared ob me, Cassius, boy? Ha, Ha!"

Why I almost for the first time since I needed diapers just about right then and there needed diapers. He continued to air jab at my body and face.

"Lookey out, now, boy. Yes, suh, man! Ah'm real fast. See dis, now, son. Ah'm so fast dat las' night ah turned off de light an' was in bed 'fore de room was dark! Yes, suh, son!" he said, coiling and then standing straight up and then coiling again like he might just catch me off guard for a second, "Ah do dat thing, man!"

He was talking to me as I was carrying my drums up the stairs to the entrance of our place on top and was still real concerned with us living on top of a crackhouse. "Yuh' sure done an' positive yuh' ain't gots no problem with dat? Ah'm just axin'. Ain't dat' right now, suh?"

I had grabbed a few things to carry on my way and was trying to balance an extra cymbal in my arms. "Oh, no, no. Fetch," (I still couldn't get David out of my mind) "me and Ross — he's my brother, he'll be here soon — why, we can fix just about anything." (I was so nervous about upsetting our new lord of the land on the first meeting, I was lying my ass off for just about no reason. Our father had raised us to fix things by buying new things, a combination of sometimes having a little extra money and all the time tending not to be so inclined to the labor of the hands. Our idea of a screwdriver was a credit card, until the corners got too worn to fit into the screws. Then it was on to butter knives and loose change.) "We didn't bring any tools with us, though. But like I said before, as long as you got some, I mean tools, just let us know and we'll be happy to fix anything you want. 'Least we can try. Where are the cracks in the house anyway? Upstairs in our place, or down in yours? Or perhaps something in the plumbing, right? Or just in some of the walls?"

Tablet slapped me on the back and started laughing all raspy — now he sounded like an old black and white radio show my Father used to talk about listening to when he was a kid. He'd start imitating it and talk in these weird, low, funny voices every time he'd head out the door to call on and go preach to one of the few and very rare "negro" families that moved into the neighborhood, trying to get them interested in coming to the church, be in the ward, maybe get them baptized — must have been a real popular and likeable guy they had on this show though. A real hero. They called him "The Famous Son Andy Show," or some damn thing like that. And who was the father of this famous son? And why was he famous? Those were the things I wanted to know. But my father wouldn't say much about it. He'd just make himself laugh when he did the voice to himself or his friends, like Johnny Standley, from the church on the phone. It wouldn't play on the radio any more though, at least that's what Father said. And that fact made me sad. Because if it had I think things would have been much nicer around our house. Maybe.

All I know is that whenever I heard Father using that voice or talking about that show I always knew that things would be good at home that night. There wouldn't be any hurting, hollering, or screams with bad dreams. No meanness. No bruises in the morning. Most importantly, Mom would be all right. She might even smile herself on just such a night. Yes, if Father was in the "Famous Son Andy" mood all of us knew right away that that night was safe. For sleeping and everything else. That was the happiest voice I ever heard in all the world. I remember at times even praying for it. Hearing our front door close, Father's measured steps, and then me closing my eyes asking God for The Voice. The Famous Son Andy voice. But it would not be a prayer that got answered much. Such a foolish thing to bother God with anyway. It seems now that everything I prayed for was all in all just one foolish thing after another (even though, to tell you the truth, there were only a couple of things I did ever request. I just requested them often).

Anyhow, Tablet slapped me so hard that for a moment I thought I had insulted him and was about to take my first beating by the beach. Pretty soon though he was coughing and waving at me so hard I thought there was some stink up there on the stairs that just hadn't got to me yet. "Yuh rock'n roll boys is allll right by me, fo' sho'! Son, every one of yuh Ah've ever in ma whole life met has had de damndest ob finest funny bones. Lookey here now, yes, suh. I don't care what they be sayin' about you white rock 'n'roll boys. Yuh always be fine by me."

I put my drums down, got my blue bandana out of my back pocket, dabbed at the sweat on my forehead, and tried to get back the breath from Tablet's neighborly slap on the back. "Uhh, yes sir, Mr. Tablet."

"Just Tabby now, son. Gotdamnit! Hee, hee, hee. Don' take it too far an' be overdoing nothing, smarty pants man. Now remember what Ah told yuh before an' make sure yuh tell all dese others, or Ah guess just yo' brutha. Jus' don' make no eye-contact now, not wid no one here on dis here ol' street. Yo' is all right a block over west toward de boardwalk. But when yuh is on dis here side, an' about six blocks in every other direction, yuh be looking straight ahead like. Always straight ahead. An' keep dem bandanas off yo' heads as well. Especially any reds or blues. Soon 'nuff de'll know yuh all be living here — an' by de way, yo' guys are living at de safest damn house in de neighborhood, yo' ain't never seen de foxes go harassing 'round dar own chicken coop now, has yuh? — anyhow, any trouble de be sideways, Ah'll straighten dem out or it's goood niiight in de morning an' get de hay back out ob de barn! Yeessiirree, yo' boys be just fine an' besides dat Ah think Ah likes yuh already. Ah've had yo' type up here before an' always had nuttin' but no trouble an' besides yuh gave me de money fo' de first month up front an' can't ever be arguing wid dat dese days in dis neighborhood." Tablet started back down the stairs. "Hey now, son, an' Ah'll let you know about mending dem cracks! Ooooooo weeeeee, gots tuh get yuh some tools to fix up dem cracks! Lookey here, yes, suh, man! Dem cracks in de crack-house. Yessirreee. Yuh boys alll right. Son, yuh all right by me A'hm goin' tell yuh dat."

And then he tapped and whisper-sang his self back down the stairs and out the door. "Jesus Chris' up dere but yo' won't find him . . . An' ol' Abraham Lincoln done down under the flo' . . . but whar's George Washington, dat's what Ah wants to know . . .

> But Casey said just before he died
> 'There's a couple more things I'd like to ride
> tricycle, bicycle, automobile
> a crapped-up cart and a Ferris Wheel
> Say you know man, it's a goddamned shame
> I'm forty years old and haven't rode nothin'
> but a motherfuckin' train.'"

I bounded quickly the rest of the way up the stairs. At the top there was a small, old bathroom mirror right before you turned the only corner, the kind you might find on the inside of a medicine cabinet. It was cracked in the middle and the edges looked black and wrinkled like a century-old will or a piece of paper just saved from a fire. It was quiet, and I was alone. I looked in the mirror and took my finger and spun it around my ear and crossed my eyes. Something I would have done to Ross, had he been there, in an effort to get a laugh. "He's a nice guy, though," I said to myself, while talking to Ross, who wasn't there. "I talked to him yesterday when I came to check the place out. Seems real honest. And a heck of a nice guy. Fetch, I couldn't breath for a minute after he hit me."

"An' keep away from Jack dar in de yard next! Yes, suh," Tablet bellowed from the front of the house. "He's a mean one. Meaner den de devil an' twice as happy to be so. Sooner stand up an' read yuh de Bible den make yo' friendship. An' believe yuh me de last time Ah tossed him De Book he done tore it up quicker den Cassius Clay can throw yuh de glove. Dat's all right, now, son. If yuh need anything put a note in the mailbox an' Ah'll make ma way up to yuh. Don't ever be knockin' down here around mine. Too dangerous fo' yuh."

I yelled back down, trying to imitate Ross's courage and instant comradery. "Who's Jack?"

"Go lookey out de back window, son. Just over de chainlink dar in de neighbor's yard. But don't be makin' no eye contact." His chuckle trailed off into the bottom part of the house until it was just a muffled vibration above some swifty, shuffling feet.

32

IV

The only back window was in the one-man kitchen on the other side of our new, little upstairs home. I hustled over to it through the two-man living room, but it was too dirty to see through, so I threw it upward and peeked down into the neighbor's backyard. It was a perfect square of dust-bowl dirt, from the back of the house to the wood and chain-link fence that separated us from one of those familiar old back alleys that were grooved like furrows through the older suburbs of L.A.

The yard was full of two to three foot craters and the beast called Jack was sleeping in the one right in the middle. As if to let me know my eyes had laid a gaze, he stood up and posed real still. He was striped a deep chocolate black and copper brown and it was those very stripes that really did make him look pretty doggone damn mean.

He was a large dog. Tall and brawny with a body that more than suggested force and a long swerved-up tail as stiff as a frozen rope. He had that obvious hound face and wore two ears flopping down in opposite directions like the motley hat of some kind of needle-nosed, four-legged court jester. I didn't know quite what to make of him but one thing I did know was that he was not one of them Rotty dogs that Venice Beach was full of.

I'd soon discover in fact that Venice was the Rottweiler doghouse for the whole goddamn world. Nothing but Rotties.

And they were everywhere. And they all looked the same. Same black face with the same oily eyes. Walking around, I couldn't ever tell which ones were the nice ones and which ones the mean ones. I'd always have to keep asking Ross.

"That one there's fine," he'd whisper. "He's fine. It's all in their eyes and how they're twitching their ears and tail. Just like the hippos at Disneyland. And just like humans as well, Wood. Ears and tail. Just like you. I'll let you know when we get to a mean one. Know how? I'll tell you to go pet him. So keeps on your twinkly-toes there, son." (He was already doing Tablet. I shook my head thinking about the new cast assembling in his wings.)

"That's not funny, Ross."

"Oh, but it is, Brentwood. It so very much is."

Anyway, Jack was bound up to a fat, chunky chain of lead that was tied to a four-foot palm tree stump. The chain granted him the perfect distance to every corner of his piazza of dust and dirt, and I imagined the next door neighbors measuring it so that his jaw just made it another six inches further beyond the holes in the fence. I felt sorry for him because it didn't look like he had much shade. Nor anything really to do.

Ross could always hear me though. "He's never had shade his whole life. A dog can't be missing something he's never before had. You miss having a dad around?"

I scratched my head like it was something I had to think about. "I guess not."

That goddamn Ross could turn a hot, shadeless dog into a metaphor for my life with no need for segue — in less than four sentences — and still sound like a genius.

And Ross would identify him right away that day. "He's a greyhound. A racing dog. They are illegal to race here in California but not in Mexico. They still race the hell out of them right across the border. I've seen them. Dad took me a time or two. You can have a real damn fine day at a greyhound racing track. More beautiful to watch than horses if you ask me."

During our first week there Jack was never let off that chain even once. Scraps were occasionally thrown out in the dirt for him to eat (and if they were thrown out of range of his chain he'd just spend hours stretching and crying and walking back and forth and to and from while teasing flies ate at their leisure, sometime just inches from him, until it just finally rotted away). And he had a small bowl of water that was empty more than it was full.

"He's just dar as a watchdog, Ross. Nuttin' more. No, suh." Tabby informed him.

Ross pressed him. "Well where the hell did he come from?"

"Well, dese people here next door. Dey get him from a guy just across de street. A man drops off a truckload every two to three months it seem. Ten dogs, sometimes maybe fifteen. Dey be comin' from Mexico. Supposed to be hauled up here for adoption. As pets is what Ah is led to believe."

"Pets? And so Jack here chained to the dirt in this yard. He's been adopted. He's their pet."

"Oh he be de lucky one. Yes, suh. De man across de street? Well, Ah puts it dis way to yuh, Cassius. Jack is de only dog I ever seen come walkin' out ob dar."

"What the fuck do you mean?"

35

"He's paid to kill dem dogs. About twenty five dollar for each one. So Jack dar. He's lucky. He a lucky one."

"Kill? How? Where?"

"Well Ah was curious about dat ma-self and axed just here a couple a weeks ago. To de neighbors here across de fence."

"Yeah, and?"

"Well he puts dem in one ob dem crates dey be used to travelin' in an' sleeping. In his garage out back. One at a time. He done cut off de top ob de crate. Put some ol' hamburger down in dar so dey go in waggin' dat tail. An' with a baseball bat and while dey be eatin' and not lookin' and even if dey could dey is already trapped. He just goes at dem with dat bat. Den in trash bags out behind in de alley and de trash man, why he just gets dem on trash day with everythin' else. Yes, suh."

Ross stared down at his feet for a couple of moments and during that time for some reason we all just stared at him, like we were all on some goddamned stage and he was late with a line. But Ross did not say a word. He just finely and gently kicked a pebble out in front of him and then turned and walked back into the house and up to his room. But the next morning when Tabby and I went to wake him up as we all had planned to go to the grocery store together, Jack was sleeping in there with him. There were some empty cans of dog food on the floor, a couple of clean white steak bones, and a bucket of water. And then Ross asleep on his mattress and Jack snuggled up alongside wide awake and growling at me.

"Gotdamned to sweety lawdy black Abraham Lincoln hisself what in de debbil is dat wild beast doin' in here!" Tabby got so

36

scared he just started soft-shoeing in place, with the accompanying elbow-swinging and everything.

"He's mine, now," Ross said matter of factly, with just one eye barely slit open. "He lives here. With us. Over the next day or two make sure you each give him some food. From your hand. And then tell him your name. And speak softly. He'll stop growling. He'll be your friend. That's all he wants anyways. Just a few souls he can call friend."

"Ross Cassius-boy. Yuh crazy giant jesus an' moses mother-humper. What in de hell am Ah ever goin' to tell de neighbors? Dey see yuh steal him?"

"You tell them I have him. You tell them not to get another. Or there will be problems. Problems from you. And then problems from me. Otherwise we can all just be good neighbors."

Tabby knew what he meant, even though he would never say it out loud. Tabby was a sweetheart of a human being but as the proprietor of one of the larger crack and coke houses around and always dressed real shiny, bright white and tap dancing and talking to himself wherever he went, well, nobody would ever really question him when he said something.

Jack followed Ross wherever he went. Right on Ross's heels as he walked and practically between his legs wherever he stood or sat. Jack himself always had to either stand up or lie down. Like all Greys he'd had his ass bred right out of him for purposes of speed and aerodynamics and if there was no room for lying down he would tough it out on all fours until he was moved somewhere else. Poor bastard (although I've met a few people in my life who if they'd had their ass bred out of them it wouldn't have been the worst thing in the world).

But it was Lizzy who seemed to love him the most. She'd look for him first thing with treats and hugs and smiles, go right down to him on her knees so that when she kissed him their noses were always even (she was the only one he'd ever let do that). And whenever she'd have to leave, with Jack it was always a real long goodbye — she would just about cry. And with a real hang-dog face on that hound was how he'd stand there once she was gone, with that motionless stare at the crack between the door and the wall as soon as it closed behind her, until somebody had to get him and finally drag him away.

In the end Jack would live with Lizzy (after it was all over she came back looking for him, picked him up from a pound where the police had left him, and made sure he was hers). His last home would be back up there in the Malibu hills with the most lovely of girls. Lucky boy. Good for him.

And the neighbors never made a peep about Jack's sudden disappearance from their backyard. Even when they saw him shadowing Ross right next door almost the very next day. Not after Tabby said what he had to say.

And that man across the street? Right toward the end, just a few days right before Christmas itself, I saw Ross come walking out of that place in the middle of the night with a baseball bat. In that moment I had no idea what he had done. But after Christmas I did. He tossed the bat down the sewer drain in the street as he jogged back. And knowing what I do now, I would just be a real fool's fool if I did not say that there is real good chance that guy ended up in a trash bag in the alley just waiting for the trash man on trash day.

V

*O*ur home on top of the house was small.

408 Broadway St., Venice Beach. Right off 4th Ave.

Ross referred to it as "the lair of the Lilliputian and one gullible Gulliver." Or sometimes the house of "Gunga Sins and Din." He'd never say who was who, though. Not that it should have been too damn difficult to figure out.

The original white paint on the walls had faded and chipped into a speckled greyish cast. Our apartment was essentially made up of one long, indoor wooden staircase that led up to a central room, a kind of living room I suppose, big enough for my drum set and, later, a lean but in its own way very green and forgiving Christmas tree. Spoked off of this central room were two decent sized bedrooms, a bathroom, a kitchenette with window to the roof, and a long closet or storage space that became Ross's room. Or at least that's where he liked to sleep when he wasn't sleeping on the roof.

It was kind of a quarter A-frame, which meant the ceilings in the bathroom, the kitchen, and the storage-space (Ross's room) went from eight feet to a little less than six real quick. Ross was about six feet and two, myself about three inches more. I always knew which part of the house Ross was in ("Fetching ceilings," if he forgot and thought David was still around; "Goddamn the motherfucker architect of the A-frame," if he remembered that he

39

wasn't). Ross never looked up unless he was out on the roof. So his head would take a pretty good and almost daily beating around the house. Otherwise his eyes were always slanted toward the earth. Fixing on the cracks in the sidewalks, studying what kind of shoes people wore, reading the saddled love of coupled footsteps in the sand and graffiti on the hallways of the city, or on rare occasions actually looking up to see if anyone would match an ogle and the challenge — eye for an eye, smile for a smile.

We both had a couple of egg-shell foam mattresses to put on the floor for beds, although Ross usually preferred the stability of the dirty hard wood, and used his mattress as a pillow and a clean place to lay out his folded clothes after he washed them in the shower with the same bar of soap he used to cleanse himself.

Like I said, Ross liked to sleep in the storage place. It was just big enough for him to lie down in and stack his dry clothes and a few books in one singular pile in a corner. It forced him to sleep like a mummy, except upside down. And when he closed his door at night his hair would leak out the one-inch crack at the bottom and remind me of one of those big, hairy dogs stuffed in a cat carrier in the mom and pop pet shop back in Pleasant Grove.

Even after we moved in, it was a week or two before he actually started sleeping in that room, though. Initially he opted for the beach and sleeping on the sand, body surfing his hangovers off as the sun rose every morning. I guess it was when Lizzy started spending the night that he started sleeping at home in the closet. At least until her presence was slowly absolved and he moved to the roof with Soda and one of his wheelchairs.

He and Lizzy had kind of been a couple since that last Christmas. She was a film student at some private ritzy-dizzy school in Salt Lake and had seen us play at a club. She just went right up to Ross afterwards and asked to put him in one of her student films (Ross always said he'd rather live on canvas, but film's a kind of canvas, right?). But I hadn't heard him mention her since about one month before we left Utah. She had gone ahead to California (her parents lived in Malibu) about two months before we did, and they were talking on the phone almost every night for that first month, then all of a sudden: nothing. Just nothing. And Ross was back to his magic drawer of matchbook-number collections and lipstick-napkin assortments harvested en masse from our gigs about town. He never mentioned her again. I didn't think much of it at the time. Ross never discussed his relationships with other people. I had never heard him do it, not even once in my life. I just assumed everyone was like that. I just second naturedly thought it was Ross being Ross, pretending that he didn't know anyone, that he'd see her when we got to the coast.

But then I heard him on the phone late one night that first week in Venice. (I realize now that he just finally gave in.)

Ross had earlier been sitting alone in his room. He was in there for quite a while. I could hear him swigging. His fancy was the most generic, cheapest, biggest (for purely economical reasons, "always shoplift in bulk, Brentwood") bottle of vodka available he'd chase with a gallon jug of tap water.

His voice on the phone was reverent and grey. Monotoned and so flattened that it was even absent of apathy. Kind of like how all those old, white, bald-headed butlers dressed in black bow ties from old movies on TV would talk when they were serving their masters — except no prissy, little misnancy British

41

accent. Kind of like those guys talked to us when we went to see Mom and Father in those undertaker buildings. Mortuaries, I mean.

"Lizzy? . . .yeah, yeah, it's me . . . yeah I know I said I never could again . . . wait, never could or never would? There's a big difference . . . I want his name . . . Therapist? Fuck your therapist . . . No, no . . . I can't see you . . . Oh, please now, lover, don't cry . . . yes, yes . . . I still love you, but that has nothing to do with it any longer. It's gone way past my love and into emotions and strange lands I know nothing about and I explained that the last time and I'm being real nice and congenial right now so don't knock down what I got going in my head and make me lose my balance and spill or else I'll say things I mean and regret . . . but it *was* your fucking fault . . . Meet? No way . . . I'm doing what I said the last time you called me back in Utah and that's the best thing anyway for both of us. But I still need his name and address . . . Why not? . . . Meet? Where? . . . No fucking way." And then he hung up.

Then he went back into his room, got his bottle, came back, lay back down in mine and started swigging again. No, actually by that time he was gulping. He was drinking like he was real thirsty. He sat in my window sill and started rocking back and forth and laughing and shaking his head and hair like a naughty old hosed down, long-eared dog. And smiling like one too. He was fleshquaking after every bolt — something I had never yet seen before. Almost like he was having to coax himself — coax himself with conviction, resolve, and plenty of decent savoir-faire — into some place or some thing he could not and maybe never would want to remove himself from. Now he was looking and drinking like a pirate. Yeah, I've seen one before. A real one. Even had a tooth missing. Chasing women around after a night of rape, ravage, and vengeance, and sitting in a window, even. When I was real, real small. On a boat. Sitting in my mom's lap. At Disneyland. Right after we escaped from the hippos. (Where was Mom's lap now?)

He waited another five or ten minutes. Then he picked the phone back up. "Lizzy, don't say nothing. There's a little place down on the boardwalk a couple blocks from where I live. It's a screwy little dive. Kind of a bar-coffee-house-dance club, depending on the night and the hour. It's called Van Gogh's Ear. Meet me there in an hour. . . No, I won't bring it up. Yeah, yeah, I promise, love. Bye."

He put the phone down and I heard him put five gulps together without a breath and the chaser be hanged. He sounded like a goddamn plunger in an unforgiving toilet. I knew that right then: he was feeling no pain. He spoke so slow I thought he was trying to sound out the words for himself to understand. I had my eyes closed. "Brentwood . . . I know . . . you're awake you little eavesdropping
. . . asshole. We . . . got to go down to Van Gogh's Ear. I cannot do it alone . . . At least not tonight. At least not yet. There are some things . . . I just . . . cannot do. Alone."

VI

$\mathcal{I}$ remember the first time he led me the three or four blocks through the blackness and white eyes of our neighborhood toward the beach and the boardwalk and the smaller alleyways that split them. The alleyways were dotted and pitted with little bars and coffee shops. We penetrated one of them and found a small mall of beer joints and hangouts known by word of mouth (because I never saw any signs) as Billingsgate's Burrow.

The first place we came upon was The Sword of Femmecles. A garish hole in the wall with painted red-brick lips for a door and a mass of garter belts hanging on a line in the one long front window. An arousing curtain for whatever was cavorting within. There were four or five rows of them, all red and black, connecting to one another dripping downwards. It might have been the front of a laundromat on the whorish side of Tijuana (please pardon the redundancy), or at least that is as Ross would refer to it on occasion.

A very corpulent, caricature-sized, bright baby-blue strap-on dildo hung over the entrance (kind of like the pair of bullhorns that hung over the entrance of Chi Chi's Fine Mexican Cuisine) our favorite Mexican restaurant back in Utah, except that instead of a huge imitation penis being the center of attention, there was a real-life and properly protruding machete. It was very shiny.

"Hey, Ross. What the hell is this place . . . I . . . ?"

44

"Comedores de la alfombra, Wood. Sappho Sirens; castaways of Lesbos. Lipstick dykes. Some of them bulls; but not all that much horny, I must say. Guys can go in. Just don't come on to a chick if you go in, man. They won't like that in there. But they do serve a good slice of pizza pie. We're going to the place across the street. The one on the corner." I never did get to go in and experience The Sword of Femmecles. But I didn't even like those bullhorns back home.

We crossed the street to Van Gogh's Ear. Corner of Westminster and Speedway. It was almost all glass. I mean the front and one of the sides were just two big drawn-out, starving windows. Each one probably about six feet tall and forty feet wide. There was really nothing very noticeable on its exterior. Just a sign that read Van Gogh's Ear above one of the windows, rather amateurishly painted with a big, bloody, fleshy-red ear sitting in for the apostrophe.

Oh yeah, there was something else: Girls dancing in the goddamn windows. Not strippers or nothing. Just normal looking, normal sized, normally young girls. Twisting and churning, coiling and curving, with normal next-to-nothing mini-skirts, normal six-inch high heeled slippers, and normal righty-tighty T-shirts with big bloody, fleshy-red ears painted on them. We went in.

Inside it was quiet. The girls were dancing in silence. But not really. I guess I mean to say that they were dancing to themselves. Like they were dancing to their own stories. Each one of them had their own rhythm and groove going on in their own little disarming, pale-faced faces. But there was actually some music being played in the place too. I first discovered it a little later that night. It took me a little while over the din of everyone talking. But I did finally detect the faintest of music trickling through the air. It was kept very soft, but played incessantly. I would later fall in love with it and I eventually asked what it was. I bought every album they ever played in that place and listen to it even today. They only played three kinds: Ravel's *Bolero*. Opera (but only Caruso). And anything by James Brown. ("It's A Man's, Man's, World, live at Chastain Park," still drives my mind right back to those comely little lasses of the glasses.)

Ross really liked those girls too. And, of course, they liked him. He'd go there often and just stand outside and stare at them and smile and lip talk and lip read and try to imitate and assimilate their dance moves and occasionally show them some of his. "Come on now, darling. Hike up that skirt a little higher and show me your world." They loved him. They'd try to get him to come up on their ledges but he'd just wave them off. And then they'd ask him to wait 'til they were done so maybe they could grab a drink or something but Ross would just smile and say, "No can do, homespun" (Ross's favorite term of endearment: "Keeps me in mind of just who is the spider and that you can't dance too damn well in a web"). He'd wink back and smile all Cool Hand Luke-like and just say, "I got myself a honeypot who is sweet and fine and I'm sort of taking care of business with her and figuring things out and sorting out the clues and well you know there's not much love in being unfaithful and up 'til today, I still have to say I am in love even though I still am sorting out the clues. But you sure have the most lenient smile I have ever seen. It's very pretty too." But they never gave up. I suppose he knew they never would.

Anyway. We entered Van Gogh's Ear. Three dollar cover. One drink minimum. Coffee, tea, espresso, incense — over the bar. Beer, liquor, cloves, weed, and all methods of medicinal goodnesses and grace — if you knew the right person and said the right words — under the bar. Everything in plastic cups. Be light on your feet, watch what you speak. Ross just winked.

And then Van Gogh's Ear. The inside was the Sistine Chapel turned upside-down and busted forward through time like a rolling, Sisyphean, settled snow globe (and oh how Ross had passion for snow globes) of iconoclastic street-urchin art gone mad-bad kitschy-camp-kaleidoscopic Vegas. Even for Vegas.

I can't even begin to account for it all.

The bric-a-brac of the divine and indigent Edgar. The prophesy of the dreadful and even more penurious Vincent. The shy wisdoms and bald-faced murmurings of James, Caruso, and Ravel. That's what it was to be contained within Van Gogh's Ear.

On one green wall, painted in vermillion blood, letters a foot high: "I say to myself, in the first place, of the innumerable effects, or impressions, of which the heart, the intellect, or (more generally) the soul is susceptible, what one shall I, on the present occasion, select?"

A pink guillotine stood in one corner where a stuffed Winnie the Pooh doll painted black like a cat waited smiling at the bottom.

A black and white checkered cross, hung upside down (or was I just too right-side up?), with a manikin painted like the sky of *Starry, Starry, Night*, crucified in a most inhumane way (legs nailed to the horizontal part at the bottom — hands clasped, covering the groin, a nail through the hands and groin, to the vertical) leaned in yet another corner.

Great Gogh sunflowers in florescent yellow and green adorned the ceiling and danced in stuttered, slight black-light, like heavenly cataracts reflecting some sun while in other parts a small girl carrying her diary stepped out of an aeroplane over the sea right into the Neutral Milk Hotel.

A very realistic painting of a great grape ape hung on another wall, its hands covered in blood, its eyes full of sorrow, a comic strip bubble-gram leaking from its mouth: "Has anyone seen my other half?" I didn't get it.

The floor was freckled cobblestone. Squares of crude, gameboarded, painted rock conjoining and melding one into the other: Parcheesi, Checkers, Candyland, Life, Yahtzee, Cribbage, Ouiga, Backgammon, Go, Shogi, Monopoly, Tic-Tac-Toe.

And in the middle of it all, ten square feet of a chessboard where in the eye of each square one of the characters of *Alice in Wonderland* was stilled and frozen doing assorted and sundry versions of the old in-and-out with Alice herself (rape-style mating by the look on Alice's face in some, except for the accommodating Cheshire, who was skim-milk lapping at Alice's lap — a generous act of unguence Alice seemed to be quite enjoying in another). Mr. Dodgson would have been so proud.

On another wall were two massive wooden doors. They seemed to indicate some other entrance or exit, into something much better or worse. They were greyish white, straight at the bottom arched at the top, kind of like tablets. I would come to spend many hours there reading them. They were handsomefully decorated from top to bottom and from one side to the other with words. Quotations, verse, phrases of every ilk and variety. Utterances, mandates, expressions, and messages from a myriad of the great philosophers, poets, visionaries, and just about anyone else deigned worthy of the door by the doors' author.

They were passionately legible. The lettering was tiny, the penmanship impeccable, the type so varied that it was rather difficult to add them all up without losing your way. Everything had been carved in red. But there were no blemishes. No attempted erasures of any sort or kind.

I adored these doors. The person who had spent the hundreds of hours dignifying their labor on this wood had done so in such a manner that licensed the mammoth doors with a command of reverence; the authority, even for that which is inert, to invoke a voice, at least for me. If Ross admired them, I never knew. But I never knew him to ignore things written down. It was only when words entered his mind via his ears that he would shut down and become disdainful. He once said to me — right after he found dead Dad — that "the eyes are soft, they are malleable, they are sweet opaque filters for the imagination, where anything and everything can be altered before it is burned into reality. But most of all, they can be closed. The ears, on the other fucking hand, are sharp, astute, and angry. They are unforgiving. They are unforgetful. They have minds of their own and never fucking sleep. I can understand our old man by what I saw. But can never forgive him for what my ears heard him say. Ears can only get hot, Brentwood. But the eyes can cry. And tears mean so much."

Anyway, each little piece of literature on the door had received no assignation as to order or category. Nor did they receive quotation marks. The arrangement seemed arbitrary, or at least feigned so, depending on how one read the doors. The first time Ross saw me staring at them he just remarked blithely, "Wood, what's the matter with you? You look like a goddamned aborigine staring at a Ferris wheel."

> *Now, as fond fathers,*
> *Having bound up the threat'ning twigs of birch,*
> *Only to stick it in their children's sight*
> *For terror, not to use, in time the rod*
> *Becomes more mock'd than fear'd; so our decrees,*
> *Dead to infliction, to themselves are dead,*
> *And liberty plucks justice by the nose;*
> *The baby beats the nurse, and quite athwart*
> *Goes all decorum.*

It is a truth universally acknowledged, that a single man in possession of a good fortune, must be in want of a wife.

"Don't you want to join us?" I was recently asked
by an acquaintance when he ran across me alone after midnight in
a coffeehouse that was already almost deserted. "No, I don't," I
said.

hey, sometime boy living on that road

why don't you cry for help?

run to the graveyard of mysteries in men

50

then climb that tower, and ring that bell.

I'm alive!

The best stimulus for running ahead,
is to have something we must run from.

Shake it, Salome

Shake it, Shake it, Shake it.

Cum, Salome

Cum, Cum, Cum

M. S. Krause was here
The girls blushed, then cheered
Oh my, that Scotty
So cunned, so naughty!

If but some vengeful god would call to me
From up the sky, and laugh:
"Thou suffering thing,
Know that thy sorrow is my ecstasy,
That thy love's loss is my hate's profiting!"

And because I am happy, & dance & sing,
They think they have done me no injury,
And are gone to praise God & his Priest & King,
Who make up a heaven of our misery.

No Se Puede Vivir Sin Amar

WOLLICOTT'S TRAVELING RABBIT'S FOOT;
MINSTRELS WENT
POACHING DEER IN NORTHERN ARIZONA WITH
FIVE NEW YORK BIKER CHICS, OUT OF CONTROL,
"SUICIDE GAL, WON'T YOU COME OUT TONIGHT,
COME OUT TONIGHT."
~The Harmless Thoughts of a London Gynaecologist~
In the Garden of Earthly Pleasures (Sam, I miss you)

The hounds of hell were coming for him;
He climbed the statue of a stylish general
On a rearing horse.
He clung to the marble thigh of the stallion.
He watched, in horror, the field below him.
The torn swans were long syllables

His name was Hallelujah, like the song, the way you could cause the
name to lilt, lingering a while in the back of your mind or throat.
Sometimes a boyfriend would call her up, usually after eleven,
while she lay in bed dreaming about the boy with a dog.

All moanday, tearsday, wailsday, thumpsday, frightday, shatterday.

My dear Clincham, The bearer of this letter is an old friend of mine not quite the right side of the blanket as they say in fact he is the son of a first rate butcher but his mother was a decent family.

You meet somebody new,
his history anything,
a big unknown story
that you only know the end of.

Hey Judas, come on!
Or I'll skull-fuck ya,
'fore long.

And on and on they went, dispensing their wisdom and their wit. To peruse Van Gogh's Ear was often to find some meaning in that winter of Venice and gain some insight into Ross's sloppy, solipsistic mind. Take a run through his unlit obstacle course of the self. I didn't realize it at the time, but I often went there in search of him. Not literally, of course. For over the course of the next few months I could find him there with some regularity sometime between the hours of three and six in the morning. He'd be out in front at a table at the sidewalk café they set up there at Van Gogh's between just those hours. I'd find him there

53

with her. With Lizzy. Always with his head to the table. He'd sleep. Pass out. She'd caress his hands and stroke his face or his hair. On occasion I'd see him squeeze her hand or touch her knee. But only under the table.

She'd talk to him. Almost as if she were talking to herself. Looking up into the sky or out toward the ocean. About what I never knew. I was never close enough to hear. And I would never let them know that I was near anyway. Or even there for that matter. No. I would stand in the shadow just inside the entrance and watch. Not stare. But watch.

And when I'd tire of this I would go look for him back inside of that place. Back at the chessboard. I would spin in a chair at the bar and look around and take in what it was to be inside Van Gogh's Ear. Where I found that its macabre, dehumanized morgue of human fallibility and comfort was lent quite kindly to Ross and the paradox of his passionate logic. Where all the chewed up, half digested, regurgitated, and spat out emotion therein he could and would at times so beautifully and crucially frame.

Perhaps that is all that wanting to be loved is: a hunting for hurt. He just preyed on the sources of his pain. A very conscious decision.

But the fact remains that there is no fact (at least that I am aware of) that Ross was ever convinced himself that he had made such a choice. His game board chose him, you see. A game called "Maiden's Rent." He was only a poor piece (ah, but then what was I?). I think he knew that, but then, with time, came to believe he could actually play himself. I mean not as a player.

Rather, as an actual piece.

VII

There were some stairs at the back of Van Gogh's that led up to a little loft that jutted out over the tables and seated bottom-feeders of the bar. It had a circle of couches and love seats, one barbershop chair in the middle, what looked to be a pair of turn-of-the-century dentist's chairs in the two back corners, and all of this surrounded by another circle of large, three-and-four-tiered bookshelves full of nothing but Gerald Foster and Bud Clifton pulp fiction. All of it dog-eared, tired, and bar-beverage stained.

It was a place for browsing, reading, and random poetry performances where people snapped their fingers instead of clapping their hands.

We went up there and waited for Lizzy to enter. Ross had a beer, in addition to his Vodka-veiled bottle of *Evian*. ("Looks even purer than water, don't it Wood.") And I had a soda (he had a rather peculiar aversion to soda, himself — unless tinctured). A sarsaparilla, actually. That's all Mom ever had for us at home. Homemade, of course. And I still cherished the flavor and appreciated the comfort it gave me. Ross hated it. He especially hated it whenever I ordered or asked for a "sarsaparilla" whenever we were out. "It's a root beer, goddamnit. We ain't at home in the kitchen no more." But I stuck to my guns on that one. I liked the way she called it.

But he didn't mind if I had it around. As long as he was comfortable as well.

We sat down and hung over the bannister from the reading loft and studied the fussy, even-flow Publins below. Actually, that first night I believe all I studied were those dancing window-gals. But Ross had his eye on the door like an owl on a rodent-hole.

Suddenly, I heard Ross say, "God for the Donnybrook Fair" under his breath and I turned toward the door. And there she was. And I must say, until that evening I had truly forgotten just how goddamn-awfully-gorgeous she was.

Every fucking guy in that den rubbered his neck when she walked in. And every girl did too. She could have been thrown on the wall herself with all the other weird art in that place and fit right in as the living and breathing, the one and the only, prototype for beauty singularly strange and fantastical.

She was apple blossom time.

She was the loveliest number.

She was what virgins from all periods of history aspired to be.

Eyes bruised so dark blue that when left open for a moment or two melted like aqua and then froze in tofana and then with every other quick blink would turn black and then again back to blue.

Eyes set like spades in an oval pussycat face above a perfectly Peter Pan-like pointed noise and a pair of the murkiest, scarlet, lacquered-on lipstickless lips I had ever seen. Her whole face just as delicate and fine as that paper made for rolling a cigarette.

She was tall, about six feet. Legs, legs, legs, Limoges — plunging to the floor like pillars of soft, scarcely bronzed light.

And her hair. Oh, man what a mane. The most carnal part of her was that which simply framed her face. It was breast length and black and was as natural as her breath. I never knew her to have to touch it other than to have it cut.

White as bonefish, her skin was perfect. Like just now descended snow on warm marble flesh, if marble could ever have blood. Her arms were also tall and she kept them pursed at her chest, with reverence, like the preacher preying mantis. She walked like sienna, breathed like milksop, and held the hourglass that was her figure with the humility of a nun and the fastidiousness of a first-night hooker. Her breasts were . . . aww, fuck it. You know what I'm trying to say here.

But wait, I will add this: she wore a mid-thigh green gown, and despite what anyone might say, was still new-mown hay . . . beyond the bounds of even the most innocent play.

Anyway, she walked in and Ross trying not to gasp said, "God for the Donnybrook Fair" and took a deep drag on his bottle. Lizzy twirled slowly, just a few times but with the energy of a soda pop. She was looking for Ross, and then for an empty table. The only one left downstairs was the one underneath the capsized manikin cross. She kind of flounced on over in a hoodwinking little swagger-stride, but with her head bent low like a peacock trying to steal away. But she could have goose-stepped her way over with fire shooting out of her ass while belting the lyrics to "Come, Come Ye Saints," and the only eyebrows being raised would have been for the impeccable daintiness of such an elevated step and the ability to sing like a cherub and blossom flames from her behind like a Revolución Mexicana musket — all so simultaneously. (Beauty is stone-blind bliss. It makes bruises look like art. Mistakes into genius. The deaf become deafer. Pain becomes euphoric. And when it's true and good, it is pure death. Ohh, that the whole world was just as ugly as hell. But then God would cease to be cruel. And who would ever believe in him then?)

Ross was busy sousing his euphoria, numbing it up even more so that he might cover it up. He could not face her naked. She was already too sweet, too hallowed, and much too delicate on the inside. To stand up to her exterior as well was even more than he could muster. That perhaps she was too innocent, too trusting, too child-like, and much too embraceable, were her only flaws. Like that rose, the most beautiful inviolate rose, with thorns both ingrown and out that pricked like catclaws curved in so much that she would voluntarily bleed herself to death in self-defense.

"Just wait here, Brentwood." Ross was fixated on the table beneath the cross. He spoke with his eyes anchored and his mouth in check. He placed his mitigating hands beneath his chin and fluttered his fingers along his jawbone like a warrior choosing and checking his weapon. "Just wait here, man. I just got to go down here and do a little bit of talking and straightening and clearing up. Conduct my business. Be about the business of my father. Put some peace of mind back into this mess for everybody. Who am I kidding? The only peace of mind on sale tonight is for me, the selfish bastard, and I'm the only fucker selling it. Can you believe that? I got what I want and I got to go through her to get it. It's a fucking mad, mad, world, Brentwood."

"Hey, man. I think they just played that song. But I don't know who was singing. You know?"

His butterflied hands floated up to his lips but his eyes didn't leave that table. "What in the feathered fuck are you talking about? I'm trying to tell you a few of my feelings here and get some kind of goddamn sympathetic ear going and you're talking about some piece of shit song that someone just played . . . are you fucking mocking me? Are you trying to juke me around with some kind of fucking jukebox talk? What the hell do you think this is? You think we're fucking driving around Utah looking for some fucking snow-cone stand on Sunday after church or something?"

He was drunk. He was getting loud. I could feel Van Gogh's Ear turning its eyes upon us. He turned his eyes upon me and they were his wide, dipso-drunk, bitter ones. I'd seen them before but never been their subject. New things were happening since the desert, every day. And they were making me new as well.

He had his right-hand fingernails digging into his chin now, and his left underneath his chair in mad pursuit of his bottle. He had become frightening. He made a pistol with his right hand and began thumping me on the chest with it. "Listen you flighty selfish little fuck, you. I didn't drag your ass down here to suck and leech and mock me like I'm your fucking old man or something." His voice began to give in to shrieking and started to split and crackle. "And if I was your old man, and yeah I might be older and have your same fucking last name, but if I was your old man I'd fucking demand the respect of Christ almighty himself, even if I had to bleed it out of you!"

Lizzy tapped him on the shoulder. She had risen to the loft without either of us noticing. "Ross. Please don't talk to him like that."

Ross went statue. Except that he took his snub-nosed hand out of my chest and stuck it in his shirt like for a moment he thought he actually had a gun and was trying to hide it. Then he just looked like a fucking Napoleon in drag trying to sit still while someone painted his picture. There were only two voices that would have stunted his growth like that. And Mom was much too cold and much too far away. Besides, in a million years she wouldn't have even sent a criminal into Van Gogh's Ear, let alone step her own foot inside.

I looked up and over Ross's black head and into the stultifying glory hanging aloft it. Her countenance was pure tragedy above him. A crude caricature of what religion was supposed to be. But by herself, she was halo, nimbus nymph, anthelioned Lizzy. She must have burned on Ross's back.

She put both her hands to her neck and fiddled politely with the silver Möbius strip and necklace that Ross had given her that Christmas last.

"How are you, Brent? How have you been? It seems so long since I last saw you."

Her voice was meek and breathy. She had more fear of the moment than any of us. But tremulously she stood there, breaking down Ross on my scant behalf. Her face glistened like frost on the cusp of a melt. I bowed my head a bit without taking my eyes from hers. "Three months. Thirteen weeks, actually." I caught myself. "Oh, it's been a while. I don't know. Two or three months, or something like that, I guess. And yes, I guess, and well, how have *you* been?"

"OK. Just OK." Her eyes sailed around the room, occasionally pausing on the back of Ross's head before searching again for a more comfortable place to land. Mine were no good as they had already landed on hers.

And so there sat stuck the three of us. Frozen.

Rub-a-dub-dupe. The three of us. Mute. For what seemed like the proverbial eternity, but what was probably the standard twenty to thirty seconds. Which probably *was* an eternity for Lizzy and me. But not for old you-know-who. A few seconds were a mere flutter of an eye for an old master biding his time across the chess board. Maelzel had made his first move an eternity ago, made everybody else's moves for them a few centuries later, made mine and Lizzy's two or three feeble moves for us that night, and was already in bed — like a baby with its nipple, dreaming of body surfing the next morning. The asshole aesthete flicking his old hand (with all his devil books tight to his chest), watching a couple of gullible greenhorns swing in the wind like helpless, shit-stained underwear — just waiting for us to dry on the line.

I dried first. "That one wall down there, the one that looks like doors . . ."

"The doors of perception." Ross now spoke calmly. He was slaked and sain.

"There's some really interesting stuff written on them. Did you read any of it?" I tried to parrot his sudden peace, but was still only his bird.

"You got one shot." Ross was crooked-grin smiling at me. He winked.

I avoided his gaze, turned back over the bannister and pretended interest in what I was saying. "You guys should go check it out. It's right over there, next to that cross."

61

He took his hand out of his shirt, still fashioned like a gun, and held it close to his side so that only I could see it was pointed at me. He cocked his thumb and let the hammer drop. "Flash in the pan, Brentwood. You are a rabbit foot's fool tonight."

I looked down at the cross and saw that some people were already sitting at Ross's table. They were a couple of guys with their dates. Typical late-night uppity-yuppity, yippity-hippity Angelinos. Wealthy, wasted WASPS — buzzing around all busy, smarmy, and snide.

I motioned to Ross with a nifty (practiced, unenthusiastic) crouch of my brow. He saw it too. He rose slowly from his chair, then bellowed down from his balcony seat. "Excuse me there kind sirs and lovely ladies but the table there at the foot of the cross is mine. I have just left it for only but a moment to retrieve the virgin from here atop and take her back to her proper place there where you are just now seating yourselves. In other words, I have reserved it."

All inside gave their attention to Ross. Even the window girls stopped telling their stories for a moment. He beckoned Lizzy forward and then held his arms out to everyone below as if to say — or maybe he really did say — "See? Cast your eyes upon her. Could you think that I would make up such a story? (Cupping his heart with both hands.) Would you think that I could lie to you?"

And then he did say, "Please, have this table up here where I am standing now. The view is divine. And this young man here is just leaving." I stood and receded on cue for some dental work in the chairs at the back. "I'll buy you all a drink for your trouble and ascension."

Places were exchanged. I sat in one of the dentist's chairs for just a minute or two. I could tell I was making the new party of four even more uncomfortable than they already were after exchanging further pleasantries with their marauding maitre d'. I kept leaning back, trying to seem all self absorbed and as crazy as he, opening my mouth, trying to imagine some bar-handled moustachio endeavoring to fit some gigantic, nineteenth-century pair of blacksmith's pliers into my head after three snorts of whiskey. One for me and two for him (too many "Gunsmokes" and "Bonanzas"). They kept eyeing me. I was as menacing as milk without Ross. Anyway, I had no reason to eye back and nothing left to stare at.

So I went outside and sat just inside the shadows a few feet from the dancing-girls window. Ross and Lizzy were sitting just a few feet behind them.

Ross had entrusted me with his *Evian* bottle ("Walk this home, Brentwood, would you please? Don't let it out of your sight and put it in a safe place") like a dying king might with his one last manchild. It was only midnight and Van Gogh's didn't close until four. I had been deserted once again. This time, after a sadistic, wholly unwarranted, and just downright mean flogging from his tongue. The thought of the silence and the sleep of "home sweet crack-house" suddenly depressed me beyond words. It made me feel lonely. Ross's hatred (wherever it was coming from, and although I knew it not to be intended for me) was, however, poisoning me with palpable melancholy. So much so, I could not even find it in me to hate him back; so drunk I was with the unconditional love usually reserved for only the best of Man's Best Friends. I, the diminutive younger brother. Droll to his Dross. Midget to his Midas. Bantam to his Boss. Ross. And me, little Hopfrog. The Tantony Pig straight at the heel of the Patron Saint of Swineherds. And so on. And so forth.

How ironic it truly is that I was very nearly twice his size. A couple of inches taller, and a good forty pounds wider. I got the size in the family. For those last several years in Utah, while Ross was lifting bottles to the health in his mind, I lifted weights in the basement for mine.

We had an old barbell set (Father, first teenage Christmas) that we had carried everywhere with us when we traveled. (Porters at airports: "Woooeee, Good god a-mighty. What you got in here, dumbbells?" Father, with slit-still eyes and church-mouth grin, hands jingling in pocket feigning a search for more tin: "Ha, ha, ha." Then looking at us: "Shut up boys.")

Mom had made me promise to never "acquire that awful taste that exists on your Daddy's side of the family." And I was faithful, never had a sup in my life and kept myself occupied otherwise, mostly with those dumbbells. Until that night.

For I was sitting lonesome outside the *Ear* and there were those beautiful untouchables in front of my pain behind the glass. And there he was behind them, supping with an angel, and I had his muck in my hand.

Everything was perfect. I was curious, wanted to know what it tasted like, how it made him feel. I could disobey him, lose it without wasting it, losing it in me. And I was bored and cupped in my soul and afraid of crying, of being like a baby, and I knew if I did I'd miss him even more. And so that was that.

It was to my lips and biting my throat before I even had time to consider the aspersions upon my covenant with earth-swallowed Mom. I'd heard a lot of horror stories about one's first good, hard, straight drink. One's inaugural prance with the prince, gambol with The Gamble. But the kindling was rather kind. I allowed its warmth to be my affection as I lay back on a fire hydrant faded pink and painted like an odd castrated cock just outside the discharged shafts of sparkled light between Femmecles' Sword and the ear of Van Gogh.

I let the window-paned women woo an invisible me. I watched Lizzy woo her nigger of his own Narcissus. And I watched The Saturnine man tug the devil by the tail.

Of course, it's all a bit fuzzy now. But here's what I believe I saw, over the course of maybe a half-hour or so:

Just below the swinging, fresh, hot panted and mini-skirted triangles, I saw Ross first slowly lean over and kiss her on the cheek.

Between two sweet onion-ripe, fondue-like, crashing little asses, I saw Lizzy blush bright — and made a fleeting mental note of her abnormal, indelible beauty once again.

Over the hills and through the bush of one very snappy, grinding number, I saw Ross filch a smile as he pushed pen and paper across the table toward her.

Through cracks that tacked and pendulums of harrowing cleavage, I saw her pick up the pen, hesitate, put it down, and pick it up again. She was beautiful anew.

Under heapish mounds split to the ground so as to make me lay flat to see through that cranny, I saw her head shake "no" and he kiss her afresh, this time on the mouth.

I stood up to see over two bodies in mesh, one straddling the other while holding on to a metal bar above, crotch in face, to see her finally scribbling the address Ross had requested over the phone.

Sat back down again, for a non-perfunctory bump and grind, when he snapped the paper from her hand.

Leaned way left around a very recent, former gymnast pretzel-posing backwards betwixt her legs, her pelvis doing Elvis while a lucky lady made lappings in her lap, as he stood and whispered in her ear.

Stood on my tiptoes to see if the two girls were faking it or not, if panties were involved (the crotch 'n kisser cabaret), when Lizzy went grey, coned her mouth in what must have been a fairly audible shriek and ran out through the door right past me, dissolving down the street.

Ross was on her tail in a dead bolt. "Lizzy, Lizzy! You can't go running off into the fucking night like that. Now just hold on you're misunderstanding me and how I'm trying to help you." He ran by me about twenty feet and I was surprised he hadn't seen me. I was relieved. Thought I could make home and refill the bottle before he knew any better. Then he stopped on a dime and hollered through his mouth. "Liiizzyyy! I'll be right there, lover. You're not safe out there without me. This Venice is not safe!" And in the same motion and even before the last of "me" was out of his mouth, he spun and pointed his whole arm at me. "What in the sam motherfucking hell are you prancing up and down out here like some fucking crazy Flipper fish dancing backwards on the water?"

"Uhh, me?" I was good-and-dumb drunk.

"No. Not you, Wood. The moon. I'm just out here chatting with the moon again. You shut up." He spotted the bottle I was trying to hide by holding it upside-down, cap off, right in front of my chest. "Why, why . . . you broke your promise, Brother Wood."

"He was a mammal. Not a fish, damn it!" It just flew out.

"What are you trying to do now? Not enough you wrestle with me but you got to wrestle with the good-hearted dead as well? Get all up in their face 'til they're looking back at you from the mirror. You ain't ready for that kind of guilt, brother. Brentwood. You're losing it, man." He spun back to the dark in Lizzy's direction, but still had his arm leveled in my direction. "I upset you. Frightened you, disturbed you. Something. I'm sorry. You're going to have to forgive me now and let me calm you later." He turned back toward me. "Get back home. Please. I told her where we lived and she might try and go there if she gets lost. It's dangerous as hell around here. Especially right now. I have to go find her."

He was pissed, but ashamed. An apology was rare. In fact, I don't think I had ever heard one escape his mouth before. Ever. I took off, zigzagging down the street like an obedient, blind bunny flushed out of his hole by fear and accountability.

"And fill that fucking bottle back up before I get home you little son of a bitch lush." He still had his priorities in damn good order, though.

He took off himself in bent sprint in Lizzy's direction. But not before turning his head one more time. "And 'he' was a 'she,' anyway. Mammal, or not!"

I've had time to research that here in prison.

He was right.

VIII

*A*nother new-found respect was born that night for Ross: His ability . . . no. I shall call it his talent . . . no. Not even that. His affinity and pure virtuosity (if it was an art, then he had formed it) to operate, maneuver, and function (most of the time) with — according to the calculations from my crucible that evening — enough goddamn alcohol flowing in his veins to render most humans as numb, listless, and useful as that bottle of blue liquid in the barber's shop.

What can I say? I just got so damn lost that night, I did not find my way back to that goddamn crack-house 'til the sun woke me up sleeping in some beach showers just about a hundred yards from Van Gogh's. I must have run and walked more than five miles that night and I ended up a football field away in the opposite direction.

I kept running up and down this street and that and every damn time just kept hitting the beach. Trying a different street every time, finding the same sand every time, and every time just muttering to myself my sentence: "I am a dead man. Ross *will* kill me. A dead man I am." And then I would about-face and be off down a different or maybe the same street again.

When drunk, the world turns vanilla. Especially in the dark. Every face the same. Same one car driving all up and down every street. Same sign in every store window. Same name on every street sign.

I even stopped once to ask directions from this old, bald, black man curled up and sleeping on a bench at a bus stop that I was positive was only two blocks from where we lived. And it most probably was.

"Excuse me, sir," I said. "The corner of Broadway and Lincoln . . . which way is that?"

His eyes were already open. "What you looking for there, boy?"

My body was slurring as much as my speech. I steadied myself on his bench. "Broadway and Lincoln. The corner."

"I know. You just said that. And then I asked what you be looking for over in that neighborhood?" He had been using a big beat-up green plastic soda bottle as a pillow. He propped his head up a little bit with it, folded his hands across his chest, and gave me a good honest look right through the eyes.

"My house. My house. That's where I live. I need to get home."

"Just you tell me where it is that you live exactly and then I'll try and help you."

"I live on top of this house. Kind of in the attic. It's on top of this crack-house."

His black pearl eyes got broad, his eyebrows spruced together in the middle, and his face got real funny. He looked like he was going to sneeze.

"Crackhouse!" His voice went up one octave.

"Yes, sir."

"On Broadway and Lincoln?!" Two octaves.

"That's right, sir."

"You! What you be trying to speak to old Soda?" We'll call it three octaves.

"Broadway and Lincoln."

"Son, don't you be messing with me like that. Can't you see an old man here trying to get hisself some sleep!"

"But, sir . . ."

He nestled his green plastic soda pillow (which I now notice makes a soft swishing sound for some reason) back to where it was and laid his head back down upon it. He closed his eyes, resting his hands in his pockets. "Boy. I can tell you be on something already. Now, if you're messing around with an old man 'cause you think it's a damn funny thing to do, then fuuuck you, and shame on you for doing such business. And if you so messed up that you think you can carry your big white ass and that puppy-doggy fresh face into that part of town and knock on the door asking for the "crackhouse," then you might as well get yourself your own gun and shoot yourself 'cause they going to shoot your white ass anyway before you get to knock number three and I'll never get any sleep tonight knowing I sent some poor, overgrown, clean-cut white boy to his grave." He knocked twice on the bench underneath him. "Now get on away from me as I be sleeping."

"Sir. My ass? Not so big?" My drunk had suddenly made me vain.

"Got-dammit, boy. Get on with yourself and leave a homeless old Soda his one time of day and peace!"

Well, I was in absolutely no condition to refute that kind of rebuke. He made perfect sense, and if he didn't I was too soused and confused and feeling too guilty to keep him from his priceless peace. (For some men those few quiet minutes just before a doze will be the only time of his life when he truly does own it. Freedom. Peace. Oh, I do know that now.) I simply turned and walked away. But before I was even half-way down the block the old guy suddenly sat up and politely bid me good luck.

"But hey, son!" he called. "If you ever be looking for a good *cracker* house, you just come back here anytime 'cause I know a good and befitting one and I'll point you in the proper die-rection!"

And then I heard him start slapping his bench and cackling up a storm and I just turned the next available corner. I'm sure he just laughed himself right to sleep. At least I hoped he did. Later, it did seem pretty damn funny.

I took a different street. And then I hit the beach again. I was so twisted and stolen in my stupor that at one point I even sat down and seriously, I mean seriously, considered and then accepted the notion that this was my punishment from God for breaking my promise to my mother: that no matter which direction I ran in, God was going to pick up the Pacific Ocean — sand, showers and all — and throw it right down in front of me until I admitted I was wrong and gave up and just went to slumber somewhere. Which of course is what I finally did. And lucky for me I stumbled upon those beach showers because I finally just fell down from exhaustion and when I looked up and saw that sweet showerhead plastered up against the dark starry, starry Santa Monica sky, well it just gave me the comfort I needed to stop worrying about the fact that God was throwing the ocean around on my account and that when He was done doing that Ross was going to kill me anyways.

I used to sleep in the bathtub off and on 'til I was fifteen. Because I was "Wetty" (Ross's title). A bed-wetter. Up until I was eight my father made me sleep in the tub every damn single night, and he was real matter of fact about it. "Hey, no sense messing another mattress and sheets. In the tub here we just hit the water and save ourselves a whole lot of trouble. It's only practical, Brent. Until maybe you stop wetting the bed."

But hell, I didn't mind. I kind of liked it actually. Laying inside those nice white, smoothly curved walls. I felt safe. I remember having then what now seems kind of like a sick and disturbing little thought (but only sometimes, because it still makes sense to me). I remember thinking, "no wonder people look so peaceful and protected lying in those caskets. Especially those nice, big, white ones." Except they didn't have a showerhead above their heads, I guess.

And there was a nightlight in there too. I mean in the bathroom. So it was never all the way dark. When Father discovered I was kind of liking it (I started going to bed earlier and earlier) he put me back in my other bed and just went out and bought me some old gluey rubber sheets (except when it was hot and I'd sweat and then they were all nice and slippery — much better — except on some occasions they'd cause me an outbreak of something on my ass-side). And then he'd have to check on me later to make sure I didn't sneak back into the tub. Especially since he almost killed me (although it occurs to me now that perhaps he was more concerned about killing himself) stomping in all in a hurry one morning late for some goddamned meeting at church.

And, to be most candorous here, I have to admit that I continued to wet the bed until I was probably almost sixteen. I'd try and hide it as much as possible (extra sheets hidden about my room, alarm clock set for four every morning — which Ross never minded, he'd even help). But there would be times when Dad would find out and then it was the belt. Ross would protest violently. Throwing furniture down in front of us to block his way. And then he'd get it too (open-palmed slaps to his ears, red for awhile but sometimes they'd just stay blue). And it was pretty bad. The both of us, pinned down on top of each other between the long narrow space between the bed and the wall. My father above flailing away with a peculiarly perfunctory and antic wildness. With a separate kind of terror. A panic that took him somewhere else (he would glaze and fix on the air between us and him — like he never saw us at all).

He'd always use whatever belt he happened to have on, never bothering to go back to get another from the doorknob where he hung them in his room. And such was the vigor of the lashing that it was not uncommon for his then beltless pants to creep down around his knees and wind up about his ankles. Ross and I would look up from trying one to get beneath the other, the both of us endeavoring the safety beneath the bed (but with each passing year, as we grew in size, so did the inevitable futility of that unending toil), and see this. And we learned to laugh. It took some time. Several years, at least. But laugh we did. We'd be crying, begging, just mewling away, "No more, please, please."

And then, eyes wet, arms red, old bruises burning new and with the artlessness of boyhood still stuck in our eyes, we would laugh.

We'd cry until we laughed, my brother and I.

We'd laugh so hard that I'd start pissing my pants again anyways.

And then one day, on just such an occasion (bed wet, Dad in doorway, belt gliding mercilessly through loop after loop), all of that changed. I had gotten a jump on Ross, beaten him to the bottom spot in the space between bed and wall and was bracing myself for his crash when, nothing. No Ross. Just quiet. I poked an eye up above the bed and Ross just stood where he was. Just looking right at Dad.

"Dad, you'll not slap my ears anymore. You'll not take the belt to Brentwood or me ever again. If you try to, I'll take the belt from you, and then I'll take it to you. The same."

Dad took two quick lunge steps in Ross's direction and he was right smack dab in the middle of his third when Ross flicked his arm toward him before bringing it back, real slow, resting his fist and then just his thumb on the middle part of his chin just below his lip. The oddness of the gesture checked my father in his tracks and he flashed his eyes at me as if to put to me a question. But of course there was none to ask. He was just dumb-sudden confused.

"And if you ever take that belt again to Mom, or raise a hand to her in any manner, ever again, I'll wrap it around your neck to the very, very last notch and hang it right back up where you got it."

74

And I never took another beating again. I never wet the bed again after that day either. I guess Ross cured two of us that day in our room.

Anyway, that showerhead above me there on the beach, especially as drunk as I was, was a sign from God. "GO TO SLEEP, YOUNG BRENTWOOD. YOU HAVE PAID YOUR DEBT. YOU HAVE ATONED FOR YOUR SIN."

Yeah, but that was bullshit too. I started paying my debt the next morning when the sun bored through my eyelids.

My mouth and throat were barbed-wired and pickled. My brain was playing the dizzy game all by itself. And my empty stomach was starving for something to heave up faster than I could consider the possibility of putting something down. It was awful. How did Ross do it? Every single, damn day of his life.

I got up, leaned up face-first against the shower wall that had just served as my pillow, and tapped my head slowly against it, guiltfully willing an even worse headache upon myself. "Sorry," I mumbled to myself. "Sorry, Mom. Never again. Never more and never again." It is a mournful and never-ending remembrance, now.

There was one positive aspect of my beastly state that morning. So wretchedly, physically, emotionally afflicted did I feel that the attack of Ross-induced anxiety — for not having lived up to his orders of the night before that should have accompanied me on my limp and meandering way back to the house — was totally absent. I simply and purely did not care. Even I could smell the pungent insouciance in my hangover. There was no wrath nor fury, not even Ross's, that could equal the consequences of the bitter swill I had swallowed that night previous.

I crawled the stairs to the upper room like a lamb to the slaughter. Except that this lamb was not only acquiescent and unafraid, but just looking forward to the comfort of a pillow, any pillow. Even if it did wait at the bottom of a rude and rusty guillotine tongue.

I got to the top. It was silent. There was no one waiting. I checked my room. Nothing. It was barely seven o' clock in the morning.

I walked back out of my room and angled over to the other side of the living room to where I could see Ross's door. It was open. On the floor at the bottom of the doorway an arm lay, flung carelessly into the living room area. It was still and bent awkwardly. It was long and thin, with just the slightest glint of downy auburn hair riding the top of the forearm. It was not Ross's. I stared at it for at least a minute, looking around and behind me a time or two as if someone might be there to confirm what I saw. Its clumsy crook and peaceful stillness frightened me. It seemed paralyzed or asleep, but only because I did not want to consider the other possibility.

I moved closer along the wall so as to gain a better angle and see into the space. "Oh, Lizzy," I whispered to myself. "Why of all the nights to break the only promise I ever made to my mother did it have to be your last. To not even be able to make it a few measly fucking blocks home and prevent this. I could have saved us all. And now we are all dead. And it is all my fault."

I edged still closer to the door. I saw the crown of her head. Closer in. She was on her back. Naked. Strokes of red were brushed and dashed and kneaded into her breasts and stomach.

IX

My stomach fluttered in a gale of blame, and the weight of my life and future bearing this enormous burden for the rest of my life crushed the air from my lungs. The image of my own blood atonement dropped and unfurled across my conscience, the white brightness of the banner blinding me with its truth.

I marveled at how the shock and sadness of all these images (both real and conjured) numbed and buttressed me forward toward this tomb. The blood, some of it dried dark and still a bit of it radiant and fresh, curled and continued down both of Lizzy's thighs. A bruise, the color of ripe plum, grew on her left hip, just a few inches from her sacred spot.

What had he done? Oh what, what, had he done! Where were the wounds? She lay so still.

And there, in that small blasphemous room, as my eyes plodded their way down her streaked and half-spread legs to the ends where lay her feet, did I find the beloved demon. The fucked-up puck of an imp: the monstrosity of what I knew and loved, called "my brother." I almost reached out. I started to mouth the words, "Ross. Ross, we can still trade places." But I didn't have the courage, still. "Oh, what a poor cowardly wretch I am," I thought. My dead suicide of a brother lay there — nothing left but an espirit de corpse, something I could never be worthy of — and still my courage, if I had any, lay dormant in an ape coffin of love.

He lay there with his eyes closed. Propped up in the corner like some discarded stick-figure drawing. He too, naked. He too, bloody. Most of it on his face. It was smeared like hurried war-paint. Especially around his mouth.

My imagination could not fathom what must have taken place there that night. The nature of the sacrifice and the reason for a crime.

I could not move my legs. Could not move myself from my spot. I came to find myself simply standing there twiddling my thumbs (something I had never done in my life before) like a dumb, little schoolboy waiting at the door of his first visit to the Bishop's office.

And then Ross moved. His eyes still closed, he moved forward toward her. He found her calves with his hands and, keeping his arms rigid and unbroken, descended, running them up her legs, hips, stomach until they rested in firm pinch upon her nipples. He lowered and sloped his torso until his mouth and nose hovered suspiciously above her vagina. He pursed his lips and cocked a brow. He inhaled. Sharply. Once, twice, and then three times. As if he were trying to recognize and reminisce an area once marked a long, long, time ago. He harked back hard.

And then his face dived into her. And she gasped. And the arm that was once crooked and still seized Ross by the hair on the back of his head and she impaled herself even further.

Ross lapped away and the sounds were of gushing and bubbles, frocking and foaming. Occasionally he raised himself for air and a swallow. And I saw the blood, pearly in spots, drip down his nose and trickle from his mouth, like a beast from *Where the Wild Things Are*, rearing its jowls from the bowels of a kill so virgin that it still breathed.

He went back down. My thumbs were now uncocooned butterflies. And he must have heard them fluttering (although it was probably my soul thrashing) because without even raising his head, his mouth still duly ensconced, his eyes yawned bottomless and glass-shattered red and penetrated me with a warning of certain and soon-at-hand hell. I expected him to growl and bare teeth at any moment.

But I didn't bother waiting for that moment. Instead, I politely, sprightly, silently shut that motherfucking door with the nonchalance of a five-star bellhop. I ran to my room and jumped into my bed and began to pray that the whole world would go away and let me dream it all up again. My mother always told me I was innocent when I dreamed. But what in good God's name had I just beheld? Had I drunk so much as to permanently derange myself with bizarre and evil sex-fiend hallucinations of death and butchery and cannibalized blood-funneled wombs — for the rest of my stoic and unimpassioned life? Or was it possible I was still beneath the showerhead at the beach and was simply lucky enough to just be having one of the worst and most decayed nightmares of my generation?

I lay there cracked and unremoved in my little egg-carton mattress until the sun finally burst even with the window above my bed in the most eastern wall of the house. Although my pain from the night previous had subsided some (by virtue entirely of the prevailing of another), I had not slept. Nor had I even been able to close my eyes since closing the devil's door. I needed the security of my wakefulness.

As I watched the shadows get longer on the wall opposite where I lay, I heard the sobbing from Ross's corner-room of the house. I recognized the sounds of Ross's double-edged rapier of a tongue and could even feel them as they deftly found their marks in the temples, groins, and jugulars of her spirit. The immortal mortal wounder. And as her sobbing got louder, the strumming of his guitar. The generous, albeit belated, accompaniment to the woeful tones of her a cappella, tremolo coda of teary-bled eyes and an already too tender heart beat badly beyond consciousness and recognition. And maybe even redemption.

Yes. He would sing to her. Serenade her. Croon her little carols of sustenance and succor. Numb her with noels of attrition in disguise. Anoint and ameliorate the lesions and sores, boils and bruises, that he had just so masterfully unleashed upon her leprotic soul. Sing with a voice so salvific and plumb that he became instantly unrecognizable. Even more so to those with whom he enjoyed his greatest intimacies.

He didn't wear a mask (so to speak) but was nothing but mask. His aspects, tendencies, textures and traits, lines on his face, looks in his eyes; forever changing, always faithful to their fountain, their original, inherent, yet mutually exclusive, definition.

It was all language to him. Using the same tools and weapons. The identical toys and music. Much like words — and the inextricable complexions of their immeasurable promise for combinations (secret and the like) — he could manipulate the

81

same components of what he wore, the same garments he donned, the very elements he was born with, to serve him faithfully in any given situation. The same skin may cut or caress. The same mouth spit venom or kiss with song. The same hands rip a heart or point to God.

It was as artless as turning a happy face upside down. Into a frown. Nothing really moved. The positions of the pieces never changed. It was just a simple turning of the board. All angles. Obliquity — then oblivion. Which side was one on now? Wait. And now?

Pure genius. Innate and artless? Yes. But only in its simplicity. Like the perfect curvature of a rattlesnake's fang, the sickly sounding sonar of the poor blind bat, or the tacit utility of the human thumb. But still pure genius. God's great genius.

At any rate, were I given the task of making a sum of Ross and Lizzy's six month sojourn in the Italian city by the sunny Californian sea, in both the literal and figurative sense, as such it would be.

The magnetic force and perversity of their fate reposed in wry coincidence. It was T. Hardy's Ruined Maid and the man named Hap and that apathetic force that swirled them together. Me, in the middle. Drain watcher.

I heard them fight and fuck and sing and dance, incessantly. Ross blast her with his poetry and lick her wounds with his euphonious little pageants of prose. I saw all their bruises. Yes, Ross would have them too. Although I could never imagine Lizzy raising a hand to him and would not put it past Ross to inflict them upon himself on her behalf.

More fighting and fucking. All of it with passion. Most of it carnal. Some of it violent.

She catered to his every quirk. He, suddenly, to her credit cards. She tried to destroy his incredulity of her chastity (for Sin had sinned, not she) and devotion on a binge of unconditional love and the fire sale of her body and mind to any one of his daily, capricious endeavors.

He tried to destroy her love for him by crashing her brand new $60,000 BMW (gift from Malibu Daddy) on a drunken toot of Sunset Blvd.-bar vodka through the plate glass window of Rock 'n Roll Denny's. (She waited overnight, alone, in the by-the-hour, cockroach motel across the street from the jail, bailed him out, and paid the five grand for fines and damages.)

He was drinking more (she, trying to keep up). Her will to live becoming less (Ross gaining strength by the gallon). And the swirl in the drain worked swifter and swifter.

Late that same afternoon while I lay still on my bed, I finally heard him drag the drunk, puckered little thing to the shower and wash both of them off. Then he dressed her. Hid her bruises. And sent her home. Told her that was it. No more. Sent her home crying. But that only lasted a day. They would soon return. The only two inhabitants of Ross's custom-made lighthouse at the end of the world. His own little private Tower of Babel.

After she left, he walked into my room. He went over and sat in the one open window, crossed his legs like the Professor of Desire, and started stroking his chin and throat with the tips of the nails on his right hand. I looked at him and shook my head from side to side, letting him know he wasn't waiting me out today. He didn't even bother.

"So you heard me and Lizzy last night heaving and tossing. Heard her fall against the drums in the living room and . . . anyway. You must have thought old Screwtape himself was paying a visit. Screwing his very own Wormwood in there."

"It's not what I heard. I've heard that plenty of times. It's what I saw."

"Really. Heard it plenty of times?"

"Really."

"Well, then. We must purchase some ear plugs."

"Fuck you."

"Yes, quite. Fuck me. Hmm. So. You made it home?"

"I'm here."

"I see that. You like the little show?"

"The door was open."

"With a sign on it that said, 'Show's free. Standing Room Only. Stay as long as you like!' Are you getting to be a little voyeur, there Wood? Something of a vicarian? Taking another vicarious vacation through your older brother? I'm beginning to find you rather offensive. That's twice you've defiled the wishes of our mother, and all in less than one fucking day's work. Peeping Tom Thumb pervert and drunk." He looked at the sun out the window. "And all before noon. You must be rather fatigued."

I raised my right hand and gave him the slowest, longest middle-finger my courage could muster.

"To the roof, Wood." He started heading for the window above the stove and the ladder that headed for the sky. "Let's go talk on our roof."

X

$\mathcal{F}$or that first month or so, the rooftop was our place. Just for me and him. We'd go up there daily, many times at night, and feel safe and natural under the cover of the sky.

He'd spin on his stool while I'd just pace and sit, walking the perimeters of the ledge.

Usually it was just the regular: get back from the Go-Gogh's or the sand or some shop-lifting down at the Herman's Herman Gourmet Deli on the Venice boardwalk and — boom — out the door and to the roof of our house with the booze and my sarsaparilla.

"How's that root beer, Wood?"

"My sarsaparilla is just fine, thanks for asking. And your vodka?"

"The *Evian* tastes good today and — no — thank *you* for asking."

We would just sit up there and quick-sip and talk. Me and my piddler on the roof. Hashing out, mincing up, and minstrelling fresh-callow and sometimes hallow unconventional traditions as if they had been around for three thousand years. All to the tune of the riddle in his head and never losing the balance on our bottles. No, not even once.

Not even when the sun came up and our world would disappear and we would watch it rise and stare at it. Trying to see who could stare at it the longest, before it got too bright, almost happy to go blind. Not even on those few nights when all the starry, starry stars fell from the starry-starry skies and wishes came true because the truth became a wish and I would come to lack what it took to tell the difference. But Ross never did. Especially not Ross.

We would speak of our first memories. The innocent ones. Before desire required lesson and suppression. Before we had hair on our groins and evil in our hearts. The oldest memories, when eyelashes are at their longest.

Ross's was the fascination of wounded Daddy Longlegs spiders hiking on his sun-sopped morning window sill at the head of his bed next to where he woke and waited to be roused every day before school, or Saturday mornings before Scooby Doo, or Sundays (tie like a bridle around neck and white shirt), waiting to go worship: "I'd pinch their legs with a pair of Mom's tweezers, one by one, just to see how they'd manage . . . limb by limb, leg by leg . . . crippling them. Until they would finally fall off the face of their own well-spun homes. Their world. Nothing left to hold them to terrible terra firma. Not even a leg to land on. What a fucking bastard I was. But others would still be there the next day. The ones that had watched so calmly in their webs. They would always return, and even walk amongst their own dead. I remember being so curious about that. They had nary a care for the corpses of their own that gathered below them, nor had they any idea of the tweezers above."

Mine was much more simple: being in the back seat of the car, driving home from the people in the steeple on winter-Sundays. Early, black evenings with each successive long, tall and wended, lamp posted road. Both of us cast and silhouetted in motion by the setting sunshine banking on our shoulders. My connected shadows running and escaping me on the car seat in front. Just watching and chasing with my hands the endless me's of the top of my heads that rose so quickly on the seat in front and then up to the ceiling of the car and then stretched like bubblegum-shoe and "oh no, gone!" and then there would come another. Like measured time. I'd reach out to stop one. You know, one of my selves. Save myself from drifting or being taken or being spread out into anonymous outer darkness. But I would pass right through me. And Ross, always on my right, would laugh. "Here you come . . . here you come . . . here you come here you come here you come and ohhh, too bad so sad you'rrre gooone. Don't worry. You'll get the next you." I would get so frustrated. Sometimes I'd cry.

And often on our roof — very, very, often — we would speak of hate.

"Brentwood, what is it that you hate more than anything else in this world?"

I always knew what he'd say when it came his turn, and so would just make up something different for myself. That last time I just said something like, "I hate that fucking 'Pin the Tail on the Donkey' game after they spin you around at birthday parties when you're a little kid."

"How come there, Wood?"

"Seems so unfair. I mean I never had a chance all dizzy and blind and I'd just end up butchering the poor animal to death. I mean they just take the blindfold off and everybody laughs at you for stabbing a poor defenseless donkey right in the eye or nose or heart. Everybody loses in that game. And when it's over the poor beast is full of holes and everyone goes and eats cake."

Ross would just stare at the bottle. Get lost in it like he was trying to find his reflection again in another dancing-girl window. "That's a pretty damn good little metaphor for what I been trying to tell you since the beginning, Wood. You might just figure this out before I do."

And then him.

"You know what I hate more than any goddamn thing in this fucking godforsaken world?"

I played like I didn't know the routine. I wouldn't call it a game though. Ross didn't like games, except for the "The Dizzy Game" we used to play in Utah. But he sure liked to go through "routines" and "exercises." I took a mean swig on my little pee-pint of sarsaparilla and cocked an eager eyebrow.

"What's that, Ross?"

"Rapists. I could fucking kill them. Put me in a room with each and every one of them, one at a time. Just me, him, and a baseball bat." He screwed the cap back on his fifth, flipped the bottle upside down, and held it out like a Louisville Slugger. He stared at it with befuddled amusement. Like he had just fouled off a pitch that should have been at least lined into the gap in left. "I would beat them into submission and then ram the fat part of the bat right through their anal passage and right up into their liver. And I would talk the whole time, nice and slow, lovey-slutty and peaceful. 'You like that. Don't you. Does that feel good? Feels good, don't it. You know you want it. Oh, you don't like it? Well then, why did you do it to her? Did she ask for it? No? Did she cry, like you are right now? Did she plead for mercy, like you are right now?' And boom, yank it out and ram it in again. Over and over. I'd lay right on top of them and do it over and over, only stopping when they lost consciousness. Because then the pain goes away and then it loses meaning. I'm not fucking around, Brentwood. I am dead fucking serious. I would do that job for free, man. For free."

He tossed the bottle right side up again, spun the cap and took a short, quick, gutter-gulp. "Never be late and never miss a day. Arrive with a smile on my face and leave whistling a happy tune. Probably that song from Snow White and the Fucking Twelve Dwarfs . . . Some 'whistle while you work' song. Shit, or was that Mary Poppins?"

"Seven dwarfs."

"Spoon full of sugar?"

"No, no. That's the lonely old woman feeding the seagulls and the Mary Tyler Moore guy dancing with penguins."

"Fucking rapists. I have no sympathy for an act that I cannot comprehend. No sympathy for the devil from me, my friend. Just poor evil desire. And this ain't no alcohol talking either, Brentwood. And it wouldn't be evil, just decent good ol' back to the Old Testament retribution — when men were men and teeth and eyes didn't always belong in your face. Satisfying . . . savory . . . justice."

We went through this routine often. But it was always for the first time for Ross. All there up on the rooftop where all the lights were. The green and yellow when-you-wish-upon-a stars, the second moons of blue, and the black and white birds only indigenous to L.A., their eyes beaming lights on all the usuals below. Only they could claim to be living witnesses to all that

89

really happened there up on the rooftop (save that one night). Besides me, sometimes.

It was all quite predictable. And that's the way Ross liked it. A creature of very few varied routines (he could be a chameleon, but never a changeling). And I'd pretend to understand and even empathize, snorting on my bottle of beer from the root. And he had a slightly different variation each time on what he would do, to the rapists I mean. Which, with more shine from the moon, was always more amusing.

That one day, though — one of my very last days (at least with him knowing) on our rooftop as a matter of fact — I had to know just what he had been doing to Lizzy down there in his room.

"What was that, Ross? What did you do?"

His smile was soaked in sarcasm. "So. Did you like the show?"

"You're getting to be a sick old fuck, Ross. I thought you were murdering the living hell out of her in there."

"Now, now, Brentwood. Just a simple part of nature that one day you shall enjoy and experience and learn to love and cherish. Granted, it's an acquired taste. Perhaps a bit more acquired than most. But once acquired, you'll find it is required. And beyond that I cannot explain it anymore, because like all acquired tastes it's inexplicable. I'd have more luck trying to explain to you the flavor of salt or what it feels like when God finally sets in your skin — you know, when they say you're born in him — a testimony.

"You know what salt tastes like, Brentwood? It's salty. Plain and simple. It is what it is and if you ran out to the beach and jumped in the ocean and swam in it and drank it and ate it and pissed it and rubbed it all over inside and out of yourself for the next two weeks you'd still come out and have the same goddamn one word to describe it: Salty."

"It's disgusting."

"So is giving birth, taking a shit, passing a kidney stone, anal sex, and wiping your wife's ass when you're both eighty years old and you're the one left with the burden of not needing a fucking wheelchair. It's all the same. You wonder why the hell you're doing it while you're doing it. Swear you'll never do it again. Yet, it all feels good and satisfyingly proper when it's over. And then you go to sleep with a smile and wonder if god really exists all over again. Well, most of us, anyway."

I was trying hard, but the fucker was making sense again.

I started climbing octaves like my old Soda, on the bench. "But what the hell is all the blood? I've never heard of there being any . . ."

He averted his eyes to the ceiling and continued to stroke his throat. "Just nature, Brentwood. You know, time of the month and all that."

"All right, all right. But during the month . . . I mean the time, the period time of the month . . . I."

Ross took both his hands and bristled all ten of his spindly fingers at me like he was casting a spell, always talking with his hands when he knew his point was already driven home, or just about to be.

"Acquired taste, Brentwood. A taste of instinct and impulse. Given mostly to those of a baser intelligence . . . and a craving for salt. It's a natural preservative, you know.

"Besides, you remember what Mom used to say when breakfast was scarce in the morning: 'Start out every day with a dose of humility and the world will feed you all day long.' Well then, Brentwood, there ain't nothing wrong with starting out every damn day with a little egg on your face. Get it there, Brentwood. A little egg on your face! Ha! Ha! That's the old pun there working at it's most finest. Spontaneous as well. Maybe not the most classy. But class can be sacrificed in the name of opportunity. Rrright on the money. The best puns are always casual. Don't ever forget that. Yessiirree! Caassuuaall as a cat and as simple as a baloney sandwich."

I didn't get it. But at least he was in a good mood. And that relaxed me. His good moods, despite their roots and reason, always made me cozy in the world. They were a great source for my peace of mind. I didn't care where they came from. I suppose that's what made me so perilously tolerant and charitable to his cause. Ultimately it was for me. Altruism be hanged. I was dependent on him and just as goddamn greedy for what ailed me. But I wouldn't say I was back to normal. Not Utah "normal."

But he was back to serious. "Time to shake a tower, Wood. Change of clothes. We need to visit a friend on the coast." He brushed his teeth and was soon rinsing with his *Evian* bottle. I was almost asleep when he popped back in my room fifteen minutes later. "Hey, Brentwood. Speaking of acquired tastes, we got some business to take care of, like I said, up the coast."

"What? Yeah, I know. We need to go post some flyers for a guitar and bass player. Or do you just want to start auditioning those guys on the beach? We might even have enough money to spare for an ad in the paper."

"No, no, no. That must come later. That will come in good time."

I sat up and dug at my eyes. "What business then?"

"Malibu." He pulled the fateful piece of paper from his back pocket and read it to himself. His demeanor went dark and his voice got real distant. I remembered the table at Van Gogh's.

"Got to check something out. An address. Maybe pay someone a visit . . . start paying someone a visit." He sucked at the *Evian*. "You drive. I need to think . . . must have a plan." He looked at the piece of paper again. "Wormwood always had a good plan."

"Sure, I'll drive. And on the way to wherever we are going you mind explaining how the old pun works there again?"

"Why," he suddenly and very politely slurred, "I'll explain it again right now, matter of fact." Another tug-a-roo kiss to the bottle. Eyes puckering in time with his mouth until one of them finally opens up right hard on me.

"Shut. The fuck up," he explained.

XI

$\mathcal{R}$oss was silent the whole way up the Pacific Coast Highway. Up until we passed the J. Paul Getty Museum. Then he turned on the radio.

"Where's a goddamn oldies station when you want one. Is this fucking town too good for an oldies station? I just need some 'Leroy Brown' right now. Anything by Croce. 'I Got a Name.' 'Roller Derby Queen.' 'Carwash Blues.' I'd even take 'Time in a Bottle.'" He wheeled the dial back and forth, wincing through the static and cursing the age of his peers and their thirst for "this sacrosanct shit called 'rap' and 'heavy metal' . . . pure bullshit bile created by only the most talentless and fuckless musical minions and lackey hacks this side of '79 . . . Johnny Cash was the first rapper anyway. But that don't mean shit to Chuck D . . . I really would like to just kill them all. Although that fucker, *Fear of a Black Planet,* is a genius goddamn marvel that just cannot stop spinning in my head." But, alas, no Jim. And so the radio was turned off with a grunt and a "We're here, anyway," and then he just pulled a map out from under his seat and captained me up a couple more miles into the cached hills of Malibu.

We finally got to the street he wanted. He had me stop in front of a house. A sunken, odd-looking mini-mansion with a long and winding driveway that dissolved into a garden of rocks and roses. He stared at it for a minute, checking the numbers on the mailbox with the paper in his hand, one at a time, over and over. And then he had me pull up a little farther and park around the corner. He got out. Said, "Won't be longer than ten minutes," and left.

"Should I leave the car running?" I was smiling. Nervous-joking, quite on purpose. But he actually paused for a moment and considered it, rapping his fingers on his chin.

"No, not this time." He donned his mirrors, jammed his hands into his pockets, and left. I watched him go back around the corner in the rear-view mirror.

I looked around at all the other houses on the block, and wondered how people got so rich. I tried to imagine myself being rich and then tried to backtrack in my mind at how I might have arrived there. But the only thing that kept coming up was that somehow I had inherited the money. Or just got lucky. I just kept seeing Charlie and the ticket with old Mr. Willy Wonka.

The concept of working hard and then being rightly rewarded made absolutely no sense to me. I guess I had seen my father and all my friends' fathers work too many damn hard days for too many damn hard years and still see them only come up with t-shirts and jeans for school clothes (two pair, max), bottom barrel bikes from second-hand stores for Christmas, freshly painted, while Santa ate the cookies left for him underneath the tree, (Christmas morning Father: "Hey kids, now you're gonna have to wait a little while longer . . . Goddamn it! I said don't touch the bikes . . . Now sons, please. Santa just painted them at the North Pole last night. They seem to still be a little wet. Mommy has some hot chocolate and green oatmeal and cookies in the kitchen. Go ahead. Get on in there. We'll be riding before noon. Just six more hours.), and trips to minor league baseball games for annual family vacations (no complaints from me on that one . . . my favorite days of summer).

I thought to myself that the rich were born that way and the rest of us just sat around and thought about it while wearing the same jeans, painting used bikes to look like new, and trying to guess which one of the players would make it to the majors so we could say we saw him once. I didn't mind the plastic spoon in my mouth. And we'd breed and beget our own, just like them, and that's the way it was — no reason to bitch and bellyache. At least I didn't give a damn. (But then again, I was raised, at least for some years, by a man of God. My father was a preacher man.)

Ross had taken way more than ten minutes, and I was getting worried. It was going on twenty.

I just sat there getting all worried and worked up as hell, my eyes swinging back and forth from the little digital glue-on clock on the dashboard to the glue-on black, metallic, rearview mirror Ross got from a totaled Shelby Cobra in a junkyard after he yanked the other one off the Fairmont one night while we were trying to keep warm in the car waiting for this opening band to get off stage so we could finally go on at this outside gig high up in the trees at the Sundance resort. We'd gotten in the car to keep warm and faced it away from the band so that we only had them nice and small in the rearview mirror (Ross always had a hard time accepting the fact that somebody was on his stage right before him . . . especially if he thought they just might be better). He finally got so mad at them when they kept playing way past their end time that he just ripped the mirror right off. And then he was calm again. The band was still there playing for another half-hour or so. But suddenly it didn't bother him. I guess maybe they were not there, if he couldn't see them.

Then he showed. Just jogging up in the mirror, Sunday-jog like, and just hopped into the car. His right hand was bleeding. "Onward, driver."

"Your fucking hand's bleeding."

"Listen. Would you calmly start the car, mildly turn it around, and then casually drive it out of here as quickly as fucking possible you goddamn moron? . . . I'm sorry." He looked behind him, and then straight ahead out the window. "Please drive. We can talk and drive at the same time, you know."

I started the car up and tried to do as I was told. I didn't mind doing what Ross wanted if I could tell he was making an effort to be polite. It really was important to him to be courteous, most of the time. And if you know families, people that are privately polite to their brothers are usually the most polite people in society. Brothers, when they're just alone with each other, can be the most hateful and vile creatures to ever drift through life. I always did notice that about him. But lately, it had been waning a bit.

We exited the neighborhood. "What happened? Your hand? What happened?"

"I had to break a window."

"Why?"

"To get in."

"Why?"

"To look around."

"Why?"

"To see what I could see."

"Why?"

"On no, Brentwood. No, no, no. You are not getting me in the 'why' game here and drive me crazy like you used to with Mom and Father. 'Why, why, why.' Why all the way from why you couldn't stay up late and watch Johnny Carson, all the way to why the earth cooled before the dinosaurs came, and all in the same goddamn conversation. You ain't doing that to me, little brother. Ain't driving me into that crazy hole like you did Father. I'll just give in like he finally did and tell you the whole story now. I broke in to check the place out and to see if it fit the description Lizzy gave to me, and to just see a few other things as well. I was checking her story out. I am still having trouble believing the little trollop."

At the time, I was fortunately oblivious to the exact meaning — well, any meaning for that matter — of the word "trollop" (it sounded sweet, I thought it meant candy, my ignorance paying David-like dividends yet again). For after witnessing what I had very early that morning, I believe I would have foolishly taken issue with his choice of words. And his state at that time might have straddled me plainly on the fence of friend or foe, which for Ross simply translated into "enemy."

"Did it check out?"

"Yes."

"Has she ever lied to you?"

"Where the fuck did that come from?"

"Yes or no?"

Ross turned and looked at me like he would never answer that in a million years and besides it was none of my fucking business. Which it wasn't. Then he answered anyway: "No."

"What if someone had been in there while you broke in."

"Then I would have taken care of him right then and there. Although I was really not prepared for it today."

"Yeah, of course. What's his last name again?"

It had momentarily slipped his mind that I knew nothing of this story, why we were in Malibu, or whose house into which he had just broken. But even through the sunglasses I could see his brain whir and grimace as he realized he was in the process of being duped by little, younger brother. His fingers went into motion on his lap, as they always did when he tried to outrace his words with his thoughts. He gnawed on his bottom lip.

"That's all the story you're getting right now, Brentwood. Maybe Paul Harvey will finish it for me one day. You are getting better though. Very fine try. Just couldn't finish it though, could you." He lowered his glasses and winked both eyes at me, one at a time. "Just consider yourself lucky. Consider yourself lucky you know that much. And consider yourself very lucky you don't know the rest."

He looked back out the window as the very fine (and re-fined, over time) restaurants, coffee shops, galleries, bars, and musky Malibluvians (with many an incestuous sycophant and hanger-on or two always seeming to have been washed up and now towed in line behind) flew by. We made our way back down the Pacific Coast Highway and into the Santa Monica lowlands and beach fronts of humble Venice Beach and the crackhouse we called home a few blocks inland. The whole way home Ross sang quietly to himself: "Consider yourself . . . at home . . . Consider yourself . . . one of the family . . ." And I listened. And it made me think about home. And about family again. And my father in the basement, my mom beneath her stone, and snow angels. And what our parents, deceased as they might be and dead as they might seem, were thinking of us now. Ross made me think a lot. He was a mighty fucking weird one. And yet, the only definition I have now for normal.

XII

$\mathcal{I}$ suppose I can say that over the next couple of months things went well and were as normal as could be while living in the land of Ross.

I cannot, for my soul, remember how, when, or even precisely where, I first became acquainted with what would become our vulture-circling of the city. First became aware of it. Or first became aware of my position and place during the ride, like the flesh-sucking filcher existing on the underbelly planet of a one-witted shark. It was so long ago and yet but a few momentary years that he asked me and allowed me to grab on to his fife. And I followed Peter Panic in, through, and around Malibu and certain other parts of L.A. In the stalking. I knew we were following something, but did not know to what end.

The Fairmont became a chariot. The whole process, my whole memory of it, some kind of wild ride with a grimacing and contorted Mr. Toad in a Stygian myth of thanatology.

I never knew who or what we were looking for, at least not in the beginning, but Ross did. For he had seen the pictures on the wall during his first visit to the house in Malibu. The man called "Sin" (from "Sinboni"). Sin always on the left in the frames (the trophies on his arms in a special screening room, the mounted two dimensional heads yet still smiling with the Sin's nectar in their hands — I imagined Lizzy's photo to be the prettiest of them all). The same place where he had cut his hand and let the first drops of consecrated oil dedicate it as a holy place. A temple of sorts. An ending place above the earth.

And so in the banana-colored car of Bacchus, conveniently boxy and shaped like old-FBI, Ross hunted, enchanted at times with the thrill of his creep and the lurk of his crawl. He was protected, he knew, by the last straw of vaporous love that he carried on his back and by the aegis of *Evian*, his breastplate bottle.

I don't know how, but we were always undiscovered, perhaps benefitting from the Sin's own indulgent, industry-induced, single-lensed solipsism. Waiting at times just a block away from his house in the mornings (he never left before ten), we would follow no more than one block behind; in traffic, two cars behind. We would go with him on his errands. Ross never let me get close, although sometimes he would mention an encounter with "somebody" and maybe words exchanged. And I only ever saw the Sin from behind, his large gravity-challenged ass catching and billowing the floral designer shirts that hung off his very hairy back.

Ross would always make me wait in the car as he would enter the buildings, stores, and wherever else his new chum might go — a fellow puck who lived now as a neighbor across the yard and just on the other side of their friendly fence of chimerical vision — and assist him unknowingly through his last quotidian chapter, researching and cataloging his certain and timely demise.

To the delis of Malibu itself for Italian hard salami, hot honey-sweet pepper-mustard, homemade in a cauldron in the back, and New York cheesecake imported from west L.A.

Climbing with him, in the great glass elevators of Century City and downtown Angeles, standing just behind him in the pantheons of celebrity and narcissism, even once picking up for him in one of those very elevators his gold sunglasses that Ross would later wear, and saying with a sly Santa Monica smile, "Pardon me, sir, I believe you dropped these."

Unsmiling and abrupt, "Yeah, thanks."

"My pleasure. Those are nice, may I ask where you purchased them."

Smirking, still no eye contact, "Milan, kid. Custom made. Forget about it."

"Of course. Oh, and I certainly will."

Ross would dress appropriately: sometimes in a grey suit, white shirt, and tie he swiped from a Salvation Army depot while jogging through Watts. Sometimes in his rock 'n roll garb that he otherwise would only use for the stage (long sleeve, untucked button-down solid-black shirt buttoned to the top, a pair of solid-red jeans, cuban black boots, his hair French-braided a la Lizzy with a white bandana tied in a bow at the end). And sometimes like the surfer — simple enough — shorts to the knees, no shoes, scaly ribs, sanded hair in his face, and a cheap plastic version, from the beach-corner plastic sunglasses stand, of those sunglasses of gold.

Ross had learned to play yet another part. The goddamn cameo role in his own fucking movie.

He followed him at night into his private little bar-haunts along the beach, watched him dine and make his deals with Bigwigs on the balconies of piers in Santy Monticay, and set his towel down next to his to steep in the sun and wax golden on restricted movie star beaches even further up the coast off that Pacific Highway.

His favorite part of the hunt though was to go shopping with him in Trudy's Gourmet Grocery Market Place, the grocery store that sat at the foot of the U. of Pepperdine and stalk the stalk while the stalker did his own stalking. That's where he met Lizzy. That's where he went the most (and so, so did we), almost on a daily basis, until after a few weeks when Ross prohibited me from joining him on the safari any longer.

I'm not quite sure, and he never did say why I could no longer come, but I think it was because he knew, saw me, that I went into Trudy's one time to follow him. To see what I could see. For it was the last time that I went with him. But he never did say that he did see me.

And inside Trudy's Gourmet Grocery Market Place all three of us followed one another. The blind following a blond (or maybe a swarthy brown, perhaps a scarlet red, whatever he was missing from his wall, whichever frame needed to be stuffed). Ridiculous as we were, it was serious work. Shopping carts in front, careful to never find ourselves on the same aisle, reading the hanging fish-eye mirrors designed to facilitate a shopping traffic evenflow (not facilitate rape, seek revenge on God, and spy on your brother), and filling our baskets full of nothings, decorating our disguises.

Sin roamed, much less concerned with being discovered by the objects of his desire (unlike us), intending smart eye contact in order to initiate his ploy with a young'un out-of-towner who had been comin' to the coast anyway, to maybe be discovered. He drove the aisles of "Spices and Herbs," "Low Fat Dairy," and

"Strictly Vegan." His empirical stalking — I mean shopping — had taught they would be there. He feigned a bit of busyness, occasionally perusing the nutritional information on the back of some tofu weenies or a quart of extra-antioxidant, organic rice milk. The tips of his lips only rising for the micro-mini skirt, or the deepest diving cleavage evenly brown to the very bottom. And then a quick nod, a maestro two-eyed wink, social civility with just a smidgeon of "just in case" fatherly flirtation.

Ross (always the economist since his years shopping with Mom) had bread, milk, peanut butter and jelly, and bologna (three varieties of each) and *Trudy's Coupon Cutters*, a weekly newspaper available at the door upon entering that looked like a Beverly Hills real estate brochure. He walked slowly, a long, lonely aisle behind Sin, checking the mirrors, watching him work, and reading the coupons as he picked up his items from the basket, comparing prices, even a few times ripping a coupon out and shaking his head. (I imagined him, despite the task at hand, actually cursing with incredulousness the prices in his hands — despite the whole absence of any intention of ever making such an improvident and silly purchase.)

And I, never really one for the art of surveillance, just kept losing them. With three boxes of *Lucky Charms* in my cart and one in my hand (always too expensive for Mom to ever buy: "Oatmeal has iron and makes you strong now Brentwood, honey. Not food with cartoons."), reading over and ever again about the prizes inside, I kept finding myself back over in the cold cereal section, looking to see if this place might actually have *Count Chocula, Cocoa Puffs*, and *Franken Berry* (They did!).

And like I said, I kept losing them but didn't see all that much and can explain it even less. But I can speak of what I did see, and then I believe I will just let it explain itself.

At a certain point I absolutely could not find them and thought perhaps everyone had left, and once again afraid for my own ass, I broke out into a sweat imagining myself heading out of Trudy's with an empty basket in one hand and my balls in the other and Ross already sitting in the car sharpening his tongue on his belt like a barber. And then I saw them, all three of them, back in the "Strictly Vegan" aisle, the two unbroken beasts and one arbitrary piece of meat. I continued on and went down the very next aisle (luckily, my *Lucky Charms* aisle yet once again) right alongside. I was even with them and could easily hear them through a row of *Honeycombs* and *Cheerios*. I cracked a space between the two and had just the flake of a peephole between breakfasts.

Sin was giving a card to The Meat. "You may call me at any time. I have so many projects I know I could get you into something right away. In fact, there are going to be a few people in the industry at my home tonight, a bit of a party I must say. A good place to P&P . . . I mean parley and parlay — oh I'm sorry, industry-speak — you know, talk and make connections. You are more than welcome. It would be a fine opportunity. Something I might recommend you take advantage of."

She gushed and oozed, emitted flush flesh, and effused. She was fresh. Still wet. Very clean. A nice cut. Her smile, appetizing. Her chest, voluptuous victuals. The rest of her quite rare. Her countenance, cringingly assailable. In fact, in a significant way, she was already butchered.

"Oh really. Yes, well I don't know. I am kind of new to all of this. Where did you say it is? Oh, I'm so stupid and blind" (hmm, no I won't say it) — "it's right here on your card."

"Yes. Right there with my number. I can even pick you up if you like. But, no. I'm sure you have your own transport. Do you? Well, nevertheless I . . ."

Ross crashed his cart into Sin's. He was dressed as the surfer. "Ohhh, man. I am sorry. I wasn't even looking where I was going. I really am sorry there, dude. I mean, sir."

"Jesus H. Christ there, kid. Excuse yourself."

Ross remained extremely apologetic. Even bowing his head. "Hey sir, man. I am very, very sorry." He backed off a few feet, but stayed right there pretending to be looking for something on the shelf.

Sin went back to his objective. "Pardon my language, young lady. I'm sorry. What was I saying?"

"Well if I can go. I mean if I can, I might need a ride, if I can."

"Well, most certainly, once again, my number is right there. Just call before six so I can make sure and have my people there . . . well they are coming anyway. But . . ."

Ross crashed in again, but this time with his voice. And it was his, not the surfer's this time, and it was just slightly under his breath.

"You got to drug them to fuck, you cocksucking rapist?"

"I beg your pardon. I mean, kid. What did . . . Are you talking to me?"

And then shifted again. "Oh, I'm sorry, dude. I was just wondering if this was lactose free, man. This *buckwheat* mix, with the *corn nuts* and *raisins*?"

Sin didn't turn at first. His eyes just hit the ground. He took in a quick breath, but just for a moment, and regained himself suddenly and pleasantly, smiling at his next young lady before he turned back to Ross. But his eyes got wide as he made the turn, the rest of his body at least maintaining composure from the neck down. The arrogance in his voice was noticeably absent, and it stuttered a bit as he tried to find it.

"I-I-I don't know."

Ross was still staring at the box on the shelf. He picked it up and turned it around and replaced it. He began to line the words on the back of the box with his index finger. He straightened and pushed his plastic gold glasses up off his nose and back against his eyes with the other, never taking his eyes off the box.

"I'm sorry, dude, man. What did you say? Were you talking to me?"

Sin looked at the box. It was a pancake mix. It appeared to frighten him.

"I don't know."

Ross shrugged his shoulders. "Yeah, man. My old lady can't have milk. You know. She's a vegan. But this will do." He looked at Sin and started to laugh absurdly. He sounded like a donkey, braying, almost trying to sound human. "Ha-ha. Hee-hee. Hee-ha. Hee-ha. Hey man, check it out. We must have got our shades at the same place. No way, dude. I mean, sir. Well, gotta fly, told her I'd be right back. By the way, you've a very beautiful daughter." And then he was gone.

I barely beat him back to the car. And we waited in the car another fifteen minutes and watched Sin and the girl leave Trudy's. Watched her get into his car and the both of them drive off together in the direction of his house. Ross just said, "Oh, my pretty ones," and then was silent the whole way home.

He just hummed. Another rendition of "Somewhere Over The Rainbow" (sometimes with the whistling part of "If I Only Had A Brain" thrown in at the end). This was from one of two movies we were allowed to see on TV every year growing up (the other one being *Rudolph, the Red-Nosed Reindeer*). I loved both of them. Ross just *Rudolph*. He'd watch the Dorothy movie but always had the same thing to say at the end. "I don't really like this movie, Mom. Nothing interesting or believable happens until the end. When the curtain comes down on that fat man, what happens then? That's where the movie should start. That's where the story should begin. Huh, Mom?"

He hummed that song and was quiet and didn't say a word for at least two days.

And I was forbidden from ever going again.

But Lizzy had been vindicated. Her story, the one that I would eventually know, and the one which he already knew, had proven true.

But the truth meant death. Now she became stuffed. Ross had seen it. She was as good as a taxidermist's dream. She was now in a frame, a life walled in, as lifeless to Ross as that one missing dimension in the photograph. And Ross could just not break through those four holds.

That was the one thing he could not penetrate, break into, the one language he could not learn to speak. And because I am

109

his brother and loved him so much and knew him so well, I shall grant him more than the benefit of my doubt and say that deep within his soul and in all of his private moments he tried, with all his will and with every energy and last fiber of any man that knows he is in his last foxhole. The one that they will just cover up, the one that if he is lucky might have a marker put upon it, the one where many (but not all) unbelievers finally cry out for God. And he did. He used to cry out (but only unwittingly; only from his sleep). For I did hear at least that. And on more than one occasion.

But he could not. He could not learn that one last language. The only one that might have served him usefully, set him free. The one that would save him from her, and save him from his self.

And he held her accountable. In his mind she was just as guilty as the perpetrator of her loss. And like sad and sullen Pilate, he only untied his fine, filthy hands long enough to wash them.

The myth was over. He'd push his precious stone up the promontory no more.

XIII

We'd had our local success. Back there in the Pleasant Grove of the honey-hive state. Before The Angels. There in the small-town pizza joints, hoary roarings, jack-Mormon pool halls, and after-hours coffee-sans-caffeine shops and delis that turned into little Mormon beehive hovering pots after dark on the weekends.

We played private parties for Brigham Young University's pseudo "frats" and "sororities" (the university wouldn't allow those words — thus, such things were against the rules — didn't approve of groups that excluded . . .the irony there thicker than Mountain Meadows flies), taco shops, secret shotgun weddings, rich kids' parties out in the middle of a nowhere pasture up in the mountains and hills of Spanish Fork canyon and the Sundance Provo River Resort (rich kids have long extension cords), and even an open-air concert right on the campus of Brigham Young himself (the *Lard's* University). I once heard Mr. Young had quite the beehive himself, hence the nickname of the state. I do know that they call his home, "The Lion's Den." I saw it myself, written and engraved right above the door where he used to live in Salt Lake City. I even went inside once. Pictures of him and all his fifty or so wives everywhere. (I remember thinking how come he didn't have any sons — 'til someone told me all those little girls in the frames everywhere were his wives. He had plenty of sons, and daughters for that matter. Apparently too many to photograph.) It's an historical monument (they're real proud of that stuff up there). Anyway, it sure had a lot of nice rooms.

And anyway again, we only played there once. At the university. We were never invited back after Ross took the bobby pins out and let his hair down (long hair also against the rules — looks too much like Jesus, I guess?) in the middle of a song and relentlessly petitioned the audience for prayer and a glass of water he could walk on. (David and Brian almost quitting again, both of them being sorely offended — the sensibility of David's beliefs being one reason, the pure disgust of Brian's wife being the other.)

The point is, I guess, that we ran our course there in Utah. And Ross had been talking for months about taking off and going to L.A. Saying that "we had the talent and what it took to compete with all the other losers who were foolish enough to pick up stakes and head off to sell their wares in the only town where it really mattered" (although I believe he was speaking mostly for himself). We all scoffed at him in the beginning, but eventually and privately got to the point where we too realized that there was nothing left for us there. And our little local fans, our "foolish disciples," as Ross so affectionately called them from his pulpit on the stage, were about the business of saying much the same. And Ross's point, and we all knew it to be true, was that this kind of success didn't come to you. You went to it.

"Yes," he'd say. "We are the parade. We are the donkey-show gala. We are the shit. But the parade don't go parading around the back streets and backyards in front of doghouses and old *hausfraus* hanging out their whites and dirty laundry. They take it down Main St. Right? And Main St. is Los Angeles. Brentwood, would you get the map out and show Brian and David where the hell Main St. is in this country."

Finally David spoke up. "All right, you fetcher. We get the idea. Flip, let us think about it."

I should probably pause here and explain that David was born and raised in Utah, where they actually have their own state-approved thesaurus for obscenities, cursing, and all other manner of naughty depravity. Some kind of dictionary for roguish-word euphemisms. In other words, "fuck" could be "fetch," "flip," or even "fudge," etc. And then it was up to one's own tact and creativity to provide the endings. I mean making it into a verb or an adjective. Slinging an "ing" or an "ed" or an "er" on the end, or whatever. Of course "hell" was always "heck." "Christ" — "Crimany," or my personal favorite: "Crimanitally." "Jesus" — some sound or derivation that rang like "cheeses." "My God" — "My Word" (which is the word for God, I mean the word "Word," or so it says in the Bible — I believe in the book of John or Luke — so I remember from Sunday School). "Jesus Christ" — "Judas Priest". (But why blaspheme his name as well? Without him Christ would have been nothing except maybe just another silly prophet dying a nice peaceful death and all these Christians wouldn't even have a cross to lie on.) And of course "shit" was "shhhhhhhhoot," with the emphasis on an elongated "sh," just to kind of leave that delicious possibility hanging out there in the air that they might actually say the real thing — kind of heighten the moment. And then there was "Good *Night* in the Morning" and a host of other nonsensicals which covered everything else that might require more than two words and still sound somewhat similar to the real thing.

They'd just invent their own words, even though everyone knew what they were actually thinking and that it meant the same doggone-diggidy-dang thing. If you're going be like that, I mean aspire to a higher standard with all of this "in the world but not of the world" bullshhhhhhhorts, why not just have the discipline and dignity to just not say anything at all — like Mom used to? Such kidders, them Mormons. Mostly kidding themselves . . . and still not getting the joke. Jackholes.

But I do remember that David was fond of the "fetch" and the "flip." He probably would have been a great "fuck" curser. Might have even given Ross a run for his money. Sometimes Ross would even try to out "fetch" David. But he could never go it very long without falling back on the great guttural "uck" at the end. The "uck" does make the whole word, of course.

Anyway, David said we should all think about it (translation: prayer and some fetching "fasting"). I said I was in right away. I had nothing else going on and had never seen the beach anyway. Brian just mumbled, per his usual softly-spoken self. But he was smiling-mumbling. That was a good sign. He was just going to have to talk his wife, The Hat, into it. And she usually didn't say much anyway as it was hard I suppose, to speak through her giant white canopy-like Gilligan's hat she wore like an umbrella and never left home without.

But I could tell we were going. It was hard enough to argue with Ross when you didn't agree with him and he was drunk. Now, he was making this argument when he was sober and saying things we either knew to be true or wanted to believe. He had us by our balls. The only one left was The Hat. She didn't have any balls. So Ross squeezed Brian's even tighter.

I knew (and I think the others could at least sense it) that Ross had other reasons for wanting to get to L.A. Utah, the small towns, just the people in general, they had all worked on him pretty hard. He had come here on an athletic scholarship to play football and baseball. The university was private and church-run. He had been told by our parents that this is where he would end up from day one. This was destiny, not a matter of choice, like everything else in his life had been.

And then one day, right in the middle of his senior year, something or someone just flipped that big, red switch in his breast. It was the "click." The click of the drink. I think he just finally reached out himself, broke the glass, pulled as hard as he could and sounded the alarm himself. He quit all his sports. Gave up his scholarships. And stopped getting haircuts.

Now, I know that the hair thing probably sounds pretty ridiculous but that was a pretty damn big thing in that town and at that school. He might as well get a big, long, nicely-manicured middle-finger tattooed right on his forehead. Ross was marked. And the people in that town — the fourth and fifth generation locals who didn't know that there were actually towns and cities in the world that didn't have a church or a temple on literally every block, and the rich kids who were flown in every semester by their parents and who knew and treated the place like another section of Disneyland, like Bible Kingdom (they'd probably prefer Book of Mormon World, with a picture of Bible Kingdom footnoted somewhere inside) right next to Tomorrow Land and Bear Country — well, all those people just either looked at Ross

115

and felt sorry for him, or hated him. Or they just looked at him and were glad they were not him. Accordingly, he was their fray-maker and reliable Friday-night flagellante all rolled into one.

Ross wasn't really considered to have any friends. But that's kind of the way he wanted it. He was trying to live on the underbelly of that place. Only problem was that there wasn't any underbelly. So I guess the underbelly was him.

I asked him once why he was so intent on trying to reinvent himself. I thought he'd get pissed at the question. That I was making him out to be a "phony," a quality he loathed and would attack whenever he sensed it in his presence. But he, I can see now, had already put the question to himself. For he just shrugged, thought for a minute and then stared at the air as one does in delivery of a carefully prepared answer. He spoke slowly.

"Your question implies that there was something clear and definite about what it was, or who I was, before. Well, if there was, I do not have any idea about what 'it' was or how it could have been possibly defined. I do know that I had never taken part in creating or inventing or even condoning the creation of 'it.' Whatever 'it,' or I, was. And that, to not know, not have any idea, and then to live 'it,' to pretend that I even had an inkling or a whisper of an idea of what 'it' or 'I' was, was to live the biggest fucking lie and be the fanciest phony of them all."

It was not until these years later that I realized what Ross was saying: his first aggression. His first assault on phoniness, or kill, or termination and execution of what he abominated so consummately and with such profound, childlike horror . . . was himself. Whether he was conscious of it or not, I believe he preyed on himself first. I call it a suicidal concession. Others, a good old-fashioned sacrifice. The Mormons even have a surreptitious, dirty little term for it (even though most of them don't know about it, and then the others try and deny it, kind of like polygamy or God not giving blacks and women the same mortal privileges and post-death rewards as all the others): The Doctrine of Self-Atonement.

I also refer to it, in Ross' case, as common courtesy.

Whatever, even lost, wandering and saturated with self-imposed guilt, a hypocrite he would not be. "Ask me that question again in five years, Brentwood. It's a good one and I just can't do it justice right now." I guess maybe I never had to ask. No, he answered it right there and then. And then played it out in Venice by the Boardwalk. It just took me five years, and then a few more, to get it.

But it did not take me five years to understand and define his interim "it." Between the suicides that led up to his jumping ship on the scholarship to the boycotting of barbers and then finally finding a voice and creating a band.

XIV

The Big Lacuna "it" (even before we got to the beach). The one he created as his cocoon, as his shell before the real show, the bandage and disguise he decorated himself with as the wounds of change healed and his ugliness transmogrified from the opacity of dumb red storm-cloud scabs into the powder-fresh faces of snowflake rainbow sails — the kind that made him destined for nets and death and framed immortality.

It was the phoniest "it" of all because that's what it was: a literal, pure and necessary, cover. A thing that was unhideable, and which he never did intend.

But oh, how lovely and gracious and self-serving and well it did serve the band, the stage, the music, and the lucky-not-too-few misses (until the mistresspiece: Lizzy) who were invited and came and knew his colt's-tooth cradle well. And all the coveting, bitter, aspirations of all the other bulls in the barn that came along with them to see what all the fuss was about.

The Rossonian "it." The wonderful, untellable, even princely, *oomph*. The smarmy, retro-seasoned *je ne sais quoi* — implying always the substructure of a creature with savage instincts in whom blood and sex triumphed over motive and need — with only a modicum of self-conferred immortality on this, or his, eponymous. *The Oomph Boy of a blood meridian.* He didn't even need volume. He could have been silent black and white and still solely relied on his own omnipotent powers of singularly ocular onomatopoeic administrations of discharge: *Oomph*, and the air being knocked out of the innocent and suspecting alike; *Va-va-va-voom,* and Rapid Roy that stock-car boy revving his engine at the demolition derby — or just the rhythm of a musical pomp and ceremony at a strip club called Babe's Roller Derby Cabaret (the kind where the girls still wear the roller-derby queen costumes); or even a *hubba-hubba* (it meant "look alive" back when The Babe still played, anyway) for a quixotic Count or Cristo incognito.

It. He was the other "it" as well. As in "This is *it*, man. "As in that uniquely American plebeianism from the fifties and beatniks, Dobie Gillis and his most unwilling bivouac Jack. Vulgar as it is. The one where design, vice, penance, impalement, casualty and then maybe the heralded hereafter come together, happen, and triumph in the shape of a remarkably revolting nutshell. "This is *IT*, man."

Glamourpuss Ross. And all with so much reverence for me. For he knew. He knew only I could see the bloody gethsemanation beneath his skin, waking and glowing, grinning in humbled and vanquished imbroglio underneath.

Oh, yeah. And one other thing. Right at the ripe old age of 23, somewhere in that same senior and senile year, Ross decided to take up drinking. Never had a sip before in all of his life. And then one night, all by himself, he just came home from the liquor store with a half-gallon of vodka and he's never been too far from it since. Just skipped beer and wine-coolers and drinking with friends and being social (and any manner of moderation whatsoever), and graduated right to the hard, clear I-drink-alone stuff in a room all by himself: "Ross. Hey Ross, we're going out to have a few drinks," his irregular few friends that did drink would ask. "Ross. Hey, Ross goddamnit. We got some quality stuff out here in the living room. Come out of your hole and have all you want out here."

And time and time again, "I'd prefer not to. I'd prefer not to. I'd prefer not to." Sweet Bartleby the Bender. Master of persuasion, never given to temptation.

Beggar's Velvet vodka and his sweet little Lizzy. Lizzy was one of those rich, flown-in kids. She was from Malibu. She said she fell in love with Ross the first time she met and danced with him at a club called The Ivy Tower just a few blocks from the University of Brigham Young. And The Ivy Tower did bring them young. (Only had to be sixteen to get in — lone benefit of the law against the sales of alcohol within a three mile radius of the campus.) But Lizzy was a good old-fashioned eighteen — to Ross's good old covenant twenty-four. Not that Ross ever bothered to ask such questions (to the ones before Lizzy). All he wanted was their beauty (until he met Lizzy). Their beautiful bodies (Lizzy had one of those, indeed, yessiree). He just had a real firm appreciation for that full-figured, inimitably feminine, the-more-curves-the-more-reckless and all the much-much-more better faculty of flesh.

Now, as far as age goes, some of them could have been younger (driver's license; maybe learner's permit), but I know too some were certainly older than he.

Regardless, and let me be clear — with nympholepsy he was not diseased — a whole host of others: lecherousy, whore-masterosy, trollopsy, even strumpetitis, perhaps. Trifling his kenotic-crotch drive, flailing them for forgiveness while just trying to raise the dead; playing Jesus all the while to every last leper in his bed, quite possibly. But whether it was Delores Haze or her mother, Mrs. Charlotte herself, requesting his presence for a dip in their lake — for Ross it was only about, or at least most importantly about, the eidetic of the hourglass.

Yes, he was just in it for the ride, finally having a good time holding his monastic mortifications under the waves of his hooch and charging them back to their graves (whenever they did mean to surface) where they had already dragged Mom and Father.

But to speak the truth I really don't know or expect that much rocking went with that ride because at the heart of all his whoring was a cauldron of mash that surely must have siphoned all his heretofore mentioned diseases to the point of mostly being as potent as never and anon.

But I could be wrong.

So maybe his drink had done him some good, been a hedge for all of those girls. Kept him pure indeed (and I know he never did nothing with the Go-Gogh's girls) 'til his Lizzy came true. (At least that's the way I'm going to tell it.)

His clear bottle of *Evian*ed booze: a grand equivocator for all those libidinous beasts (as beautiful and as bounteous as they were).

Funny though, they still would aspire and bid at his door — keep coming back for more — until he'd scare them away. On purpose of course.

I guess, well of course, his conversation was that good. (Oh, but it was!)

I saw all kinds trundle in and out of his room. Their ability to truckle had nothing to do with the length of a certain largess tooth. And that was only for a brief period anyway (relatively speaking). Because soon enough his Trojan came a-knocking and that mare of this knight was bearing love and charity and then things that not even she could have known were only for Ross. And after Lizzy, there would be no more.

She once told me, while we were both sitting on the beach waiting for Ross to come in from a morning of body surfing and hangover management, that she first fell in love with him *not*, she said, "because of how he looked, or even because of how he spoke. It was his scent. The way he smelled. Always like fresh milk. Fresh, warm milk. At least to me." And then as she paused, her hand still making hidden hieroglyphics in the palimpsest sand just beside her feet, she took her gaze from where he was in the water and instead fastened it on one of the kiddie rides, the Carousel I believe, at the amusement park down on the pier that was just getting warmed up for another amusing day. "And then I just kept falling in love with him . . . over and over and over again."

And this was odd to me (perhaps smell has more to do with what one desires inside the protection of love, or in defense of it again, when words, images, and memories simultaneously smack together in a synesthetic anesthesia lost ad infinitum on the mind in the end) because to me he always just smelled like Mom. Which is to say like orange juice and rubbing alcohol with possibly some very old *Chanel No. 5* thrown in.

See, while in Utah, when sipping, Ross always chewed this high-priced, designer, imported from somewhere in fancy-fucksy

122

french-tickling France, tangerine-flavored bubblegum he'd buy from the gay-*París* concierge who worked at the gift shop at the airport hotel whenever we went in to Salt Lake (although he drank the goddamn cheapest, grotesquely generic, plainest-label vodka he could get his gangly little grubbers on — something a few grades above filtered *Listerine: Baron Rothschild*, could it have been?). He thought the gum killed the odor (I guess he wasn't all that smart about everything).

She really did fall for him, though. A lot of girls fell for him. I guess I just never looked at the others as girlfriends because he'd only have them over at night on the weekends and always made sure they'd leave before the next morning. They weren't allowed during a weekday or night. He called that his "inaccessible" time. "I apologize," he would say, "but I'm afraid I am, well . . . inaccessible at that time."

What he actually meant was that he was drinking and reading. Because that's mostly all he had in his room. Books and booze. And his guitar and a whole bunch of record albums. Besides, Mom — before she went — would always call on weekend mornings to check on him and he never felt comfortable talking to her with some naked girl staring at him from his bed. The first and only two times it did happen he made the girls hide under his bed with their fingers in their ears until he was off the phone. It would have killed Mom to know stuff like that, even though there was no way that she could know. But that didn't matter to Ross. All he had to do was hear Mom and see the other. That was more than enough to ignite his guilt. And the guilt — no matter if he was still drunk the next morning or not — really caused a lot of commotion with his soul and whatever little peace

123

of mind he had either scavenged or salvaged somewhere there inside.

He could never remember the girls' names anyways. Just had a big drawer in his desk where he'd throw all their numbers (little pieces of paper: ripped corners from the Bible he still kept, title pages from novels, junkmail envelopes). No names. Just numbers. And then when he'd get all lonely and glum just stick his hand in the drawer like he was playing the lottery and start calling away. He didn't write their names down on purpose. He'd just pretend to recognize them when he saw or spoke to them and rotate a few pet names and ferns of endearment into their conversations, which he kept to a most bare minimum. And when they'd catch on or when one of them would accidentally open up the drawer, well . . . if they were smart they'd figure out his game or what he was up to and a lot of times decide to stay on anyway because he was so unusually blithe, or so devil-dog handsome, or just the rebel with his own sauce (or maybe the even more peculiar and costly medley of all three) that was so rare there in Happy Valley. Or they would remember what their mommies had taught them and indeed turn the other way and run for their own handsomeish little lives. Either way suited Ross just fine.

Until he started with Lizzy. He really did like her for some reason. She had drawn a different mark on his heart and Ross had dared to look down and see it.

Until there was Lizzy. The last straw of hope he would heft onto his humped back before he headed into the desert. It had not been in crusade of crude gusto that he had been periling life and legacy — and sanity of reason — I dare wager. It had been in the desperate attempt to flee from torturing memories, from a sense of insupportable loneliness black-rooted in the crushing realization of all the mythical proportions of his religious training and a dread of some strange, impending doom. And here came the sun. Jack-long-legged and all. The most improbable *Zeusa deus ex machina* to ever creep out of a bad example of a good idea in any or all of the greatest stories ever told.

She was his worship of purity. His end of the rainbow. The spirit of Christmas. His star on the tree. A cottontail on the Peter Trail that transcended any denial in any resurrection. Feminine beauty initially disjointed from any proffer of the sentient physical sex he had so rebelliously thrust himself into. A symbol of the two things he had forsaken and forgotten about, in terms of the only woman he knew he should know. An emblem of inspiration and care. The consumptive angel who prefigured all his past dreams. A chance at a redemption that would cause the graves that he visited, and the cold angels he did forge, to finally make for him some sense and sublimate his conflict.

I was not there when the two of them first met, nor did Ross ever bother to mention it to me. It could have been as simple as an arbitrary appointment in the aisle of some austere grocery store.

They were together always when Ross was not with the band. Always and alone. The company of others unnecessary and distracting. I cannot say that during that time Ross became like some piteous humdrum, broken horse. Instead, he was galvanized in such a way that his tongue, hand, and step inherited purpose, control, and power. His chaos, never abating, became useful. The entropy on the dip-stick of his dipsomania, noticeably low. And his eyes weren't as yellow either.

All was getting pretty peachy until that one phone call. The one she made to him from Malibu after she had headed out West a month or so before me and Ross. The one that froze him on the line, bled him like a corpse before make-up, and poached his voice for three days while he paced our house like a spirit sentenced to never lie down.

He never even hung up the phone. It lay on the floor for all those days. Right where he dropped it. I went in his room and hung it up myself when he finally broke out and went for a run in the park around the corner from our house.

I wonder how long Lizzy waited before she finally hung up hers.

Before that, well, I saw them from a distance often and shared crowded rooms with them frequently. Ross always walked ever so slightly behind her (always on the side of traffic in the street), never let her open a door, whispered in her ear often (she'd favor a concealed smile, crinkle her nose, and cast her eyes at the sky), and (this may sound a little weird, and I don't think even Lizzy ever noticed this), no matter where they were — at home, inside a restaurant, fast-food drive-thru in the car or standing at a hamburger stand in the park, he never took a bite of his food until she began eating hers first. No matter how long or for whatever reason she waited to begin, he waited for her. (How undone and odd am I for noticing such a thing!)

And Ross kept his goddamned tooth in his head for that one four-month period of their impenetrable fastening as well (it remembers from some time around all the empty Christmas tree lots and Bing always singing, to sundry bunnies of chocolate and colored-egg dreams of vinegar and Mom, yes a little after that

Lizzy had gone hopping down her own trail). He kept it all shiny and clean, even tending to the glue on his gums as well.

I was actually alone with them once. Actually spent the whole night with them. And they didn't even know I was there.

I was doing the unforgiven one night. That is, hanging out in Ross's room playing his guitar, as I would often do when Ross would spend the night at Lizzy's place. I heard the Fairmont pull up, both doors shut, and the key jiggle the lock down the hall of our tiny two-bedroom house in Utah.

The dreadful change of plans.

He always kept his guitar in its case, at a certain angle, under the farthest top corner of his California king-size bed. To replace it in any other position would have been to place an obelisk under his majesty's mattresses.

And so it was fine and back where it belonged when they entered the room. But I was trapped and not where I belonged. And so I lay there right next to it.

They didn't say a word. Just turned the light out (which Ross always left on while he was away), undressed, and went straightaway to bed. I, in those few minutes, had already satisfactorily resigned and talked myself into a comfortable night of sleep beneath those springs, realizing that escape at that point was foolhardy and suicidal (I could not bear one of Ross's tongue-whippings in front of Lizzy) and that my only hope was that they left early in the morning, without Ross reaching for his guitar, after which I could finally beat my safe retreat.

Several minutes passed in silence, and soon thereafter I heard several soft, rhythmic breaths in sweet succession. The stainless sighs of sleep. It was Lizzy.

Ross tossed. Ross turned. He had always been one hard to fall. Sleep for him was haunting. It simply waited for him, like a mad curse or demon, until he was defenselessly fatigued enough where it would then pounce and beat him with vicious odes to his past and very real visions of an ensuant future rooted chiefly in death and marked blackly by loss, loneliness, and the image of an always dying but never quite dead dog, chained, as it were, to the center of the earth, while handsome men in dark suits beat it over and over again, until it cried and howled and suffered so loud. And then they would leave. Until the hound was almost healed, when they would come back again.

"Lizzy!" he whispered.

"Yes, Ross."

"What am I?"

"You are my only love."

"Your only love . . . what?"

"My only love forever."

"And then what?"

"My lover-love, and only boy forever."

"And you, Lizzy. What are you?"

"Your only girl, Ross. *Your* love. Your love and only-only girl forever."

And then Ross sighed, "Yes, yes."

"Ross?"

"Yes, my love forever."

"And what will we do?"

"Why, we'll hang this world, of course."

"And then what?"

"Then we'll set the trap for the sun."

"And then what, Ross? What then?"

"Then we'll break our chains and write our names in the night."

"No, Ross. That's not how it goes."

"Well how should I know? They're your words, not mine. Remember that, love?"

"I know *you* remember. Now say it right, please."

"Write our names in the *sky*, not night. Of course. I'm sorry. I always forget that one," he teased.

"And then, Ross, we'll throw our arms around every star in the night. Yes? Promise me we will."

"Of course, my love. Always. That is what we will do. That's why we're so good together."

"Of course, Ross. I can't wait. I love you. So very much."

"As I, you. So very, very much."

"Can you not sleep, Ross?"

"No. It's the same. Like always."

"I'll kiss your ear. Give me your ear, love. I'll nibble until I know you're sleeping. That helps you."

"Yes. Yes. I would like that."

"And, Ross?"

"Yes, Lizzy."

"My wrist."

"Butterfly kisses?"

"Yes, please."

"Where?"

"You know, Ross. Always underneath. And then up and down. Yes, there."

"Of course, I know."

And soon thereafter, with her and I'd have to say at just about the same time, he made the very same sleep sighs too.

XV

*A*nyway, the decision was made. We were going to Californ-I-A. Now, how to get the money together. The poorest guy in the band was the one most hell-bent on getting there as soon as possible. Ross. And none of us had any extra to loan. (I would always give him a few — hey, I was his brother.) But he still came up with a way to get some quick cash by devising one of the slickest, most fascinating, best, beat-all, world shakin' yard-sales I've ever had the privilege to witness. Right in front of our old rehearsal space on the corner of Main and Center. Smack-dab, center stage, downtown.

  Our plan was to leave the second weekend of July. We had four weeks. The sale was planned for the Saturday before, July 3. The Mormons would be celebrating their freedom the day before the fourth, on account of keeping the old sabbath as holy as hell (no fireworks, hotdogs, or baseball for Jesus — just baseball on TV after church behind the walls of home, where Jesus can't see). It was going to be in the parking lot of Peter Dishy's Odd and Exotic Pet World. Peter was a good friend of ours. And a great friend of Ross's. Over the years Ross had spent hours in there cooing to the King Snakes, rubbing noses with and winking to the giant rats, and perching and posing a Praying Mantis on each of his shoulders and then one on his head, all the while discoursing away with Pete every last creature that might pass through his door. I would often ask Ross why he never got something or took one of them home. "Oh, no," he would say. "I like to come and be with them. Here, in their place. All together. All at once."

And then there were The Geese.

There were the geese that Peter Dishy kept behind his store, in the backyard. In the yard with much of his pet-shop accoutrements; some for future use, others never to be used again. But instead of a junkyard dog for all that stuff Peter had something even better: A might fine fucking family of geese (excellent watchdogs, by the by). And Ross loved those geese. Loved, loved, loved them.

Because of: The Geese. As I just stated (and I don't mind quoting myself here, that is if you don't), "And then there were The Geese." The Geese. The Geese. The Geese.

The Geese (all the mommas), the Ganders, and the many, many Goslings. White Chinese Geese — a very domesticated bunch of more than finely feathered friends. I heard "The Geese" a lot growing up. But only from the mouth of Ross. I'd catch him up deep into the night, long after we'd turned in. When we still shared a bed. I'd turn over, stirring a bit I suppose, and then something would wake me. The thing that woke me I believe today was simply Ross in his silence. Even as silent as he could be, barely even making his own breath, he could somehow in his distilled absence of lugubrious sound still bring me out of some of my deepest slumbers. There he would be, just inches from me. Just staring at the ceiling. That vacant, vanilla, deaf look, not all that unfamiliar to his face, just swallowing up his eyes in severe, extravagant thought.

"What is it, Ross?"

"The Geese. Go to sleep."

Even when we finally got our own beds (on account of Ross not wetting the bed anymore and me showing signs of only getting stronger) I could still catch him from across the room doing the same on certain nights. His open eyes were always easy to see in the dark. If the moon was full and Mom left the shades open. His two eyes would grab that light so big and bright and then hold it until it was like he made it his own. His light. I even wondered sometimes if the moon was trying to steal some of it back, reflecting off of him instead, in an effort to keep up with all the stars that seemed to always get so much more attention when it came to matters heavenly and of God. That jealous moon. And when I'd say, "Ross, you awake?" he was always real calm. But not collected. "The Geese. Brentwood. You go to sleep. It will be alright."

And in later years, walking around the house in the middle of the night. Pacing halls, stairs, and even streets. Regardless the weather. Even when he finally learned how to take cover inside of the drink. It would still be: "The Geese."

But only at night. And only to me. No one else ever knew of those words. And we never did get around to talking about it. It never did seem to have the lure of discussion. For either of us.

It was only one summer in Arizona. Down on Uncle Will's farm where Mom and Dad had sent us away. He was ten and I was eight and it must have been when they decided (or maybe Dad just finally gave in to Mom's beggaring his imagination and sense of moral duty) that they needed some weeks, a couple of months or so, some time anyway, to go to some kind of counseling provided by the church, with a Bishop (who had no training whatsoever in these matters — probably never even read a Reader's Digest on the subject — but was also indeed in possession of a powerful imagination and a mighty sense of moral duty). The intent was to try and work things out, I suppose, make them better at least (but if I remember correctly it really just made things worse; for when we returned Dad suddenly lived in the basement, with his own entrance from outside and Mom by herself in their old bedroom on the second floor). Anyway, it was thought best that Ross and I visit the old Uncle and Aunt for a bit. Who lived on a farm. Who had no kids. But lots and lots of animals.

And The Geese.

Of all the animals they had — the horses, the pigs, the parakeets, cows, and ducks — Ross spent most of his time chasing around with The Geese.

And yes, White Chinese Geese I believe they were, too. He'd spend hours out there just trying to be one of them.

They honked real loud and could be real pissy if you knew how to push certain buttons. And so the Button Pusher went to work straight away.

And that's what Ross must have figured out, regarding the pushing of the buttons I mean. That although (and indeed) these geese did have those buttons, their buttons seemed to have little to do with them individually. And this fact (or should I say discovery) fascinated him to an endless degree.

All animals (I include the human animal here as well) have their own individual buttons (of course) to be pushed (or not) to the point of honking and tantrums and general dismay. But not The Geese.

No, their buttons somehow bled outward having more external connections than in. And these connections made each one unique, but in a uniquely connected and most unindividual way.

You see, these geese mated for life. And the life of their mate was all there was of life to them.

Mother goose would sit on her eggs (and yes, I did check and no, none golden) and the gander would go out in search of food and Ross and I would be just as tongue-tied and befuckled as could be at what we would then observe. For every time we gave that gander what was the most coveted corn of the barn (the better to fatten him up, of course, just like Uncle Will had instructed us to do) that goddamned bird wouldn't have any of it. Oh, he'd take it. Yes. And then strut it right home like only a goose can strut (and believe you me they strut a lot faster than any eight-year-old could ever imagine in his "this goose-could-never-outrun-me" meager mind). To his one true, blue, and always coming home to, only you . . . *love*.

And then make sure that she not only ate first but ate every last bit of it. Until she absolutely refused to have any more, before he would then finally go out looking, with standards much lowered mind you (oh, mind you me) for himself to feed.

Three times while we were there we slaughtered The Geese. Ross and I had the job of locking the barn door and then chasing around some one-hundred or so terrified little honking souls until we finally caught one. And then we would hold them up by their wings and walk them out to the chopping block while they screeched for mercy and desperately protested. All the way to the chopping block where we held them down for Uncle Will with his big cheery cherry smile and his axe very sharp and covered in blood quite a ways up the handle.

The Geese always knew something was very wrong before we'd even get to closing that door. They would gather in a mass all huddled together in the farthest corner. And then run amok and shriek in terror as we approached. And then as the rest shuddered to a dull, white noise the one in our arms would cry even louder and struggle that struggle of the one last lying hope.

All the way out until its own most personal and intimate earthly finality.

On more than one occasion a goose (male or female — it made no difference it seemed) would step forth from the horror-struck flock. With every feather a-quiver and its head diddering slowly and widely from side to side and then to and fro, as if to say in the calmest, most polite possible way while even soiling itself simultaneously: "Please, please, please! No, no, no?" As such it would step, with a tremulous almighty bravery, right up to Ross. And sometimes me.

It would be the mate of the one we had plucked from the flock. The one we now had in our clutches. It would even make eye contact with us (this had never happened before). It would remain very nearly fixed and almost unmoved before us, having embraced the worst fear life had to offer.

And if we paused and stopped there with it, yielding as it were, if but only for a moment, it would just about still itself entirely. Save a wispy, remaining sway of its neck and a low, anguished hink-a-honk cuing. And then the one we held would still itself as well, and begin to cue in kind and do the same sway.

It stood there before us to comfort its lover and stand there with it. With it until the very end. Until we marched its love away.

Goosey Goosey Gander, wither dost thou wander?
Upstairs, downstairs, in my lady's chamber!

That's how Ross would greet the geese behind Peter Dishy's. And chase them until they were honking up a storm and had all coupled up together. And that made him happy. He'd find his biggest grin and stand there with his arms across his chest and shake his head in wonder. It always made him very, very happy.

And Peter got a real kick out of it too. More out of Ross, though. He, of course, never knew what Ross was really thinking.

And, of course, Peter welcomed our use of his store front and parking lot that day. He was having a sale on ravens anyway. And he thought that weekend might be the perfect chance to maybe raffle one away.

XVI

The four of us plus The Hat made plans in the office (rehearsal space) one night after practice.

Ross, per usual, was maestro. And we, per usual, were his fiddle to tune. "We got to sell all in one damn day, boys. All sales final on Saturday. Next day's the Sabbath. We don't want any menacing Mormon Jesus's turning our money tables over and getting all holy highbrow on us in front of Peter's." It was this type of talk that really pissed David off. The only thing that David would never put up with. Ross knew the Bible very well. We both had been weaned on it. Ross even taught himself how to speak Spanish when Father was sent to Mexico for a few years as a preacher, and as a teenager he had read the Bible in Spanish, twice.

The Bible and bullfights. That was Mexico. Dad loved to take us to the bullfights. Right after church, in fact. Wherever he preached he took us with him. Tijuana, Mexicali, Juarez, San Miguel, San Andres, San Pablo, or even the wondrous Mexico City itself. To church for some worshiping and then to the stadiums for . . . really much of the same (just with a tad more death, it seemed). Why I don't even remember going to church in Mexico without seeing a bullfight either before or after. We'd watch dad preach in some old chapel and then head to a stadium and watch bulls get murdered and then quickly dragged out of sight by gallant men dressed in the same indigo and gaudy almagre as the whores in *la zona norte* Tijuana (or whichever city we were in) with whom Dad would always later share tacos and tequila and then with whom he would soon disappear (the whores; not the murdering bull-butchers, I mean). "For some personal preaching," as he always took his scriptures with him (which I guess made sense: first the sacrament, then some sin, a little bit of penance, then do it all again).

The bulls had their *querencia* just as my father very much had his. Ross did too. And hemmed into them so did poor mother and me. All of us herein always and unknowingly only facilitating (or is it honoring?) that sullen psychopomp who carried the blade.

All this while Ross and I sipped our own little *bebidas requeridas* (he, *Sangria*; me, *Jarritos Tamarindo*) from dusty, old highball glasses and black paper straws while seated at the bar or at very small, square tables. He'd leave us with a big plate of tortillas and a few coins for more drinks and the jukebox (*"Ay, Ay, Ay, Ayyy, Canta Y No Llores!"*) and instructions not to move unless we had to piss (he always pointed out *los baños* for us first thing) and we'd wait with our bullfight programs from the day, reading them as much as we could in Spanish, studying the pictures on each page and watching the rest of the women dance, dart, and hang around the other men like sweetmeat-striped hummingbirds at their feeders. They'd always exchange a pleasantry or two with us. Even flirt, I suppose. You know, a few hugs. A couple of kisses (I believe Ross even caught some tongue a couple of times).

"*Cuantas orejas hoy, mis hijos tan hermosos!*" (How many ears today, my beautiful sons?)

"*Solamnente una.*" Or, "*Muchas!*"

That's how Ross would reply, referring to the ears sliced off the dead bulls and awarded the *matadores* (Spanish for *killers*, of course) if the quality and style of their killing that day made it so. (On occasion an ear would even be made a present of for a special lucky lady by the killer himself.) But that's all Ross would really ever say after the fights and in the cantinas. And during the fights I don't remember him really saying anything at all. He was always still and silent on those Mexican Sundays. But not so bored. I wouldn't say that. His eyes were just as intense as ever and maybe even scared (it is always hard for me to tell the difference between the two). And with his Spanish-English dictionary, a pen, and as many bullfight programs as he could beg Dad to buy, those days were as piquant and precious for Ross as I'm sure they were for my father.

And yes, on days when the programs were few, he'd read the Spanish Bible too. And, like I said, not just once had he read it. I'm talking cover-to-cover, twice. Now, that's in addition to at least several in English. Like a goddamned novel he'd read it. Ross even used to translate for Father when he'd travel to give sermons in church meetings in chapels in all those cities. But Ross was the star of the show. Everyone thought he was a real Mexican teenage boy that Father just dragged around with him because Father's Spanish was just so *mierda* (that's "shit" in *españolie* — one of the few words I know). Santa (that's españolie for "saint," by the way) never made good on the gift of tongues for dear old Father and me. Plus, Ross's accent was real good.

Plus, he was a lot darker than our blondie Father, and a lot better looking. (Blessings from Mom . . . for whatever that's worth. I just remember those Mexicans really appreciating handsome devils.)

And that Spanish would come in good and handy later too. For nowhere was our band more popular (in most places we traveled not even known at all) than just right over the border from San Diego in Tijuana. And it was with Ross's Spanish that he would first get us those gigs in those most prestigious TJ clubs and then get our songs played on the local radio and in the jukes of all the local bars *por la Avenida revolucíon* and eventually well stocked in every single little Mexicali cd music store.

Tijuana was in love with The Hinge. And The Hinge loved right back. We'd play there several times a year in the two biggest rock 'n' roll clubs in that Mexican town: Señor Salamander's, Jose's Sweet Suenos, and La Black Knight. We'd have either place packed every time (upwards of five-hundred in attendance: a mixture of locals and the weekend Californians under twenty-one who crossed the border to drink and play like they were three thousand miles from home).

Those gigs were just big parties. Almost like welcome home parties just after the first few times. And we would ever have the most interesting and famous of guests.

Bonnie and Clyde would show up. Nabokov and even a Kundera. With them always we'd see Dr. Jekyll searching frantically for Mr. Hyde. Then there was the Grinch. Oedipus, of course always with mammy at his side (*y que mamítas calientes también*). A few guests right out of the Bible itself (including God and Satan himself). And we were never without a whole stable of porn stars (each one with their director) and more deadly sin than contained in the *Confessional Cathédrale de La Ville Lumiere de Notre Dame.*

"Good Together" was the song we always opened the show with in TJ (right on the heals of The Mills Brothers' "I Don't Know Enough About You," *por su puesto*). It was a good, hard, bluesy rocker just slow enough to let people hold and feel one another and trade partners on the choruses but just fast enough to let them swing and dance like mad as they all sang along. Everybody knew the words by heart and it was in consummate costume (oh, what garments quite camp) that many would attend (I loved the ones who came as Christmas the most).

Yes, bound and determined they would be in front of The Hinge. To not only honor their that-night chosen character but also to completely fulfill their role with every unhallowed bump, grind, and low-center-of-gravity thrusted wriggle they could muster and mobilize at will.

We could be so good together
Hanging this world and setting a trap for the sun
I'll be Bonnie, you can be Clyde
I'll let you Jekyll if you let me Hyde
Ol' Humble Humbert and Lovely Lo-lee-ta
I'll be the Savior and you be Iscariot

We are so in love with each other
Breaking our chains and writing our names in the sky
I'll be Thomas and you be Teresa

You be the Grinch and I will be Christmas
I'll be the son, you be my mother
We'll make ol' Oedipus so jealous

I'll be gluttony you can be pride
Five more, hey we got all night
You be Samson and I'll be Delilah
I'll be your porn star and you my director

We are going to live forever
Throwing our arms around every star in the night
I'll be God, you can be Satan
All the details we can work out later
You down on me, now I can go lower
And if we get caught, we'll just call a "Do Over!"

We'd play two nights at one club and then come back months later and play two nights down the road at another. And on the second night of each leg Ross would always open the show by saying (after the lights went down and our Brothers Mills had bowed out and the crowd was hushed and waiting):

"*Anoche, fue la primera cita. Esta noche . . . nosotros . . . HACEMOS EL AMOR!*" The place would then explode.

And then the first few bars of "Good Together." And what with the last line of the song we sometimes would play it over and over and over. Until Ross would just stop it himself and say, "*Basta, mi gente. Se emborrachan mejor con muchas botellas, no solamente con la primera, mis amores.*"

143

Mom and father would say Ross had the gift of tongues. But Ross just sneered and grimaced at that as he got older. "Gift of tongues my white Mexican ass. I lived in the streets with a notebook, a pencil, and a tape recorder. And at night recorded myself talking until I could play it for the *hermanos* down on the corners and in the chapels until they couldn't tell me from the other locals I used to walk around recording. My gift was being bored and a bit fucked in the head. I just couldn't stand the fact that I could walk around and have people talking without me knowing what they were saying. Drove me insane, Brentwood. Absolutely fucking insane. I mean, they could have been talking about ME. And as a matter of fact they were, quite often. But I sure put a stop to that, and speaking it better than most of those goddamn natives." I do remember Ross seeming pretty happy and friendly back then.

Oh, man. Anyway, Ross knew his scriptures better than most I came across. A whole hell of a lot better than David. And David knew it. So Ross would throw it around whenever he wanted to make a point to David. Or sometimes simply just to amuse his own self. Especially when David would try and stifle his swearing.

"*Verily, verily, he went into the temple, and began to cast out them that sold and bought in the temple, and overthrew the table of the money changers, and the seats of them that sold doves. And would not suffer . . .*"

"Fetch, Ross. Man, come on." David would try not to look up. He knew he had a better shot with Ross if he avoided eye contact.

"What is the matter, David?" Ross, as customary, would get all timid and innocent. He'd put on his best little-kid veneer and start hunting down David's eyes.

"Yoou knooow. Hee, hee, hee." David would tug at his pants, start monkeying with the knobs on his guitar, and try his damndest to simulate a sense of humor about it. "Fetch. Hee, hee, hee."

"No. Really David. Share with me this time. I really do not. I mean you were not planning on . . ."

But David would have none of it. He hated the mocking. And he knew when he was being baited. He knew Ross was only playing. Being friendly. But it was still mocking, and it really did pain him. David wasn't what one would necessarily call the keenest arrow in the quiver (but his axe was sharp — man, he could play guitar) and had never really had the knack for cracking a book. Even if it did come in black and promised "holy" on the cover. He was born and reared there next to the dead sea waters in Utah and, like most where he was from, his father had done all the reading for him and David just did as he was told: "Believe. Have faith. Believe. Don't question. Believe."

But he did know when to walk off and what was worth what when it came to contention. Especially between friends. He was the opposite of Ross, really. But for some reason — a reason that anyone who knew them both could never figure out — they had been friends for years and defended each other to the nail to anyone else. It's funny now that I think about it, but almost all of Ross's friends sat around a lot looking at each other trying to figure out how the other could stand to be around him so much. And yet, there they all were.

David slammed the door to the office behind him. He fled quicker than usual this time. I could hear him take the one flight of stairs down three steps at a time. Ross went over to the window and waited for him to get to his car. He barked down, "You weren't planning on selling any fetching doves now were you?"

David pretended not to hear. And he probably had no idea — or if he did, just a very vague, fatherly, mention of one — of what Ross was referring to. Ross wrinkled his eyes, puckered his lips, forced a smile, and then looked over at me and winked. Then he turned back toward the window and followed David's car out of the parking lot. His face went back to blank. "Doves."

"Doves?" I said.

"Yeah. I wonder if they were the white ones."

Then *I* pretended not to hear.

The plan for the great yard-sale was to have all our stuff set up on the corner in the parking lot of Peter Dishy's Odd and Exotic Pet World by six o'clock Saturday morning. Even though me, David, and Brian had enough funds put away between the three of us for gas money and some rent until we found some jobs in L.A., we still had some stuff we could unload at the sale for some extra cash for the trip. The sale was really for Ross. I don't know if anyone really had any idea of his actual financial situation. We knew he hardly worked. He delivered pizzas occasionally for some of the pizza joints where we played. He used the old roughed-up, white-walled '79 Ford Fairmont that Father let him have when he went home for Christmas once after two peripatetically imposed years in college. It was dingy urine-yellow, dented on three of four doors, and as square as a mousetrap. It looked like old FBI from a rear-view mirror. Inside, it was zitted with cigarette burns and dull vodka dye. It too smelled like orange hawkweed gum.

On other occasions, some old buddy of his who ran a pyramid scam out of his house would let Ross come in whenever he wanted to cheat old ladies over the phone for minimum wage an hour selling souped-up snakeskin soap and shampoos. He called his business *Skin-New* (slogan: "All of the good. None of the bad." How fucking original is that?). He'd get minimum wage and, if he wanted, the freedom to phone up all the friends he ever had (and of course family too, that was especially encouraged) and hoodwink, network, and then labyrinthize them into some pretty fine, bootlicker commission for himself. But Ross hated that, "I hate fooling people I can't look in the eye, just doesn't seem all that damn fair — reminds me too much of praying."

But for the most part, he had spent at least four of the last six months there in the company of Lizzy. Just living off of whatever he had cached away before then. But she had been back home for going on two months now, and Ross was having to make new holes in the one black belt that he owned and wore everywhere.

But no one was really surprised when he didn't show up at 6:00 in the morning that day to help set up the signs around the block and the tables in the parking lot. It wasn't unusual for him to show up for gigs seconds (literally) before we were supposed to go on. The rest of us sweating on stage, fiddling for time and tuning our instruments for about the fifteenth time while an angry manager or owner paced, cursing his ass off in the wings. We finally figured out that Ross was actually always on time.

That he was there, just unseen. I mean just not on stage. And would suddenly just seem to materialize as soon as we played the first few notes to the very first song.

Ross always liked to appear on the scene as if he'd been hiding up someone's sleeve (sometimes even his own). Once we figured that out, we'd just start playing the first song right on schedule and Ross would appear out of some doorway or hallway. A bathroom or closet. Or occasionally he'd just stand up from where he'd been sitting behind a guitar amp, in the shadow of a curtain just offstage or — if we were playing outside — a bush or a tree just a few feet from us. After a while we even stopped looking around to see from where he would appear and just waited for the sweet — or sometimes maniacal (depending on the song and his mood at that moment) — sound of his voice on stage. Most of the time it would drive the others absolutely nuts. But I kind of relished those little game-playing trick entrances he used to make. I've never seen someone so in love with and so adept at entertaining themselves. Everyone else in his world bored him so terribly.

But he always made up for it afterwards, though. He'd carry everyone's equipment out to their cars for them. Always drive back to the practice office with the rest of us. And insist on carrying all of it up the stairs by himself. Of course we never let him carry it all, we'd have been there for hours. But he came pretty damn close a few times.

Like I was saying, we weren't really expecting him at that hour on a Saturday morning. On Friday nights he was "accessible." Which meant Saturday mornings he kind of wasn't.

What did surprise us is that when he did show up — at around just before noon — crashing up on the sidewalk in his old, faithful, piss-colored pumpkin and sending The Hat into a brand new partition of her Gilligan, we could tell he had been up and working all of the morning, if not a good part of the night as well.

The four-door Fairmont was full and stuffed to the ribs. Busted and bursting, top to bottom, with boxes, clothes, a broken down bed frame, and more clothes and boxes. He had tied his old oak desk, the one that our grandmother had given him from her attic when he first got to college, to the roof of the car. Its legs shooting straight up to the sky, the second-hand Sears swivel chair minus one wheel parked loosely in its upside down cavity. All four windows were rolled down and hangers, shirts, towels, blankets, and even a couple of lamp shades poked through and hung and fluttered in the back-breeze of his landing on the sidewalk. The trunk was open and its lid forced to its maximum height where even more boxes and a coffee table I had never seen before were crushed and choked so tightly that the removal of one would have meant the collapse of the whole creation.

On the hood, tied down with the same combination of fishing line, bungee cords, and weather-tattered clothesline rope and wire from some apartment building in back of our house, were two hand-push lawnmowers and an old black and white TV with the tin-foiled rabbit ears still arched and straining for reception. The TV was straddled by a mower on each side.

The car and the imagery of Ross actually packing it so amused me that it took me a minute to finally realize he was yelling at me to come over. The apocalyptic vision of his car, in all its beautiful destruction, kind of made the world go mum on me for a minute. Plus, Ross was trying to yell with his stuck-open butterfly knife in his mouth. He looked like some sundown junketeer just back from looting the night away.

I walked over to his side of the car. He was clamped in by two boxes he had wedged between him and the steering wheel. The veins in his neck were bulged and blue and he couldn't unplug his arms from between the boxes to get the knife from his teeth.

"Where in the hell did you get all this stuff?" I bent down to get a closer look at the dam he had built in the back seat. Two microwave ovens were sandwiched between a complete set of Encyclopedia Britannicas from 1976. All the way from A-Z. The microwaves, though, looked brand new.

"Get this damn box off my chest, man." He was wheezing a bit, just barely making intelligible sounds through the teeth and metal in his mouth. "I haven't taken a breath since I left the house. Hurry up, man. Fuck, I'm serious."

I reached in and started pulling. There was no way in hell. "Brian, David, get over here. I can't budge this and Ross's face is getting kind of purple." They were both still laughing as they circled around the car, but got real serious themselves when they saw the expression and the color in Ross's face. His face was really blooming. "Here," I said, "somebody get around to the other side and start pushing. David, you go. Brian, start pulling on this box with me."

And then things just got worse. As we loosened one of the ropes tied from the front seat to the back and keeping a couple of ceiling fans from flying out the windows during the drive, it got caught around Ross's neck and was pulling real tight. Everyone then started sprinting. A regular, old chinese fire-drill. Ross couldn't talk anymore, and for the first time in my life I was the one giving the orders.

Frantic David cleared out the other side of the front seat and started pushing and kicking stuff off Ross's lap with his legs. Brian grabbed at any part of the box that would allow a grip and started pulling and scratching like someone was dying while I tried to loose the rope around his neck. First, he tore the top of the box off, and then the sides. Everything inside just spilled out onto the ground. It was all books. Must have been about fifteen of them. Big, thick ones too. David was still on the other side — his ass in the air in the front seat and his face to the ground just outside the car door — huffing and puffing and just kicking away like an old, insensitive mule. Books flew up and out the other side door as if the car itself had decided to vomit the spoils. A couple hit Ross square in the nose as he turned to face David and the bucking of hind legs. Finally, with his arms free from being pinned by his literature, he took the knife from his mouth and cut the rope from his neck and dove out on top of where me and Brian had fallen into the gutter.

"David! David! We got it, man. Stop! He's out! He's out!"

He couldn't hear us and still felt something at his feet and just kept going. Finally Ross said something. "Jesus Christ you goddamn donkey. You're getting my books all dirty in the fucking street!"

David heard that. He rolled out on his side of the car and came over to where we were lying. "Hey! Fetch, man. You can't be yelling that kind of talk in flipping public. You . . ." Ross stood up. His face was bleeding pretty bad. Not only had David managed to boot him a few times in the nose but it looked like the knife had left a nice slice on the left side of Ross's mouth, right where his top lip met the bottom. It's kind of ironical when I think about it now, but David just took the last straight thing on Ross's handsomely twisted and hound dog jagged face and made it crooked too. He probably should have got it stitched up at some point that day. But Ross didn't like hospitals — nor people all dressed in white for that matter — so of course he never did. And anyway by the time he learned to keep his left side still enough so the scar wouldn't open up again and bleed, some time around Halloween there in Venice I believe, he was already well addicted to his new look. I don't think Ross ever even tried to smile straight or talk the same again in his life after that. At least not since the last time I saw him.

David got scared. He turned whiter than an angel. "Oh, flip. Ross, I'm sorry, man. I really am sorry." And then he just shut up because Ross started walking toward him. David was standing next to the Fairmont where a lawnmower was hanging off the hood. Ross saw his knife a few feet away, walked toward it, and bent down and grabbed it out from the gutter. He looked back up at where David was frozen, kept his eyes laid right into his like he always did when he was on the verge of getting real serious and urgent, and walked the rest of the way up to him. He got close enough so that he could kiss him. He was still a little hoarse. Or maybe he was whispering.

"David?"

"Yes."

"Do you know who the king is in the land of the blind?"

152

David flashed a fidgety glance at me, then Brian, and then faced Ross again. He said nothing.

Ross smiled. "Why . . . *Me*, David. Who the hell else?" One of his big, certified, Ross smiles. So big that the blood spilled thick and free from his lip. And then he really did it. He gave David a kiss. Just grabbed both of David's shoulders and forced a big, hushy-mushy bloody one right on his cheek. And then he took the knife and started to cut the line off the mowers on the hood. "David, you're just trying to help. You saw me in trouble and did what you saw best to get me out of trouble. Not many people do that as quickly and as fiercely as you just did." Ross went around to the other side and started cutting the rest of the stuff free. "You're my best friend, man. Now how about you and the other two guys standing over there give me a hand and get this crap up so we got some money for this little excursion to L.A. Hey, Brian. The Hat got a band-aid or some cream or peanut butter or something to stop this bleeding? I don't want to get too used to the taste of blood." Ross smiled again but flinched suddenly at the pain. He covered his mouth with his butterfly and tried to hide a cringe.

But that was nothing.

"David, now you remember what we planned. After we get this all unloaded I'll park the car a little more nicely here in front of the store, right in front of Peter's. Just set up your guitar and amp on the other side of the Fairmont. Grab an extension cord and plug in over inside of Pete's. He's expecting you. "Right, Dishy? Hey, Peter. Come on out here!" Ross motioned at Peter, who had been watching all of this on the other side of the big plate glass window in front of his store. He came sprinting outside with a big, wide smile on his face, a big, black (but wing-clipped sadly) raven on his shoulder and a Chile Rose Tarantula he was still lovingly caressing between his palms.

"Can I hang it up now, Ross? It's all ready. I just need to jump up on your car and hook it from both ends so it hangs up real nice and high above the window and all the birds!" Pete had a banner for the Raven Raffle.

"It's all yours, man. As soon as we unload and I re-situate the Fairmont you hang that bastard banner up there nice, big, and high. What's a third of July celebration without a yard sale, some hymns nice and patriotic, and a fucking Raven Raffle. How many you got?"

"One to raffle and twelve to sell, man. All still perfect little juveniles just craving a home. They are so magnetic. So odd and magnetic. And they're discounted way down, man. These people got to know about this sale, man. You won't see ravens flying this low ever again. I promise you that!" And there they all were in the window behind the car at that. Each one on its own little perch. All quite pretty and as shiny black as new polished Sunday shoes.

And then the banner was unfurled. And then the banner went up:

AN ODD DISHY RAVEN — GIVE ONE A HOME TODAY!

XVII

$\mathcal{I}$t took us about an hour and a half to unload Ross's car and get it all organized on the sidewalk and in the parking lot. He finally explained to me where all the extra stuff came from. "Storage, man. I've just been collecting it for the past several years and putting it in storage. You know, thought it might come in handy one day. Just like today. A lot of it I've been picking up cheap at yard sales myself."

"And this new stuff?" I asked.

Ross flittered all ten fingers about six inches from my face. "Unload and set it up, Brentwood. Just unload and just set it up."

And so that's what I did. Shut up. Just unloaded it. And just set it up.

By mid-afternoon, our little sale was actually going pretty good. There was a decent stream of people milling around downtown, most of them waiting for the fireworks to start at the park catty-corner from where we were set up on Center and Main. Brian and The Hat had sold a couch, a love seat, and some pots and pans they said they didn't use anymore. I sold my ten-speed, figuring I could always buy another one and not planning on using it much on the beach where we were going. And David was having an extreme amount of prosperity selling all his old record albums. They were vinyl and the kids liked the big pictures on the covers. Mostly Led Zeppelin, Ozzy Osbourne,

Jimi Hendrix, and anyone else he had once idolized as the young and undefiled teenager.

And Ross was out working the crowds and passerbys in the street like Mr. MePhisto himself. He was the mirror-ball man. He took snake-oil salesmanship and tossed in a little black and white Andy Griffith and turned himself into a brand-new *It* all over again. He bobby-pinned his hair back all nice and secret, put on a white shirt and tie, kept his mouth full of an extra piece of spicy orange *mélange* and even a dash of Listerine, and snorted his *Evian* bottle as warily as a wily coyote. Because he knew. He knew that *this* stage wasn't so elevated, that he'd be a little more equal with these people, and that his performance would have to be elevated in other ways.

He knew they'd all be there that day, their fourth of July. The venerable retired couples, all shuffling and squinting. The hard-working middle-class, all too pridefully humble — with their small, snotty, precious, second-hand smoke for children. And even the usually cautious cavalier who hid higher than the others and built lavish homes in the foothills and mountains on the upper levels of the valley, so as not to flaunt his blessings of wealth on those below and feel badly about it afterwards. He knew they would all come down to dwell in the valley that day, for one day, to be with the common man on a common holiday. They'd all look the same anyway. Everyone wore plaid on the fourth of July in Utah.

Obviously, as individuals, everyone in a crowd is very different and distinct. But, as crowds go in terms of congregation, well, I'll let Ross finish his own thought: "Let's just say a herd of sheep, by any other name, is still a fucking herd of sheep. And,

156

verily verily, I reveal unto you, Brentwood, Brother of Ross, you may even dress him, whom they call their shepherd, in silk. But he still smells the goat."

I could never be that profound.

So, in other words, if I may take the liberty to again put Ross's words into mine (because he can't do anything about it now anyways, I guess) they weren't out for a good time, or to feel better. They were just out to feel like they were better than somebody else, which, if I may now contradict myself, was their way of having a good time and feeling better. And that meant they just spoke a different language. And Ross knew that. That is why they were there. And, I guess, of course, being the day before the fourth of July, there were going to be some fireworks as well.

When the dusk settled, Ross had everything that had not been sold set out in front of the Fairmont's four-bulbed high beams. He had about thirty minutes before the fireworks would start. He went over to David and whispered something in his ear. David went back to where he had set a chair up a few feet back from the Fairmont, picked up his guitar, flipped the switch on his amp, and gave a thumbs-up to Ross. Ross then looked over at Brian who was standing next to a stack of speakers where Ross's mic was plugged in, and nodded.

Ross hopped up onto the hood of his car, slowly spun around as if to check his bearings, and then skipped up to the roof.

He had changed out of his black tee-shirt and jeans and was now wearing a long-sleeve, button-down white shirt with the collar tucked all the way in and the sleeves buttoned down to the wrist. On top of that he had slipped on an old, dark black suit coat (it was tight, about three sizes too small), except that he had

157

put it on backwards with every single button done up his back. The very edges of his tucked-in shirt collar rimmed just discernibly enough above the coat in front.

He had also somewhere found and was now wearing a pair of generic, black Buddy Holly-type reading glasses. They perched on the tip of his nose and the thickness of the glasses themselves made his bloodshot eyes look like a pair of polished, cheek-bursting, jumbo jawbreaker balls.

He held the microphone in his right hand, placed his *Evian* bottle at his feet, and held the big, black book (black electrical tape on the cover to hide those two words) in his left hand like old Pablo Bunyan might have done, full of vengeance and just heading back into the woods.

Good gracious god, I thought. He's the preacher man from hell. No, he's the preacher man in hell. No, no, no — he's the preacher man that's sucked so much hell out of the world he's been preaching in, that now all the hell he's sucked is instead inside of him. A preacher man who could never just get the hell out! He looked as scary as Father after a row of preaching to Mom.

People actually started to gather in front of Ross. And there were more than a few. Yes, I would say much more than a few souls that were now looking his way.

Ross played the part to the ham bone that he was and never even looked up, instead licking his finger while paging through the big black book with the conspicuous electrical tape and then finally readjusted his glasses.

"Now if you will kindly pick up your books and turn to page 222, we'll ask you all to sing. You'll find your books on the backs of

your seats." (People actually looked for these books on the backs of those seats.) *"Are we ready? Everyone, 222 let's really enjoy ourselves, let's live it up. Let's have a happy time. Let's feel it with a great exuberance, it's not raining inside tonight. All together, thank you kindly kindly."*

David started playing the guitar. He was playing softly, but loud, just kind of picking and chunking it. The chords echoed and lingered with a singular, nimble timbre. He had a one-second delay on his effects box that made for a nice fat twinkle through the parking lot. They were simple chords. They were the notes to the old southern song, "Dixie". He played those for a couple of minutes, and then went into the chords for "Battle Hymn of the Republic," for a couple of minutes, and then back to "Dixie" (indeed, the minstrel meets the monarch). People were turning around. A crowd began to gather. David could play beautifully. Now he was just staring at Ross, waiting. He didn't have to wait long.

"Ohhh I wish I was . . . in the land of Ziooon. Old times there are not forgotten. Loook awaaay. Loook awaaay. Loook awaay. Zion land. Ohh I wish I was in Zion. Loook awaaay. Loook awaaay. In Zion land I'll take my stand. To live and die in Zion. For in Zion land. I was born. Early one December morn' . . ."

He was singing it. And his voice was even softer and louder than David's guitar. He stood motionless, his eyes staring over the nose-perched glasses that he'd never worn before, right down to the sidewalk like he was reading something in the cracks. He was an odd as hell sight for sure. And whether for that or for the fact that they liked his singing or just recognized the song and were bored staring at a dark sky with no pyro-panoplies, he was getting their attention, and a congregation was really starting to collect.

"*Glory, glory, Halleluuujah.*" David hit his chords harder, then paused. "*Glory, glory, Halleluuujah.*" David even stronger, then pausing. "*Glory, glory, Halleluuujaaah. His truth is marching on.*"

And then David just went back into the background just like he began and kept the music faint and tight while Ross jumped down onto the Fairmont's hood again and pushed his big Buddy Hollies up on his nose like a good old quaint and fashioned preacher-man who might have after all had some familiarity with sermoning atop his only method of transportation. He put a finger on the cut side of his mouth to check for blood and remind him to keep it still:

"*Ladies and Gentlemen, I want to tell you a story about my mother. My mother who died on this very day exactly two years ago and whom I goes to visit as often as possible but especially on this day. And I want to tell you why I go there. To my momma. I want to tell you the story of why I go there and what I do. And . . . I want to tell you that after I visited her today . . . I'm of a mind of never going back. Even though I do, and always will, love her ever so dearly.*

"*I used to go there at least several times a month to pay my toll and respect and to seek sanctuary and also because I had to because that is what she had requested of me before she died.*"

Ross jumped off the hood and onto the sidewalk and walked along that imaginary boundary line that a crowd won't cross when they sense they want to be entertained. He paced it up and down, careful never to cross it himself, for that boundary must be respected by he who entertains as well, except in the very special

160

cases. Never losing eye-contact, occasionally extending his right arm like he might want to shake a hand and shuddering his shoulders down to his hips, all wet-dog like, he cocked a high brow (as supercilious as the preacher inside him would allow — which was actually pretty goddamned high), faced the people again and proceeded to work his crowd.

"'Goshdarn it now son,' she used to say. 'You best make sure you visit me at my stone at least once a month or thereabouts. You come and spend a night with me now, you hear? You come and talk to me and let me know how you're getting along and if you're still consorting around with little fourteen-year-old girls or I will come back and I will visit you and I will ruin you and surely make your life hell, so that you will want to go to hell just to get off this world. Ok, now sugar? You do as your momma says.'

"So I went to the stone, but I preferred to go at night, in the winter, especially after a rare snowfall, so no one could see me make snow angels on her grave. So that no one could see me talk to her, or lie face down on her, trying my damndest to penetrate the ground; to conjure her; to evoke her. I even built a wall around her so that on that delicate and precious chance, when she rose up to spit her disgust, or kiss her affection, no one would see.

"Some months later, I painted the headstone Cadillac blue . . . because that was my favorite color. And I began each visit by outlining her letters and numbers with expensive vanilla ice cream from a cheap store-bought cone . . . because that was her favorite taste. I loved to watch it drip and run down the stone 'cause it looked like tears, or sometimes rain — and even on occasion blood. But these are the sweet kinds of drip and I liked to lick them off her cold, metal, blue face. It is my favorite taste now too.

161

"*And even if it was real cold outside, that is to say too cold for the ice cream to cry, it didn't matter. Because then the ice cream smear would freeze and with one of the many rings on my fingers, which I now have forsaken forever, I could scrape the edges and make the letters and numbers even, and proper.*

"*Prostrating before the stone I would recite to her First Corinthians Thirteen and recount the most recent events of my life and extol the high status of my charity and proclaim my pure love and how it was that I excelled and exceeded almost all else. I complained about my Zion plight and swore I wasn't smoking any hash. But my mother wasn't buying any of this.*

"'*Son,' she would say to me, 'you still ain't nothing but a white-trash bumper-sticker from where I'm looking. You are just like what they called you from the beginning. You always was and still are the white nigger. You're still a disappointing car-crash piece of shit. All upside down and your wheels still spinnin'. And were it not for Johnny Cash you'd be a flippity-fetchin' sissy to boot. I don't give a Mississippi mud-shot if you do fight Hitler, worship Christ, and conspire with Nixon.'*

"*That's right my lovely ladies and fine gentlemens, I have met with Nixon.*

"*And then she would continue, 'They can put you on a goddamn U.S. postage stamp for all I care. Now I don't even want to hear none of your lip talking back to me this time. What's wrong with you, son? What's wrong with you yellow-boy, you high up in the banana tree again? You just best hold that tiger and come and lay down and sleep with me and maybe we will make that love work again.'*

"*This made me ever, ever so sad. So I did what I knew she would like even though she swore she wouldn't. And I'd hum the Battle*

162

Hymn of the Republic. And then with all the force I was capable of calling upon I would belt out the chorus and this always satisfied her and then we could connect and she actually and physically held me as tightly as possible. And then I gave her an autographed color photograph of myself to take back with her because now, this is the way, that I say, 'I love you.' In fact I even have a few extra here with me tonight, should any of you be interested.

"Most recently when I went though, she wasn't in the mood to respond and I calmly circled the grave. Circling and circling and circling, with my hands clasped behind my back, just sitting myself there at the table of the beggars banquet and pleading to old yeller hisself, right there where her red fern did grow, for her forgiveness and acceptance. She is, and always has been my god. But she did not come out. 'Momma,' I said, 'please now Momma. Ain't none of this my fault. The little girls follow me everywhere I go Momma, and they're so pretty and lovely. They're just like you, Momma. And I just try and show them the proper attention. Look here Momma. I done brought you a TV to watch. Actually three of them. I got them all hooked up to a battery that I'll have recharged every other day and these here TV's will be on all day and night long. Twenty-four hours. And I'll have them all on different channels. That means, Momma, you can watch three different channels at the same time.

"'Anyway Momma,' I said, 'I brought you some roses 'cause I know Momma loves the roses. And I know I need to get better friends, I mean some real friends,' I explained, 'but I pay these people and I just have a hard time trusting a real friend. Would you like me to sing to you? Please come out Momma. At least say something. Please Momma. Here Momma, hold on. I'm going down on you again. I'll lay with you again.'

"Ladies and Gentlemen, I was the center of gravity in the world she lived in. But with my mother I was still just the sweet innocent loving failure that was dead and buried right at the exact same day and time she was. Now listen, I knew what she was capable of if I didn't please her. I tried my best. But I was weak in the face of her needs. Even more so now than when she lived above and our space was equal.

"I lived in fear for my life because of this. When she tired of my begging she simply started to say, in a nice low invidious monotone from deep beneath her stone and even further from her heart: 'Hey. Hey you, hey you white-trash, Zion-flash. Quit running circles round my bed trying to make me melt like you some old powerful Sambo. Now you get your goddamn fat county-fair, blue-ribbon, hog-ass out of here. And I only need one TV.' That's right! She said, 'ONLY ONE TV! You're always overdoing things these days. That's not the way I reared you. Not at all. I'm watching you, son. I see and hear everything you do. You disappoint me any longer and I'm liable to just take leave of this ground long enough to drive you down here with me and put your little hooliganisms and horse-shits to a stop quick and lickety-split.'

"That was today, ladies and gentlemen. I left in shame. Full of reproach, I silently conceded defeat to myself. Each time it was getting worse and I knew that I could not turn back, that I could not but continue to disappoint her.

"I sensed that the end was near and I left for that very one and last time. I closed the gate behind me. I told the groundskeeper, 'Hey groundskeeper! You there, groundskeeper man! You best get ready for the tourists. THE TOURISTS!' I said. 'They will be here 'fore very long.'

164

And without looking at him, Ross flicked his fingers at David, and he started to play louder again. Surely, they must have rehearsed this. *"And now I am here to tell you all tonight. To you my friends and foes of the county of Utaaah. Get ready for the tourists! You know who the tourists are. You know why they're coming and what they'll do. That's why I'm leaving here tonight. Driving right out of here tonight. To gather back my family in California. To gather them and bring them to the truth and to prepare them for the tourists. That is why I have all of my and my dear mother's left-behind belongings out here before you. Not to be beholding to you. But to simply leave them with you, as generous offerings. And if they might be of any use . . . well then, the exultation of this patriotic day and self-made man of Zion and God that I so aspire to be, is more intent in me than ever."*

And then (and I'll swear this on any holy Bible that ever existed — even the real ones — though I know it sounds as sappy as hell and if I was a good enough liar I'd make something else up, but I'm not) the fireworks started going off right above his goddamn head. I swear it. It even caught Ross off guard 'cause he obviously wasn't done with his discourse, and he dropped his bottle and had to scramble and crawl back up on the roof of the Fairmont with the mic in one hand and stopping the blood on his lip with the other.

The Friar's Lantern could not have come at a more fortuitous time.

And behind him the birds — fine, fine ravens all — (what is it they are called, when ravens all get together?) in all their perfect blackness, in sudden front of a purple curtain, in their fantastic total absence of light. Each one reverent and still in their half-

165

moon perches save for their heads which cocked and bobbed curiously at all the ferment and disorder in that night. And oh, how their blackness captured and confined, in mercurial feathered silver, all the quilted colors from all those stitched-up fires low-shot and yowling in the sky.

Ross then pointed long and hard at the banner as he promised Peter he would, straightened himself all up and took off his Buddy Hollies and raised them as if to toast all the burning hubbub up above and then went right to the end of what he had come to say. *"And this pretty little lady sitting down over here, that's right, the one with the big white hat pulled all the way down to her waist, the one that our sweet, dear mother used to wear, sitting next to everything that our family has left to its most honorable name. This is my sister. If there is any contribution you might be able to part with to help us back to our family out on the great West coast of this great country. Well, we would really be very grateful. It truly would be gracious of you. And I would thank you."*

Then Ross wheeled and gave the sign again to David and belted out one last verse of the Battle Hymn while the fireworks were still in full force.

And I don't know if they bought all that shit for the truth, if they just liked a good story and a good singing voice, if they thought it was some kind of comedy act hired as a surprise by Peter Dishy's Odd and Exotic Pet World, or if they just felt sorry for the pitiful lunatic standing on his car during their third of July celebration and the next day was Sunday and they didn't want to feel guilty on the way to the church-house about not being good, generous Christians (or even worse haughty-naughty Mormons). Or even if they were just wishing he'd get the hell out of Dodge before morning and never haunt them again (I imagine it had to be a combination of everything), but I'll be a sucker myself if not only was all that shit carried off but The Hat was taking money faster than she could say thank you and pull her Gilligan hat down over her face at the same time. She even finally put the damn thing to good use and took it off so the crowd had a place to put their donations.

We didn't know what Ross had just said or done that night, least of all me. And sometimes when I think about it now, I don't even know if he knew. Crowds and how to read and speak them, that he knew. Like a farmer knows what he grows in his field. Maybe he didn't like people so much. But know them, like a doctor knows his ills and pills? Oh, yes.

We made over seven hundred and fifty dollars that night. About five hundred of it due to Ross. It was more than plenty to get us all to L.A., and combined with the rest of the cash that everyone had already thrown into the pot, enough to spare for at least two month's rent.

The old Fairmont was now empty, and Ross asked that I drive me and him home. He was counting the money next to me in the front seat.

"How much, Ross? How much we got?"

"Just a good tad over twelve hundred buckaroos. Not bad. Didn't even have to pay for the fireworks. Ha-ha!"

"Twelve hundred!" I swung the wheel toward the money and just about impaled both of us on the Polar Bear in front of the Arctic Freeze. "I thought we only did about seven, maybe eight hundred."

"The road, Wood. At least one of your goddamn eyeballs on the road . . . the money does us not much good freezing in hell." He wadded it all up and shoved it down the front of his pants. "I got The Hat to give it all to me, including what everyone had already pitched in. Told her I'd stop by the bank early Monday before we left and get us all some traveler's checks for the trip before we meet up at Brian's. You know, told her it was the prudent thing to do. She didn't put up much of a fuss with my lip bleeding and considering all the people that I got to stuff money in her hat. Just handed it right on over. Quick, even. Almost like it was infected or something."

"So, we're leaving Monday afternoon then?"

"Nope."

"What, Monday morning, after the bank? Just meet at Brian's house like we said. Yeah, it's probably better to get an early start."

"Nope."

"When, then. When do we leave?"

"Tomorrow morning. Bright and furry." Ross waved at some young wife out in front of her house hanging laundry.

"Sunday. I thought David and Brian wouldn't travel on a Sunday. Besides aren't the banks closed on Sundays?"

"David and Brian . . . and The Hat for that matter, will not be joining us."

"What, they're coming a day later?"

"We go alone, Wood. We will do it alone."

XVIII

$\mathcal{D}$id I mention Ross loved to run? Not away from anything, or anybody, or out of fear or loathing. No, he'd run toward those things, like a lost dog to his dinner bowl.

Running for the sake of running, that's what he loved to do. He'd had scholarship offers for football and baseball to just about any college he wanted west of the Mississippi. Mom cried when he originally didn't choose Brigham Young University. So that's how he ended up there (some mothers' tears are bigger than others).

He quit the teams after a couple of years. Said he couldn't take all the time standing around waiting for "a bunch of has-been asshole coaches telling a bunch of wannabe asshole kids how to use an instrument they already knew how to play in the first place or else they wouldn't have been there anyway. I respect preachers and ministers more than I do coaches. At least they're smart enough to blame God for them having to punish you when you fuck up. And at least they don't pretend to be God themselves."

But what he did love about the playing was the running he had to do in practice. He'd fuck up or talk back or go the wrong way just so he could get condemned to some extra laps or even miles and take off and run and run and run.

And the running never left him, even after he quit (not too long after Mom did her quitting). We had a park in back of the old house where we lived in Pleasant Grove. Liberty Park, probably about half a mile running one time around. And I would go look out the back window of that house and catch him running around that park at the oddest times of almost any day of the week. Even six a.m. on a Sunday, hung over as hell from drinking all day the day before.

Sometimes he'd stop alongside the stream that ran down one side of the park and eventually ended up as a river some ten miles down in the Provo Canyon. Fathers and their kids would fish in the park during the summer, and Ross would just heave and gag his lungs and all his poisons out right into the water. Then just keep on running. "Sorry sir. In training. Tough workout today."

Sometimes he wouldn't stop by the stream. Just turn around, backpedal a few strides, and stream it out behind him like old Hansel marking his trail in case he got lost. He ran when he felt good too. On those occasions he'd take a bottle of vodka along with him and swig it whenever he got thirsty.

"Nothing like the sweet buzz of running with a Russian," he'd wince. "All that adrenalin shooting through your heart and brain in that nice warm glycemic index (whatever the hell that was) of an eighty proof bath. No such high like it on earth. Gives brand new meaning to the term 'feeling no pain.' Hmmm, or even 'no pain no gain,' now that I think about it . . . fucking coaches. Once ran two miles under eleven minutes doing that. Only problem is I can never get it so I can remember the third, fourth, and fifth miles. But it's still a good workout."

That's right. He'd run around the world with a bottle that said *Evian* on it. And then run around his track with the genuine-labeled McCoy.

170

No. He ran like he was chasing something, never like he was being chased. Never looked back, never checked his bearings, his eyes on some prize always ten strides ahead and just barely escaping around the corner. Chasing something in sweet, boyish, and faultless futility — perhaps that reputation, the one that always would precede him — like a child chasing its shadow: the puppy and the tail.

Chasing, and then disappearing through a dale in his mind like old Rin-tin-sin. To bury or dig up (or maybe even both) his weaknesses. The things that he did and then hid. And then missed, and have to dig them up again for a good lick-chew and a suck until he was properly reacquainted with the reason he buried them in the first place, and then bury them again. All of his giddy gluttony — cleaned bright, shiny white. Good for sharpening his teeth. His sinbones.

He would run in the winter in two feet of snow, sometimes sliding and skidding on the ice. Didn't matter if it was light or night. He ran mostly in a pair of red or black cut-off sweats and some expensive running shoes he'd always manage to find at the Deseret Industries downtown. No shirt, unless the ground was frozen (and then only in a long-sleeve, red and black flannel lumberjack number), and then sometimes in jeans and his black Cuban-heeled boots and a button down solid shirt if it was right before gig time.

Sometimes he'd run to our gigs. Sometimes he'd run home from the gigs. Sneak away and do it. He wouldn't advertise or talk about it. "My personal time, Brentwood. If anyone asks just tell them I'm talking to God and shrug your shoulders. Keep them away from me in the park. You stay away from me too in the park." Always had his stopwatch with him. Kept his times written in some tattered, old book called "Prefontaine" which Father had given him right before he went. It used to hang on the wall behind his clothes in the closet.

He even ran a local 10K once, because he was sober enough one Saturday morning, since I had just bailed him out of jail after two days on a DUI he got trying to find the hospital where he was born. Wouldn't run a 10K hungover or drunk, though. Wouldn't race unless he thought he had a real chance at winning. But run every day otherwise, he would.

And that's my first memory of Ross in Venice. Running.

I was sitting on the beach in Venice, the day after I arrived at our new place just a couple of blocks from the beach itself. I was lonely and making up games for myself and pretending that David and Brian and even The Hat (no arms now, just legs sticking out) were a ways down the sand playing their guitars and enjoying the sun and not hating us for the lie. But my pretending wouldn't last and so I looked the other way and found the rim and the spokes of the still Ferris wheel on the Santa Monica pier. I let my eyes drift down to the surfers shooting it underneath. And then I saw him. The lie himself. Jogging through the forest of pillars underneath the pier, his black hair bumping off his head, and chasing seagulls on the wet part of the sand, right at home like he was back in Liberty Park. Except in Liberty Park he'd usually chase the grasshoppers.

It had only been a couple of weeks, but he looked different already. He was skinnier. I could see his ribs even in the distance. He had a brand new black eye (surfers, territoriality) and a fresh new tattoo of a bright green apple just under his left nipple. He'd

172

let his sideburns go — lambchop like — and he was red as a lobster except for two white circles around his eyes where his shades usually were. He looked like some big old beat up, scarecrowed raccoon that had been shaved and boiled but had hopped out of the pot just in time to save the hair on his proud head.

He had his shorts and running shoes on, his sunglasses embedded in his mop, his Cubans in his left hand, and his *Evian* in his right. He studied the sand as he ran. He ran right by me. And then he ran by my imagined others.

It was then, I think, that my own plight ceased to be a tacit one, and I for the first time could actually feel it poking about my fringes and teasing me with doom. Like the great wide water in front of me, dauntless, now just barely feeling my feet, edging closer as I sat still there in the sand at the hem of the Pacific.

I looked down at the water circling and sinking my feet as I too sank down into my mind and asked myself the great questions: Who was I? What was I doing? And why? But it was Ross. I was still inextricably sewn into his shadow. Or maybe I was his shadow. Sometimes in front of him. Sometimes behind. A reflection of himself in the cracked rear-view mirror of his perverse animality. Standing idly by, watching and following and I believe at times even leading him through this obstacle course that he had conjured from within himself and — even more ominously — for himself. Like some great self-inhabited specter ship intentionally navigating the most shallow and perilous of waters, challenging its own invisible but still very vulnerable underbelly on the sharpest rocks.

He picked away at the scabs on his soul and seemed to take pride in the sight of their new growth while nursing them only with his anesthesia.

My own self-pity puzzled me as I wondered who was using whom. Who was the devil and who was the angel? And just whose shoulder and which side were each of us sitting on?

Mom had told me once that it was Ross who found Father. Found him naked and on his knees, his bloated body angled and leaning down against the strain of a belt tied around his neck and fixed to the doorknob of the bathroom in the basement of our then house in Mexico. And how he just stared at him, for several hours she said it must have been. Even sat down next to him, cursing him for what he did to her, and for always missing his baseball games, and for tying a belt around his neck, and for not being able to go out back that day and throw the baseball around one more time. Until she finally got home from her work that night at the church-house and found them both down there in the basement. And how she knelt down next to him and just put her arms around him and told him not to cry even though he wasn't. It was her that was doing all the crying, and Ross put his arms around her and picked her up and apologized and said, "You were not supposed to see this, Mom. You were specifically not supposed to see this." Because Father had told Ross that morning to hurry home from school and come down and help him in the basement (I guess he thought I was too young to see, and he'd already hurt Mom enough).

And then Ross walked her back upstairs and put her in the swing in the backyard while he went back down and untied Father and put his clothes back on and called someone from the church to come and "do whatever you guys do." And then they took care of it and I never heard Ross mention it again.

But I lie. He would mention it in one sense, I guess. Sometimes he'd say, but only when he was sober, and in a very calm and reverential manner, "Never trust the people in the steeple, Brentwood. They killed him, those motherfuckers. Gave him the guilt so bad that he thought he was already dead and just a curse on the family. Like they or no one else had ever made a mistake and still been able to reckon it with this God. They brainwashed him. Brainwashed him with so much shame and injected him with so much unforgiving sorrow. Forced him to read those cock'n shit scriptures, and all that doctrine. So much that he finally bought in to that self-atonement sacrifice doctrine that they try and hide under branded rocks on hills called Cumorah. And then went crazy with it. Told him he'd never have his family again in one of those fucking holy-roller kingdoms of Oz, and made his heart into a pungent pit of reckless and self-serving remorse. Just strangled him with gutless, fucking guilt. He thought he was doing us all a favor. And then, afterwards, they covered their mouths so politely and whispered so thoughtfully while pointing at the heavens with one hand and undoing their pants with the other to piss on his grave and keep his memory alive, worshiping him all the more for being such a whore — like some suicidal dunk-tank clown, their coward of the county — loving him for knowing that they were always better. "He was once a great man of God," they said. "He had it all. All the knowledge. He had the testimony. A man with that much should have known better," they said.

"And poor Mom bought all the bullshit the whole way too. Don't ever tell her that, though. I promise I never will."

But those years that wear away promises to reveal the more sensible beds of rationalization and wit would never need to come, as she too saw it right in her plight to follow the same fiction and choke on God's guilt.

Yes, Ross got to find her too, home for Christmas vacation his first year at college. "Misread her prescription," he said. But I'd seen her. Watched her in those years since Father left. The color of Father's bruises replaced by the waxen, spider-webbed mask of the hidden flask. ("The doctor says I should drink plenty of cranberry juice. Can't ever have enough of it, he says.") Bright, bulbous W.C. Fields nose and all.

I witnessed her seesaw extremes — two shots of happy, three shots of sad — every day with another pitiful, plastic, dixie cup in her hand, the kind that had a different knock-knock joke on each one *(Knock Knock.* Who's there? *Arthur.* Arthur who? *Arthur any more jokes here? —* HA!)

Never leaving the house. Drifting footless and muted, like a Disneyland Haunted House demoness finally finding flight at the end of each day's long journey, in a house that wasn't haunted (too lonely), in the same long wedding gown that she confused for her pajamas.

Heard the sandy scrape and tap-clink of cheap bottle tops on glass, behind closed bathroom doors. Saw the toilet tanks, the lids put back on crooked (I'd straighten them later, when she'd forget). Smelled the spill of drops missed on the floor.

And I knew no one prescribed that. There was no misreading there.

And I figured out why her long-sleeve cuffs were extra long in the casket. And why she was found in the bathtub when she had never taken a bath in her life. And I kept it to myself and never asked questions, and played dumb. Dumb like I was good at, like a good brother.

And Ross, like a better brother, took me in to live with him right after I finished high school. Let me bang on the drums in the basement where the band practiced, when the other drummer wasn't there. 'Til after a couple of years the little drummer boy got good and grew up. And Ross let me in, and let the other guy out. And I guess that's kind of how I came to be sitting on the beach that day.

XIX

And it was clear to me that day on the beach — just as he went trotting on by, in fact — that Ross by then had finally chosen his own course. Or created it, like I said before. And I had no idea where it was headed or if it was headed anywhere at all. But I always thought he knew. Until now. Until right there on that very day when I saw what should have been just his apparition running down the Santa Monica beach. And he had that sassy, insouciant look of contentment and ease on his face, like an animal does when it chooses and finds its place to die. But what kind of death did Ross have in mind?

All of this did occur to me, and I did wonder much.

And it was then that I got the first inkling that maybe he didn't know. Maybe he had no idea at all where this was all leading to. But whether he did know then, or not, I'll never know. And presently . . . well let's just say he's in no condition to tell. Not only is he so gripped, biting and southern in the ground, as well as so high in the sky (either beneath or below me, I know not) that even alive, if he cried, his mind would have been so fractured and mumbled by now that his versions and deconstructions of his past would have just drifted and gallivanted through his brain like light refracted through a splintered and jaundiced, green prism.

Just about any combination — of charming but foul, vile yet confectionery, or highly fictional although somewhat based-in-fact memories — would have been capable of nothing less, and then maybe a whole lot more, than just being bent and twisted, before they were sent and sifted through the rambler of his mouth — the withered woodpecker of his one good, *raconteur*, black crayon-colored hole.

I'd like to think that he knew what was at the end of his tunnel. That his canary-paved road, weaving and weepy as it was — was as he knew it to be all along: the end of his straightened and attenuated rainbow. That he'd had it all planned out and was simply reading the map and waiting to get there. But his jaded, worn, beautifully bold crap-shooter face would never give away a thing. I think he would have bedeviled even himself had he looked in the mirror more often.

I must confess, that in sitting there and thinking about all of that — about Father, about Mom, about Ross and whether or not he was his own red herring, or his own glass of hemlock — that I probably only fell in love with him more. But now the love was different. It had taken a turn. The dew had dropped, and drifted just a little outside the boundaries of blindness. Even somewhere darker. (Could it be true? That love is blindness?) It became a bit more profound, and a little less understood. It put sweat on my brow, and wanted me to start looking over my shoulder.

I looked back down the beach. The son of a bitch was talking to the others. No, he wasn't talking. He had picked up one of the guitars and was playing and singing to them. And the fact that I knew it wasn't my aped David and Brian and the little white Hat,

179

made me madder than hell. They were strangers: Ross was already making friends, without even addressing me yet. And already had more friends than me, who'd been sitting lonely on the beach for days. Ross had pulled us up to the very first house we saw in Venice with a "For Rent" sign in front, got out, walked off, said he had some thinking to do, as he handed me a fistful of the money from his pants. I hadn't seen or heard from him in nearly a week.

They were all smiling their asses off. Even applauding. Even the one who was wearing a hat. In fact, I think he was singing to her. The bourgeois General Bacchanal. His stride in perfect pace, voice in perfect pitch. He hadn't lost a step in his march, nor a beat in his cadence. In fact, he had probably gained on both accounts. Why not? Boot camp was over. We were in the trenches. He had taken me and landed on the beach and we were — or at least he was — ready to finally translate his training into the purer war of hell (and maybe even heaven, but I'll never know).

He had gone home. Gone to a home he had never been to before. But it was still home to him.

Some say home is where the heart is. Ross's heart was dark and lush, sad and certain, logically chaotic, a knightly knave for his own selfish raping and enlightening, and innocently forked by its own enchanted hunters. It was lured by the perilous magic of his past.

Ross was always home.

He finally put the guitar down and started jogging toward me. He pulled up about twenty yards from me and just walked slow, watching me, waiting for something to react to. But I said nothing, and met his stare evenly. He sat down on my left side. I ignored him. He threw sand on my feet. And then he cleaned it off.

"Where you been?" I said.

"Rattlebrained and nuts." He started to take his running shoes off and put on his Cubans. "I've been through a hitchhiker's hamper and maybe even used her bloody tampon as a pillow."

"You're disgusting."

"It's a fucking figure of speech there, old Brentwood."

"From where the hell did you get that?"

"From me. Where do I get anything I say? Why? Does it matter?"

"Never heard that one before."

"Yeah, well I've been thinking a lot the last week, you know. The desert will do that to you. All that flat antiseptic sand and wide open oblivion. It can hustle a soul into a lot of thinking. I loved it. I loved it dearly. I almost didn't leave. Where the hell you been, anyway? I've been sleeping on this beach for almost two nights now."

I turned and looked at him. "What! You loved it? You've got to be lying now, man! I drove through that desert myself and it was the biggest and most barrenest wasteland I could never have imagined. I kept thinking I was lost the whole time. Just one big, long, dirty brown anxiety attack. You had me drive through a nightmare. You must have slept in the back seat through the whole damn thing."

"Yep, maybe. But I went back. I walked it for quite a few miles, and even a few more hours, actually. I was hitchhiking.

Even napped for a bit one night under some sign that read 'Last Chance Casino and Motel — Fifteen Miles.' Decided to save my last chance for here, though. Ha-ha-ha." He clucked his thick tongue and winked, took his sunglasses out of his matted hair and put them back in place over the white splotches that were his eyes.

"What's up with that shiner you got?" I said, nodding with my nose at his one black eye.

"Not all the drivers were as friendly as most. Let's just say I had to get myself out of a tight spot real quick. Had a row with a couple of guys who let me crash in their motel room. A little disagreement about gender and intentions and what I use my ass for, while I was trying to sleep. I had to defend myself, you know. Anyway, cops came. Bracelets on in front of my back, the whole shit 'n' shaboodle, just like the good old days. Threw me in the backseat of their fucking car with my knees in my ears and my nose in that cage, even though I told them I was claustrophobic. They didn't care. But I controlled myself this time. Didn't bother with that Houdini thing where you force your arms over your head and dislodge your sockets for some great fucking escape — I got to stop believing everything I read. Anyway, I just let all that salt in my sweat sting my eyes and I closed them and I went running. Must have run about twenty-six miles sitting balled up in that backseat. Ended up spending the night. They just opened the kennel and let me out in the morning. Didn't say a word to me. How are you?"

I got up, put my back to him, and started to walk off, making sure he could sense my disbelief. I yelled out to the pier in front of me. "How could you love it! How could you sit there and lie to your brother, who thought up until now he could trust you like you've always told him his whole goddamn life, and tell him you loved it! You are a lying son of a bitch!"

"Brentwood," he said. "Brentwood. Turn around and look at me. And I will tell you."

I didn't want to turn around. But I did as I was told. He was lying on his back now, his big mirrored shades fixed in my direction. But for all I knew, his eyes probably closed. I pretended he was asleep, and a strange, barbed, pity pierced my soul. I looked at his face, and it was not the face of the brother in Utah. But that it was the face of my greatest and only friend, I was unable to deny. Perhaps he was not telling me the whole story. And perhaps I would never know the whole story of anything he ever said or did. I looked at him stretched out on the sand. His arms splayed with palms to the sky and his bare booted legs eagled, like the boys I once knew who made snow angels in the cemetery at Christmas after running and laughing through the graveyard (always just a hop, skip, and a plot from loved ones). The two last bats in the belfry, stealing memories and swearing they'd be together until the day they died, right next to our mother's grave in sacred Pleasant Grove.

I weighed the mutiny of all those new emotions that had been aligning themselves those last few days, and even a few minutes, before. And felt ashamed for their betrayal. Why was I so quick to be so false? Such an eager apostate. So immediately inclined to judge and forsake? Or was it true? Was I the fool? Had my will been voluntarily required?

My eyes moved over to the bottle of *Evian* that Ross had let fall from his hand, and I watched it roll down to the water where

183

the milksop waves foamed and tried to carry it away. "How easily could that be me," I thought. And how many times in Ross's sad and sudden life did he not wonder to himself and even cry out loud when he thought he was alone (for I did hear him) — in his mind on runs in his parks, in his head incubating in nightmares in his beds, or in his soul from his rock 'n roll stages, reaching out and hiding behind the bluff of a band and a big, tolling, please-take-*me*-out-to-the-ball-game belle of a voice — asking that someone trade places and release him from the lot so arbitrarily cast his way. And how wretched and unworthy it made me feel that not in a million years could I, nor would I, ever take his stead.

I walked up above and behind his head so he would not see the tears that crept upon my eyes. If he could see me cry, I thought, I would hate him. And if he never saw me cry, I thought, I would hate him even more.

And then everything flickered away and the world shut down and it was just me and him and the sand back in the Nevada desert and I felt that same last-chance sign above my head and the sand was so much whiter but this time didn't burn my eyes like the dirty, brown sand when I drove the first time through. But now we were alone. And not even the thought or possibility of anyone else being alive on this whole earth existed. It was just me and Ross. And for the first time in my life, loneliness was comforting. A bitter peace of mind. But peaceful, still.

Ross looked up at me. His mirrors were now gone and he began to flap his arms and legs and the sand got whiter and whiter. And then the sand was snow. "You know why I loved it, Brentwood?" And then he stood up and was turning around and looking in all directions. And then, I too was turning around trying to see what he could see, until we were both spinning, just spinning in this new bleached-blond wasteland like a couple of tops set in motion from the beginning of time, unable to stop unless the world itself stopped spinning and threw us right off, sending all the laws of nature with it. "You know why I loved it, Brentwood?"

"No, Ross. Tell me. Tell me why you loved it!"

We started to spin faster. Like the dizzy-game we used to play when we were kids, to see who got the dizziest and fell down first (of course, it would always be me), but I didn't feel anything now and I just kept spinning and I kept yelling even louder. "Tell me Ross. Why did you love it! Why did you love the desert? Why did you love to be alone in the desert!"

And then he fell down. Him, first. He crashed into the sand head first. And then, but only for one moment (though it seemed like a season), I saw him from a great distance. And he was red and black, red blazing in the center of the sand, a roman-candled desert rose. Suckled and *sub rosa*, defying the sun and following its fire across the sky, while all life around him wilted and ebbed in the heat. I stopped my own spinning. "Tell me, man. Aren't you going to tell me?"

He got up on his knees below where I stood. Prostrated, he shook his head dog-like, trying to get all the sand out of his hair. He looked up at me, and then right through me. "'Cause it's clean, man. It's just so fucking clean."

XX

$\mathcal{S}$oda always had a bottle of green juice with him. A bottle that no one else would touch — even when we were playing our game, *Whose Blues*. Not because Soda wouldn't offer, he would. But for whatever reason, no one would even care to give that bottle an eye-graze of consideration.

Soda would nurse on it now and then, pacing it like a little kid with his all-day sucker. And when Ross ran out of his own stuff or intentionally lost it to the other guys, during a round of *Whose Blues,* he slowly learned to bite, finesse, and eventually prefer it himself. But I never saw Ross buy or steal his own — and where he would have found it anyway, I don't know, for I only saw it in that battered plastic *7-UP* bottle inside of Soda's bag. He just always got it from Soda.

Soda also had something else that made him walk real funny (and I didn't think it came in a bottle, although at some point in his life, it most probably did). Like he was always trying to screw his right leg into some gigantic wine-cork in the ground. Seemed like he was really trying hard too, because his face had the look of mighty pain and perseverance every time he put it down. But only the right leg. When the left went down his face went flaccid, almost kind of like drooping with comfort that he'd been able to lift it at all, and then it wrenched back up again with the right. He was so skinny that you could almost see the strings underneath the skin on his face that went directly down and were directly connected to that twined and rigorous right leg.

I even tried to make a joke the first night he came walking up on us by whispering to Ross. "Hey, who's this squiggly-mark of a cripple coming up here with the white shirt?" And Ross looked out over at him and then peeled his eyes to the side at me without even dignifying my comment with a head turn, and just gave me one of his patented death mask looks. I had forgotten about his soft spot. It had been a while.

I never knew if Soda had been in some kind of accident or caught some kind of disease or if he was just born that way. Ross seemed to know, though. Because just a week after we met him, which was plenty of time for Ross to get endeared to him, we went down to the hospital right there in Santa Monica.

Right down to the emergency room. Ross walked in there brazen as can be, right in the middle of the day. Was only in there for not more than two minutes. And came out pushing two nice, shiny, clean wheelchairs (one for traveling and one for the roof). Just stole them. Not even a drunk-and-oblivious-to-the-real-world Robin Hood would have had the same bulk of balls. "Soda will need this soon. He's getting worse. Besides, we can take him for walks in it around town, take him to our gigs. Ohhh, shit." He looked down at one of the chairs. "Damn," he said softly. He fluttered his fingers on his temples and chin like he just walked out of the grocery store with everything but the milk. "This one doesn't fold. It doesn't fold up, Brentwood. We need one that folds up so we can put it in the car. And him in the car, of course, whenever we go somewhere in the car." He marched back in and returned in even less time. He had the milk. "This one folds. Let's go."

One night, as the season of the year was just ginning itself up to swell the yuletide, Ross and I were hanging out just a block or so down toward the beach from Van Gogh's Ear in a cul de sac at the mouth of the Boardwalk in front of a swank and fopperish little blues club called St. Luke's Blues. I say swank on account of Ross and I could never go in because it was just too damn expensive. Fifteen bucks just to walk through the door. They had their own valet service and everything — even though most of the people that pulled up there were doing so in stretch limos and expensive convertible taxis driven by all kinds of funny and foreign chauffeurs and crowned with hood ornaments I had never seen before.

But the music was always loud enough that Ross and I could sit down at the end of the corner in front of the big, black, curtained window on the other side of the band, and smoke bedes and cloves, sip on some beverage (*Evian* and sarsaparilla), and take in some of the best blues that was ever played live.

Ross loved loved loved the blues. Not like everyone else that says they "love" the blues. Especially all the chummy musicians and misanthropic clichéd lead singers on all the talk-shows and in all the magazines. I mean he loved them so much he was scared of them. Tried to avoid them most of the time. Run away from and not talk about them until they finally reached out and grabbed him by the balls from some strange radio in a car on the street, an open bedroom window around a corner, or a club he just happened to be walking by due to boredom and poverty.

He'd been like that since he was a very small kid, since he got his first record player when he was eight. A little thing no bigger than the big, black Bible on the living room table that said "Hey Mouseketeers!" on the outside and had a real Mickey Mouse arm with the needle coming out of his index finger. Mom used to drag him to garage sales all the time and when he discovered all these old women unloading their husband's and grown-up children's 45s, 78s, and 33 1/3s, well, from age eight to twenty-four he had amassed quite an impressive vinyl-blues collection.

Mom had taught us, inadvertently, how to barter and be bold on the garage sale circuit. For years from when we were still in strollers until we were about six and eight she'd have us in tow and she mined every suburb within a hundred miles for her very most favorite thing in the world: *snow globes*. She'd call them *water globes* and *snow domes*, too. She had them all over the house. In every room. It snowed whenever we wanted in our home and we'd spend hours with our eyeballs as close to them as our little-boy eyelashes would allow: full of wonderment at these perfect little statues in their perfect little miniaturized wintry wonderland glass-sphered scenes.

Ross would spend hours with them holding them up and turning them to gaze from all angles and in different shades of light at night with the electric bulbs or candles or even just in the moonlit dark and of course during the day in all the degrees of the sun. Shaking them. Staring. Like he wished they were crystal balls. Like he wished he could get inside, even if it meant having no motion in life. It was the silent things that I ever saw most make him smile.

He'd shine them for mom and make sure she had always had her favorites by her side. The ones with angels.

She liked the ones with angels especially in the spring by her bed with the rosebuds she'd once a year buy and bring home from the market.

We knew all the regulars real well. The ones that always had their garage doors open, that went out to surrounding towns to bring stuff back and sell. Most of them older couples. And they knew us as well. Real well. But not by name, I must say. I tried to introduce us a couple of times in the beginning but Ross punched me in the kidneys both times and just hissed at me to shut up.

"What do you think you're doing, Brent?"

"What do you mean, man? I'm being polite. Introducing ourselves. Like Mom always says we should."

"No."

"Why not?"

"You give our names, they'll know who we are."

What he meant was, "They'll know who our parents are. And then know who we are." The sons of that poor woman. The mother who never went to church. Seen at the grocery with heavy make-up on her arms and face. The one you could occasionally catch wearing big hats to the state liquor store, darting through the parking lot back to her car. Married to "you-know-who." Who never missed a church meeting unless he was traveling and speaking at other chapels.

I didn't know that's what he meant right away. But I eventually figured it out. And so we were simply known as "the two little boys who never comb their hair." "Why look, here come those two little boys who never comb their hair. Hi, boys.

How are you today?" Which was interesting because at home we were known as the "two little boys who never say their prayers." As in, "Don't you boys go to sleep without saying your prayers now." (Mom like a great, faceless, amorphous shadow night-gowned in the doorway of our just darkened room.) "You don't want to be the two little boys who never say their prayers, do you? You know what happens to them?"

"No . . . I mean, what's that, mom?"

"Well, God can't hear them unless they call out and get his attention . . . and then if they don't do that why then he'll just ignore them. No matter how much they might need him. He has many, many little boys to attend to. But only the ones who say their prayers."

"Mom, when do you say your prayers?"

"Right after you two fall asleep and then right before you wake up. Goodnight, my beautiful sons. I love you." And then she'd slowly shamble up the stairs, her gown picking up a bit of light from up above along the way, one hand on the banister and the other death-gripped on a bottle. Until we finally — some nights it seemed almost an hour later — heard her footfall in her room right above us.

I always tried saying mine. Kneeling down by the side of my bed. Just trying to do like Ross. But then he started saying them while he was kneeling down in bed. And then he would say them lying down, under the covers. And then one night it was obvious he had just stopped altogether (although for Mom he did fake-pray; sustain a perfunctory kneel for a moment or two when she came by to say goodnight). And I don't think you can really blame him much either. It's just goddamn hard to pray when the

191

world above you is so full of hurt (you know some ceilings have a way of grabbing the softest of protestations and cries and directing them right down to vibrate in the springs of a metal bed — covering your head with a pillow just makes them even all the more clear).

On the other hand however, with the hair, well, one day Ross had simply had enough of that and started combing us both before we ever left the house. For many years he did that. He would comb his. Find me. Comb mine (and he was pretty good with a comb too). One wouldn't say a word to the other. Just comb and be combed. "OK, we look good so let's go."

You know, there were some days (just a few, really, not that many) up until the very last, when out of nowhere and without saying a thing he would still do that. And even then, nobody would say a word.

We spent many a cherished Saturday, he and I, trolling our neighborhood on our couple of used Santa-painted Schwinns, looking for buried treasure until the sun went down and our legs finally hurt too bad. But those nights of discovery and open communion with a brand new voice and somebody's bleating, broken heart were always more than well worth it.

And all I ever had to do was ride with him on Saturdays. Hell, he rode alone every morning before the sun came up year round for more than a decade — flinging papers for money at ninety miles an hour and pedaling his bike not much slower. Climbing hills, dodging delivery trucks, and giving the finger to the garbage men (they got a kick out of it) just to have the Saturday ransom to buy the goddamn things. (His coaches were always in shock for the first year whenever they saw him in action. But it was never a mystery to me why when Ross got to high school — even though he had never played on an organized team in his life — he could run faster and throw a ball harder than any other prick in the state who had been coming home after school practices and getting in extra work with their Dad in the backyard ever since they were old enough to say "raise in my allowance.")

And then when he was out of high school, with his supervisor's borrowed station wagon for picking up the paper at the printer's, we'd shoot out, slowly but surely, into the surrounding towns and counties. Just garage sailing our happy little asses off. Checking out pawn shops. Used book and music stores. Deseret Industries (the Mormon Goodwill) and thrift stores. Anywhere where somebody might have left a dirty old disc, some unpolished and carved, black bijou, or a priceless old first edition written in a language they just weren't born to understand. But Ross was.

Then everything else changed. Somewhere there in his early twenties. When he quit sports, took to the drink, buried Mom. Started playing the guitar, dreaming about Father, and making love to women. Started growing his hair, running in the park, and making love to more women (and must I say, "not necessarily in that order?").

Then suddenly one day he took all his records, hundreds of them, down to this high school next to the park where he used to run and gave them to this math teacher. His name was "Hoooaaahhh" Doug. He was also a track coach.

Doug used to watch Ross running there at night in the park out his classroom window and, I don't know how, but soon he

193

was running with him. I think he saw something lonesome in Ross, could tell he was kind of lonely. I never knew what they talked about. All I ever gathered from what Ross said was that he used to live in Hawai'i, ran marathons for the National Guard, loved to surf, served two tours in Vietnam, and brought back a little kid from an orphanage there even though he already had four other little ones waiting at home for him and just on a teacher's salary. I've never known Ross to have more respect for any other man. "He's a fucking intense man, Brentwood. A devout Mormon. The kindest and wisest man I've ever met."

Doug died a year later. Heart attack. Two months after he sub four-houred the Boston Marathon. Doctors never detected it because he was in such good shape.

"Local High School Track Coach Dies." We both saw it in the local paper at the same time while waiting at a cash register in a 7-11. Ross just went back to his bedroom, put on his running gear, grabbed a fifth of generic vodka still in the bottle, a book (*Lunar Caustic,* I do believe), and headed for his park. On his way out he glanced down at the paper again, raised his bottle to the sky, took a polite, sacramental sip, started to walk off, then looked back at me and said, "If God isn't dead, he's dying. Or at least stopped wearing his suit of lights." And then he broke into a trot.

Anyway, he had given all his records to him and just said, "Put these, a few at a time, on a table at the back of your class. Don't ever point them out. But if any of your kids ask about them, you know, sound interested or anything, just say, 'Take one. Go home and listen to it. It's yours.'"

194

Math teacher Doug ("Hoooaaahhh") took them all. Told Ross what a smart, enterprising guy he was. And would tell him every time a kid would take one home, and especially about the ones who would come back looking for more.

Aha! The question: Why the hell did he give all his records away? I don't know. Because he couldn't take any more erotic suffering: the simultaneous betrayal of both men and women? Because he finally realized and felt sorry for the state of women: that they are compelled to marry beneath themselves because the worst among them is yet better than the best among us (dare I speak for all men, let alone Ross)? Or was it that he finally came to this conclusion: that for which we can find words . . . is already dead; all the "I Love You's" he had ever heard or said, were meaningless? Or, was it simply that finally fancying himself a bit of an artist he felt paled and-oh-so mortally humbled by their loyalty to the soul? The voices on the vinyl — the first modern owners of bowel-howled, soul-mirror blind reflection of the human condition. He had either had enough or could not take any more of their beauty and destruction, what he often referred to as "The Beautiful Destruction," in the face of his own feebly perceived attempt to reflect it in himself.

Or, even more simply, was it because of all of these things, and a pungent and useful desire to go away within himself and dream it all up again? But this time, for the first time, on his own. Sensing that his reliance on these circular and plastic forces of nature and their power to inspire had run its course and become impotent. A weakness. A crutch.

I don't know. *"Doug died."* I don't know. *"God is dead."* I don't know. *"Hi. I'd like you to meet Lizzy."* I don't know.

195

What I do know is that we used to have a damn jack-dandy and jimmy-crack-corn-I-don't-fucking-care good time outside of St.Luke's, actually listening to live versions of all those records. It had been a few years since Mickey Mouse and we had never before heard these songs played live. And Ross couldn't resist. And I was happy for that.

He'd bet his bedes, slugs of swill, and clove cigarettes against the small change and homemade hooch of our newly discovered real good friends in a booze-jockeyed version of *Name That Tune*. The hooch usually came from somebody's bathroom and the small change and even the occasional greenback or two from the real fine way they dawdled, worked, and bided their time with us outside the club on the corner.

They were the window washers. Their work was to wait and converge on the rich and sometimes famous as they drove up to be dropped off at the door of the club. They were homeless, had squeegees, all of them old sore-backed black guys (the bouncers chased off the young ones and anyone who was white). Nowhere to go, a squirt bottle of blue water and a rag. Had to wear a button down-white shirt — buttoned up all the way to the top — (bouncers again) and would start washing the windshields before the cars had even stopped. The dupe of implicit compensation obligation. They made enough every night to buy some wine and a liquor store sandwich. At least one of each every day.

Ross's game was: "Name the song before the first fucking chorus and then the original artist — I got three cloves, a Marlboro, and a swig off this bottle for the next one." And boom, off they'd go, all of them snapping their fingers, swinging their hips, and clicking their heels. All of them trying to get back home.

Ross called all the old guys "Cassius." They loved it. And they called him Cassius right back.

"Commit A Crime." "Boll Weevil Blues." "Look On Yonder Wall." "I Loves You Porgy." Howlin' Wolf. Leadbelly. Elmore James. Billie Holiday.

"Goddamn, Cassius," Ross would roar. "That's three out of four, now. I am kicking all y'alls black asses beet red. Let loose with the juice or give up some of that honey-money."

"Coffee For Mama." "Dusty Road." "Sad Letter." "I Ain't Mad At You Pretty Baby." Lightnin' Hopkins. John Lee Hooker. Muddy Waters. Gatemouth Moore.

"Awwright!" they'd gravel back, "we breakin' even now, Cassius, boy. Breakin' even now!"

"Catfish Blues." B.B. King.

"Yes. Yes. Yes. A swig for the pig."

"Wee Baby Blues." Joe Turner.

"Comin' back, boy. We be coming right back at ya', Cassius. Get them smokes out of your dirty ears, now. Out, son. Out! Why Cassius, you do swing them hips pretty damn good for a white boy. Where your momma from? Naw, Naw . . . That's Roy Milton. I know that one like the goddamn Bible is black. I saw him play that myself in New Orleans in nineteen and forty nine. It's goddamn Roy Milton, hip-shaker boy. Roy Milton!" And Ross would fall down laughing so hard he'd be pissing tears.

If it ever got too heated (as all the Cassiuses, or "Cassi", took their blues pretty damn seriously), Ross would start to lose on purpose. And if they were taking it well, in other words, if tips were good that night and they didn't mind losing too much, he'd still get them all good and drunk and give them all plenty of cigarettes before the night was over. But he could always kick their ass. And on some nights (but never that many) he did make away with a decent chunk of that change.

I do believe that earlier I said all the guys there were *old* black guys. But I guess I lied. Again.

There was one that couldn't have been any older than me. And that would be Soda. And yes, it was the "old Soda," as he liked to call himself. The Soda from the bench. And he did look a whole lot younger by the light of St. Luke's — less the shadows and shards of a good drunk in his eyes. Although, there was something aged about the way he held himself. Something dainty and doddering in the angles of his arms and fingers. Or was it the other way around? Was it really just something youthful in the old? Like refreshing new homemade wine in bottles well worn with the labels long scratched off. That certain agerasiatic condition a few of the lucky are cursed with?

XXI

*E*veryone else called him Soda as well. I guess because he liked sweet stuff. I think they let him work there with everyone else because of his condition. He was kind of crippled. And a bit slow as well (I mean not just physically). Ross had a soft spot for both. I mean a real soft spot. A sober one. He had many soft spots, all of them varied and wholly interchangeable, while under the lap. But I hadn't seen a sober soft spot since ol' Doug died (of course Mom was in a category by herself).

Soda had a sweet tooth. Loved sugar. Always had some kind of sugar he was carrying around. Sometimes cubes, sometimes in a little supermarket box, and sometimes just in those little coffee packets like you can steal from the *7-11*. "Sugar Sucking Soda," Ross would call out to him. He was always either holding on to it or playing with it or mixing it in to his bottle of green juice that he kept in a dirty old plastic grocery store bag tied to a belt loop off the side of his one pair of black pinstripe suit pants he must have found at the Goodwill.

That and his Plastic Jesus. Which he carried and cradled around in one arm or the other wherever he went.

Ross really took a liking to that plastic statue of Jesus too.

"Soda, boy. Where'd you get this thing? It's beautiful. Where in the hell did you come upon something as elegant and useful as this? And what used to be inside?" Ross unscrewed the everlasting father's head and promptly stuck his nose right down inside him.

"Well inside of there come sweets real fine with . . ."

"Chocolate," Ross chortled, arching his right brow real high proud.

"As a matter of fact there, you is right Ross. Had me some real good sweets inside ol' Jesus. *Kisses, M&M's,* and little chocolate licorice pieces."

"But he's empty now, Soda. This savior's got nothing left to offer. What you still lugging him around for?"

"He blesses me, Ross. 'Sides, how you gonna throw away Jesus anyway? How do you ever put Jesus in the trash? Even though that's where I found him."

"Where?"

"Behind the candy store, all the way down there by the pier. Someone just left him, man. Left poor Jesus just a layin' there under the trash. Believe that, man? So I took him out! And then I ate everything he had inside. Had to before it went real bad. And now of course I keep him with me. No way throwin' out the lord."

"Where is this store? What kind of store?"

"Candy, man. Candy store. I used to go everyday but the man inside caught me walking out with a pocket full of *Bible-Verse Buttermints* — you know with each one you get a free scripture. Kind of like them Chinese cookies I seen. I just forgot to pay is all. Now I'm not allowed back in ever since."

"Well goddamned Soda, just tell me where it is and I'll get that candy for you. I'll get it for you whenever you please. What's the name of the place?"

"Delilah's Just Desserts. Just ask for Dee-Deé, with the accent on the last Dee, not the first — 'cause she'll tell you first thing anyway, that's Delilah. She's real nice. Still likes me but it's her husband that don't want to see me around no more."

"Really?"

"Yes, I first knew her as a stripper when she used to dance down at The Tender Trap. But then she found god, changed her ways, married one of her best customers she'd been seein' for years as he was tryin' to talk her out of dancing anyway, and then one day they just struck a deal between the two of them. The deal bein' she'd quit and marry him if he would put up the money for her own business. A candy store business. He had some kind of inheritance comin' to him from some dead granny or something. Anyway, they struck a deal and with the help of god she quit strippin' and with the help of all his money they put up a candy store business. And it's all Christian candy. She keeps god in everythin' she does now. Although she did keep her stage name so all her old customers would know where to find her. And the husband, as you can well imagine, he wasn't real happy about that. But she said that's the way god wanted it and he just lived with it. He's a real pissed off guy anyway. Just sits in the backroom of the store drinkin', grumblin', and typin' away at some novel that he can't ever seem to get published."

Ross suddenly felt the need to do some chiming on the topic. "Well maybe he'd be a lot happier consented to the fact that what he's got to say just ain't worth a shit anybody wanting to read. Perhaps then he could start to get happy!"

"I know, I know, Ross. I said as much to him one day myself, meanin' to be helpful in a most kind way. But then he stuck his finger in my chest, poked me real good leavin' a bruise that lasted more than four or five weeks, said somethin' about the publishin' people not knowing their jack-off hand from a copy of *Moby Dick*, and then challenged me to tell him any different. And then I told him sure, I would, except I don't really have much time for readin', mostly 'cause I can't read — but I didn't want to admit to that, and then, well . . . well all I know is I ain't ever been allowed back in since.

"I must say though, regarding Delilah, or Dee-Deé — with the accent on the last Dee, not the first — 'cause she'll tell you that first thing anyway, she's runnin' a pretty good little business down there by the pier with all that sweet candy. And I do miss it. Miss it much. Done digged behind in the back in the trash. I miss it that much."

"Sure, Wood and I will get some of that soul-saving sugar for you first thing tonight. What time they close?"

"Oh, yeah, open least 'til midnight."

"And the husband works there?

"Oh yeah, but he just stays in the back and goes to bed real early. Probably 'cause he starts drinkin' Thunderbird every day right around noon. I don't think I ever seen him after dark in my life."

"Very good. Shall we, Wood?"

That was always a rhetorical question, and I was three strides ahead of him before he even finished asking it.

"Just got to pick up the backpack from home and we'll see you right back here in just as soon we can."

"Ah, Ross, you don't have to do that."

"But I do. I do. I do. I do. Do you know why?

"Wellll, no. Why, Ross?"

"Because we're going to make a little deal, you and me. I'll get you all the sweets you need, anytime you need, if you just let me have, no, no, just borrow, your Jesus for a while."

"You take good care of him?"

Ross just smiled, the big original one. And Soda smiled back. While handing Jesus over to Ross.

"*El Sagrado Jesús Plastico. Ahora es mio. Gracias al honorable, Soda!*"

Ross held it tenderly for a moment. Maybe two. Looking down on it with a whole lot of pride. Then he unscrewed his head, filled him to the top of his shoulders from one of the bottles of booze veiled in brown bags, and skipped right ahead of me.

"Lets go, Wood. Let's go get some candy-coated religion down at Delilah's Just Desserts. We'll be right back, boys. Right back, Soda. Lickety-nickety split." Then he just took a real long (and I'll have to admit even for him just a little bit immodest) greedy guzzle on what I can really only describe as the body of the baby Jesus. Preserved in plastic, of course. But for some sudden reason, a reason which I could not reason, boozing up Jesus just rubbed me completely the wrong way.

"How can you do that, Ross? Fill up something like the baby Jesus with your filthy alcohol and then suck it down like it was one of Mom's bottles of that *Night Train* or *MAD DOG 20/20.*

"What you be talkin' 'bout there Wood? What you think the savior, the big baby Jesus who once was the little baby Jesus, did when he turned that water into wine?"

"Obviously, that was for something holy, sacred. Like the sacrament."

"At a fucking wedding? No, Wood. It was a *wedding*. He turned that water into wine because he was going to a goddamn wedding."

"What are you talking about?"

"Ahh, that's right. You've never been to a wedding."

"So what."

"Wood. He was off to a wedding. He needed that wine. He needed that numby-num-num. Trust me."

"Fuck you, Ross"

Ross was in the middle of an even greedier guzzle. He laughed so hard at my saying that, which I must say I had never before said (well at least not directed at him) that he blasted his little adult Bethlehem beverage out of every single hole in his face. Even his eyes. When he recovered he just put his arm around me and we both started walking on down to the beach. Him giggling still like a little girl, me not so much.

"Well played, my brother. Very well played!"

And they were all still there when we returned that night. I mean not just Soda. But every single one of them blues-balling window-washers as well. Apparently they were all quite familiar with the "just desserts" you could find down at Delilah's, and not really ever wanting to waste their money on chocolates and such (first booze, then bread, then, well then more booze), were willing to stick around for this rather rare opportunity on this particularly special night.

And with Jesus three-quarters empty by the time we even got to Delilah's, and with Delilah herself having remained in quite honorable and praiseworthy stripper-form, and still dressing the part, and taking quite a striking liking to Ross right away . . . well, let's just say Ross and I returned with almost two of everything from the store and the backpack busting full. Ross paid for half of it with the money he'd won in *Whose Blues* that night and the other half just seemed to flow in free of charge as Ross and Delilah walked around the whole store, most of the time arm in arm, as he delicately picked up, palmed, and in a most involved and interested way, queried every piece of Christian sweetness in there (including Dee-Deé herself, and more than once I do believe). And she in kind was as twee-tickled to answer (in great depth, I might add) as any god-finding (and now fearing), ex-stripper with a potent vitality for chocolate and candy could ever possibly pray to be.

And so the generous distribution began. First to Soda, who immediately made as his first request two *Strawberry Mary's* and a *Pontius Pilate Popcorn Ball* (which was so deliciously thick and sticky with caramel and chocolate that unless you washed your hands right after eating — everything you touched afterwards just got fucked).

And then the shouting and charging began. All in good humor, of course. For how could it not be when the sight of a bag of candy turns old, grey, grown men back in to broad-eyed, greedy-grabby, and great big grinning nine-year-olds.

"Gimme some of those goddamned *What Would Jesus Ju-Ju Beans.*"

"I takes me one *Crucifix Candy-Cross Necklace*. The one with all the different colors."

"What about them *Candy Adams Apples*. You gets some of those?"

"And *Ave Maria Mary Janes*. A good gotdamned handful!"

"How's about some of them *Lazurus Life Savors*."

"Hold on now." Ross finally had to take back control. "No more just reaching in this here bag and calling out for stuff. Let's all go back behind St. Luke's by the back window where there's a little more light."

"But they see us back there and chase us out before we even get in a proper circle to choose," blasted Soda, as if Ross were about to drive us all off a cliff. "And then they just take the candy. Like the bouncers always be doin' when they catch us back there with our hooch."

"No," said Ross. "They just put a big, monster of a Christmas tree up there in that window. I saw it last night when I snuck in to see the band. It covers the whole goddamned thing. So not only can no one from the inside see out but with that tree with all them fucking lights shining, why we'll be able to see exactly what I got and what we got to choose from. We're safe, man. Let's go. Oh, and when we get back there one of you roll out your blanket and I'll set every piece of what's in this bag on there nice and orderly for everyone to see and we'll divide everything up evenly and real fair. Like Christians should. Especially at Christmas. So gird up your yarbles everybody and let's get to going!"

"OK, Cassius. Let's get to fuckey goin' then," one of them said. And each one of the others all agreed in unison by either nodding a head or just turning and jogging on ahead in front of me and Ross and wheels-turning, hard-charging Soda.

"But I still get all the *Judas Jelly Beans*. Right?" Soda yelled into the night without even looking behind. "If they still have them. Do they, Ross? Right?"

"Yes, Soda."

"You know them beans is joke candy. Right, Ross? It's funny funny. Real funny."

"I know, Soda."

"You give it to someone and it makes their mouth all black and tastes like goddamned salt and vinegar. It makes a face do things I never seen before. Ross, Ross. That's for me. Right?"

"So Dee-Deé informed me. Yes. And she made sure I took some just for you."

Back behind the club they had a tough time deciding who would get what and when and how until Ross finally convinced them that they each just take turns and pick one at a time. Of course, then there was a great debate about who would go first, then second, and so on. So Ross then just had them all pick balled up pieces of numbered paper from the then empty backpack and that was the order final. No discussion further.

The blanket rolled out. We each took a place on the edge and knelt reverently either on one knee or two. And then once all laid out on the blanket, spread out evenly by the hand of Ross like a pile of precious stones for their first time exposed to human sight, it was a most glorious confectionary consecration and display.

Foiled candied conserves. The colors gold, green, red, blue, purple, and silver. Each one crackling and electric. At times spinning with heat and then cooling in an instant as their colors changed to the rhythm of the blues-washed Christmas hymns echoing evergreen through the tree above us in the glass.

And it was the ember-ensconced shadow of that tree which made those pieces dance and burn that night. A shadow so great that at its foundation from where it sprung it seemed not even to have a beginning. Yet, as it rose it ascended on both sides unto itself in a continuum that one would have assumed might have an eventual endpoint and connection. However, it did not, and instead disappeared into the darkness and out onto the beach behind St. Luke's and perhaps still ran and ran and ran itself, drowning in the purling arms of the ocean.

Its edges, hued mist pink and steamed a black green from all the heat and luminance swirling inside the club.

But it was from within the shadow and all on its own that came the big, hot glow.

And it winkled and it blinked. A very strange shadow with its own adornments of metallica and a reflection upon the blanket that tickled all and beguiled us not just a little as it burned to life the booty before us right before we divided it amongst ourselves. Right before we took it to eat. Right then. And of course some for later. For other times. Of our own choosing. And not just because our physical hunger made it so.

All those tasty treats in the shadow and shade of St. Luke's easily rivaled all the Halloween pillowcases Ross and I ever emptied and threw on our own blankets at home. Ever. Even all combined.

And Ross and I halloweened serious and hard every year. Like a couple of scarlet, sugar-hounded harlots — that's how serious we took it.

Come to think of it one year we even went trick or treating as Jesus and Judas. It was the last year, actually. Ross knew that

that particular year would be our last in costume (we were both just too tall by his junior year of high school, we were taller than the parents escorting their kids) so he really wanted to do it up good and proper and go out with a little bit of our own personal bang and touch of peacockery and swagger. And more than anything else he knew it would irritate the crimany out of all the locals there in Pleasant Grove and be seen as blatant, shallow blasphemy.

And so we did. As such we did festoon ourselves. Carefully and with more than a little attention given to detail. The thing was, however, that everyone just thought both of us were Jesus. They could not (or would not?) recognize Judas (and there just is no Jesus without Judas, is there?). We tried to explain that one of us was not. But they could never tell the difference between the two of us (and just between you and me, I never could either). So in addition to getting chewed and harassed the whole night, and going home with the lightest of pillow cases in our Halloween history, no one even got it. Which really, really frustrated Ross. Much more than anything else. In fact, I might say he found it even to be tormenting. Even to his last day.

Anyway, it was never "Christian" candy we dumped out on our blankets all those years. I mean out on that blanket that night everything was very specifically and legibly labeled. Not only so pleasantly foiled. I mean (as you shall right now see) that Dee-Deé did have quite the theological wit for takeoff and dressing . . . she was a stripper, after all.

Before us that night was everything from *Bible Verse Buttermints* to *John the Baptist Jawbreakers. Apostle Paul Pixie Stix* to *Healed Leper Licorice. Gethsemane Bubble Gum. Resurrection*

Rock Candy. Walk on Water Watermelon Taffy. St. Peter Push Pops. Sermon on the Mount Sour Balls. Candy Coated Chocolate Crosses. Calvary Hill Cotton Candy. Matthew and Mark Milk Chocolate Malties. There was even something called *Noah's Nutrageous Peanut Butter Cups* — and you better believe that they only came in twos. (Only thing there actually from the old testament I happen to notice, now that I think back on it. Which makes sense, I guess, as technically speaking that would make it a Hebrew sweet. So it really didn't belong in any good "Christian" candy shop anyway.)

To sum up, we all went home that night with one of those once or twice in a year (and for some just once or twice in a lifetime) curlicue busting grins on our faces. The kind that reveal that men are all always just harking back to being little boys again.

That rare kind of smile that has no mask or veil or misdirection of any kind. The kind that has its shell cracked from the inside. And lets some of that rare light shine out and in. To the world. Revealing that it can feel good to feel good about a good feeling. Not sheepish, mature, nor damn sure ashamed.

Me and the window washer blues boys each carried home enough candy for at least three days. Days filled with that wonderful type of malady that while you groaned in pain you still reached for just one more (as you pleased and at your leisure) until finally there were none. Which made you very sad (for they were finally gone). But also very happy (for they were *finally* gone).

Soda got his extra bag of *Judas Jelly Beans* to pass along to all he would meet for that very next week. Making some new friends along the way, but mostly just enemies. And then tell us about each one with a laughter so roiled in his soul that it made him almost pop right out of his own bones and bounce up and down like the spring in his spine came from the toy factory in a clown-town evil and down under. A veritable black jack in the goddamned box. One that I promise you never would really want to meet.

Oh, and let's not forget about Ross. He got to, from then on until his very end, always sip his spirits from the always aborning body of plastic Jesus.

Yes, even the little baby Jesus himself.

XXII

When me and Ross would finish our fun there outside of St. Luke's we'd usually head back up the street and get our table up in the loft at Van Gogh's. We'd always get the same table next to the railing. Ross had to have the catbird throne at all times. Anything that was elevated. He loved the stage for more than just performing his songs. He liked being above. He liked looking down.

If his table was taken, Ross would either sweet talk the girls out of it that were sitting there ("Now, see now here you two little honey bunny vixens. It just so happens that I have this table reserved for the evening on account that my mother is flying all the way from Nuuu Yark to see me, and me and my brother here and . . . well she's a bit of the claustrophobic type and you know, doesn't like to be down around and in the middle of where so many people are sitting elbow to ear all crunched up and breathing on each other like at the bottom of a cemetery, besides here's a couple of tickets to The Whiskey for next weekend, and for your trouble . . . really now, you wouldn't mind. Would you? She'd really be fondue of you for doing something so generous and sweet like that"). Or, he'd just belly up to the table and act a little bit fucked in the head if there were guys sitting there ("Hello, my name's Johnny Cash. And this is my wife, June" — putting his arm around me — "We're getting married in a fever. Hotter than a peck of pickled peppered sprout"). And then

212

launch into whatever Cash song happened to be washing through his head at the moment. Pounding and slapping away the beat on the table, scooting and sliding everyone's drinks all over the damn place: *"I hear that train a coming/It's rolling round the bend/And I ain't seen the sunshine/Since I don't when/I'm stuck in Folsom prison/And time keeps dragging on/But that train keeps a rolling/On down to San Antone/When I was just a baby/My mother told me son/Always be a good boy. Don't ever play with guns/But I shot a man in Reno/Just to watch him die/When I hear that whistle blowing/I hang my head and cry . . .* Come on June, help me out here. And where's my goddamn harmoni-cay! "

Several times, not being quite in the mood for Johnny and me, the boys would want to take it outside. Johnny would just sit straight up, get all somber and sad and start slowly marching down the stairs balladeering away, *"The old home town looks the same/As I step down from the train/And there to meet me is my mama and my papa/Down the road I look and there runs Lizzy/Hair of gold and lips like dizzy/It's good to touch the green, green grass of home."* About half way down the stairs he would look back up at the gaping mouths of the poor saps sitting at the table, "Come on fellas let's get to going outside. There ain't nothing wrong with singing and swinging at the same time. Hurry up now. I need to get back up there before anyone else takes my table and finish proper my show." And they would get up, furious as all hell, of course, and move to another table. Either not drunk enough or just plain smart enough to let rabid dogs lie.

Only once did a couple of guys step out into the street and down an alley with him. I tried to follow him but he waved me back in and just said, "What the hell are you doing, June?

Somebody's got to stay here and keep the table and the others entertained. Get your ass upstairs!"

He came back up about fifteen minutes later. Hands in his pockets. A bloody mess. Nose leaking, lip spilling, asphalt crumbs embedded in his forehead. He sat down at the table. I felt sorry for him. I knew he was bound and deserving of a suitable ass-kicking. But I didn't like to see it. I just shook my head. "You just won't learn, will you?"

He was staring at nothing in the air, just kind of tonguing his mouth, sucking and bathing at his blood. "What do you mean by that?"

"Look at yourself. You got the horseshit banged out of you."

"Just hand me my *Evian*, please."

I rolled my eyes and said it again, my pity for him bolstered my courage and made me somehow feel dignified in my righteous signification. "It was bound to happen. You just won't learn. Will you? Why can't you just be like everyone else and learn a lesson before you get killed or crippled. Always got to be kicking and kicking against the pricks."

He shook his head right back at me. A little too tired to argue. So he made his point quickly. "Pricks make for good kicking. And those guys were pricks, some of the prickiest, indeed. Besides, they deserved to be kicked. Besides, there isn't anything wrong with getting killed. That's already on the horizon for all of us. The noble "when"s and "where"s of when it happens is all you have left to control . . . except for whom you've left behind, maybe. If you want to leave someone behind. Now, getting crippled. No. That should never have to happen. That I do not like. I would lose sleep over that. You would have to kill me then, Brentwood."

"Not even if you deserved it, I will not."

"Get crippled? No animal has, will, or shall ever deserve that." And then he grinned to himself and lapped some more blood from the lip gash. "Always remember, Brentwood: No greater love does a man have for his brother . . . than to kill him when he is crippled." And then he looked at me, very peacefully, and saw that I was confused. "No greater fucking love," he said.

"No greater love?" I pushed his bottle toward him across the table.

"Nope. Not in this lifetime."

"You still got your ass beat down pretty good."

"Mmmm. Is that right? Where are those other two guys?" He feigned a quick and mocking search of Van Gogh's. Looked underneath our table. And even asked me to empty my pockets.

"I don't know." I played along.

"Where am I?"

"Right here."

"Doing what?"

"What do you mean?"

"What am I doing?"

"Sitting down."

"Where?"

"At your table."

He finally took both hands out of his pockets and two-fisted his bottle for a drag while keeping both his eyes on me like he was waiting for the sun to shine right through my cavernous little noggin. The knuckles on both his hands were shredded and torn.

The skin lifted up on a few like rounded-out, flawless little flaps on the shiny white coral underneath. I stared at them for a moment or two, Ross holding them there for me to see and adore, and I tried to imagine the other guy's faces, but could not.

It was I who still couldn't learn.

He then held them out at full arm's length — put them out in front of his own face like a goddamn woman inspecting her fresh, new, fancy manicure. "We shouldn't hang here long tonight. I don't imagine they would, but those guys might come back with The Badges. Coppers, man! Let's go back to the house. I need . . . damn! The Hat's no longer. Brentwood, what did she used to do for my cuts again?"

"Tell you to close your eyes and then spit in them."

"You're very witty this evening. Well, whatever it was, it worked. Do we happen to have a bottle of that red stuff she always had on her that she would pour in me until I had to pretend like I was laughing to hide the fucking pain. Mercurochrome? Oh, wait. That was Mom. The Hat had peanut butter and butter cream. Wait, which one was for actual open wounds? No, yeah, wait, it was that red stuff. We got any of that?"

"If not, I believe your bottle of the clear stuff might have very similar ingredients."

He looked at his bottle, and then thought for a moment. "You know what. You are once again being witty, but you are probably exactly right. Fuck that red stuff. Although I hate to waste this stuff on a bunch of open, little wounds. Bah! We'll find something. Let's get out of here and get home. My knuckles feel like a goddamn wet hornet's nest. And people are still staring. My

216

god, man. You sure know how to make a scene there, Wood." He winked at me and proceeded to promenade down the stairs and out the front door with his two bloody mitts held straight in front of his face, palms inward, knuckles out, like some fiendish, freshly-scrubbed surgeon calmly making his way to his next surgical procedure.

His nurse was right behind him.

It got to the point where when we walked in to Van Gogh's, and if there were some people at Ross's trellis in the sky, they'd just start moving before we even got to the stairs. Most everyone there were regulars anyway, and knew us. And Ross would always comp them for their unwitting kindness with future tickets to our never-to-be shows on the Sunset strip. Or, if they were lucky, some free drinks, actual coupons he'd coquet out of the Gogh-go girls who were only supposed to give them to people who came in for their first time.

I ended up only having to be Johnny's wife two or three times. And luckily, never had to sing. I never had quite the same affinity for Johnny Cash as Ross did anyway. Much less his wife.

The first time we met Soda, Ross just *had* to take him to Van Gogh's. Soda spoke in shrill, soft, dry staccato. He had an accent that was both very odd and yet very familiar. It took me a while to figure it out, to determine it exactly. Actually I never did. It was Ross who heard me talking out loud to myself one day, trying to imitate Soda and finally put a finger on it. I suppose he had discerned it himself after only moments of meeting him.

"It's not *an* accent, Brentwood. It's *two* accents. He's got two fucking accents rolling off that prophetic little tongue of his."

"Impossible," I protested with confidence. "Even if he did have two accents, the combination of the two would create a whole other one and it would still be one accent. Not two. Even I know that."

"Yes yes yes. I know. But he trades off. When he jumps and skips and leaps his thoughts, his tongue lands in different grooves and goes back and forth between some kind of white, rural, Midwest prairie flair and some real deep, proud, inner city, negro-speak. But both are pure and unmistakable, even when he does it from one word to the next. It is subtle, but yes yes, very discernible."

As I thought about it, replaying Soda stereo in my head, I could hear it. "Well how the hell does that happen, I mean unless he's doing it on purpose. Where the hell's he from?"

Ross winked his fingers at me. Abracadabra-ing me to comprehension. "Nary a fucking idea."

"Now how in sam shit hell is that possible? You're practically his best friend . . . the only friend he talks to. You talk to him all the time. How could you not know where he's from?"

"Brentwood. Unless a man is wearing a white shirt and tie, never ask him where he's from. It's just plain rude. That is information that should only be offered by someone who chooses to share it. It's like asking someone how old they are. Or what God they believe in. Or how many times they fucked their best friend's wife. It just isn't done. Just not proper. I realize that doesn't sound so very damn common, perhaps even a bit peculiar . . . Here, let me give you an example . . . No, I'm tired of scrapping for metaphors and similes in our conversations. I'm ruining them, they're almost becoming cliché. Just trust me . . .

but not as far as you can throw me. Besides, most people just lie anyway. Tell you where they want to be from. It's better not to know. Least not until they tell you themselves. And then they're still probably lying their fictitious little asses off. Anyway, I don't know where he's from. But if you want to ask him, go ahead. Just keep it to yourself."

"So two accents, huh?"

"Probably has something to do with his disease as well."

"What disease?"

"I think it's palsy. Cerebral. Mind and nerves all going to hell in the worst way. Slow. Or maybe even some kind of muscular dystrophy. I can't really tell because either way his mind and body are both fucked up real bad. But he could just be born retarded and have his body eating itself away with a variety of God-given diseases. Or it could be all of them just spun into one. I don't know. Don't really like to think about it. Either from birth or from an accident or just getting knocked in the head an awful fucking lot when he was a kid. I mean a small kid. Like a baby. I've been reading about it down in that bookstore on the boardwalk. It's something that just keeps getting worse. Either way, he won't be around much longer."

"Hmph," I snorted, impressed with the opening of yet another one of Ross's "personal and unutterable unless the time presents itself" dispensations of wisdom.

When I think about it now I just wish I had taken a few of Ross's statements a little more seriously. He never lied. He made his confessions and requests early, often, and as literal as possibly could be done. He just hid them well. Camouflaged them in their own frankness. Disguised them in the brightness of their own honesty. Like all great storytellers. And liars.

Soda also had a very distinct gravel in his voice. And he stutter-paused at weird places between his words. Like he had some kind of notion that a complete sentence just wasn't natural.

These were two things I did not pick up that first time I spoke with him on the bench just a month or so before (did my drunk make him seem so normal?), but two things I did begin to catch the first time I heard him at the blues bar. And then he just kept getting worse.

His voice just kind of lay there at the bottom of his throat. Sounded like he was trying to swallow sand. It sounded like static. In fact, it kind of reminded me of Ross's old Mickey Mouse when the needle would get real worn down and start skipping all over the records (it always took us a while to save up for a new one). At first I thought he was just excited to go with us into Van Gogh's because no one had ever invited him anywhere before. But he always talked like that: a bouncing, bargain, old record player born with no bass and just a little bit of volume. You kind of had to hang there in the air in suspended vexation, straining your ears, waiting for the next skip to come, waiting to see where the needle would land.

Soda was real excited about visiting Van Gogh's with Ross and me until Ross started explaining and bragging about the special reserved balcony that we always had, and then suddenly Soda couldn't go.

"Sorry, man. You know I. Just now remember yes. I do I. Just now remember that I have to be down at. This other place. I cannot. Go."

Ross shut his mouth and studied Soda's face. "What do you mean you can't go, Soda. Just a goddamn second ago you were in love with the idea of joining me and Brentwood and now . . ." Ross shut up again. His eyes shot down at Soda's chair and then he scratched his nose and I could see he was calling himself an asshole inside. "Soda, man. We don't got to sit upstairs. There's plenty of tables downstairs. It's just a little closed in and claustrophobic is all, like dead fish in a barrel. But that's workable. Let's just go check it out. Now that I think about it a little bit more and accurately, I seem to remember an elevator. Just that me and Brentwood never have given that a real try as yet."

"I. Can't go. Upstairs, Cassius."

"Maybe. Maybe not."

"Can't. Do it. Cassius."

"We'll see, Soda." Ross put one arm on his shoulder and with the other started rolling him along in his chair.

"I'm telling you, Cassius man," he started to giggle and twitter, all that sand in his throat trying to get up out of him. "I know. What I can and cannot do. And stairs and me had plenty. No good pain in the past together. I . . ."

"We'll get it, Soda. We'll get it."

And off we went and walked right in. And Ross led him over to the stairs but Soda shook his head instead and so we sat beneath the upside-down, god-is-Pooh-Bear-cross. And on the next night Ross had him at the stairs again and Soda shook his head again and so we drank again at the foot of Pooh Bear's crucified little head. And on the third night he led him to the stairs yet again, and again Soda said noda. So this time we ate with the ape.

And this went on for a week. I kid you not. A goddamn week Ross led that poor, crippled, sugared-up and always with his green juice and just-a-little-kind-of-slow bastard, to the stairs. Yep, seven fucking days in a row. And on the seventh Ross just picked him up and carried him like a baby to his favorite balcony seat, Soda screaming the whole way up, and sat him down at the table. And then Soda started crying. So Ross shared with him a big, long green sip from the old *7-Up* bottle. And then Soda started laughing.

And after that first time Ross carried the cripple up those stairs every time. And Soda never minded at all.

And after that, when he wasn't pushing him in his chair, Ross carried Soda everywhere.

And they together shared that lush, glowing bottle always.

XXIII

Absinthe. It was no average juice (the oldest of wines sucked from the newest of bottles), this masterpiece of some august alchemist. But the emerald elixir was Soda's subtle bane and Ross welcomed its ravages upon his own heart and mind. The imminent residuum of Ross compelled an outlet of even larger proportions. His alcohol, he knew, was his amulet. A talisman, necessarily wheedling and tyrannical — and its powers still required enhancement.

And thus he plumed his lance head, a quivering gallantry, and leaned upon it as well.

The word is from the Greek "absinthion." It means "undrinkable" or "undelightful" (he galvanized his paradox as well!). So bitter beyond human pluck is a cup that it must be aromatized and soothed with a bouquet of herbs and still be succeeded by a sugar-suck. But nothing mellowed its bitter effects on his enough-already sourballed soul. He had finally found the savage sacrament that he wanted. The one that would glass his inner eyes with sufficient horror, and gloss his outers with more than enough testimony, facilitating what I now know he had known for quite some time in his fantastically planned and richly-so-sadly rhymed life.

And so now with the help of Soda and Soda's soda, this absintheur of Sparta — a new member and uncommon aesthete of the emerald city underworld and olive drinks with no olives — surrendered his life starkly and lovingly to the task.

And Ross and Soda would sit and sip the steely opal. Ross had endured 'til the end. Until all things had changed senselessly and wooden before his eyes (and him changing with them) 'til he became as God, knowing the difference between good and evil, and that they were one, and how recklessly and baselessly they might be separated by the thin, opaque veil of vengeance.

He had finally learned how to translate his myriad martyrdoms into indisputable expressions of life and death. I cannot imagine it.

(It may be a long time before my veil lifts.)

And so Ross and Soda were soon close companions. And perhaps even before the happenstance of their first meeting were an unknown union to all — except to Him, who does the carving and the whittling in preparation for the proper fits in human coalescence. If you believe in Him. If not, just call it corny coincidence — their convergence, like an iceberg and a boat.

Old Soda did now always need the chair. And Ross wheedled and rolled him around the shops, stores, sights, and sounds of Venice with the fury and huff-puff of an old-world occidental rickshaw race. It had been so painful for Soda to walk around since his being bussed out to the West coast that all he had been able to manage was the few hundred yards from the homeless shelter where he lived to his place of labor and handouts on his bench near St. Luke's.

But Ross showed him the world.

Ross propped him up and danced him like Geppetto with the Van Gogh-go window girls. And Soda did more than wax a wooden smile.

Rolled him next door to The Sword of Femmecles and introduced him to a matriarchy of kind and benevolent lesbians who loved him like a brother and awarded him with androgyny.

Ross wheeled him agog up and down the strip of Sunset, finding friendly favors with the working girls (trading trite tricks for a skinful of sinthe), and gaining free access to just about every bar and club on the boulevard with the bait of the lame and the duping of a devil.

With Ross, Soda was unleashed. He was actually quite the charmer, even rivaling Ross at times, and the pair of them — the bald, black, bag of bones sitting in his shiny, stolen chariot and pointing the way with a box full of sugar cubes, yelling, "Cassius. You going. Awaaay too fast for me now don't. Kill me let's stop. Stop and talk to those girls those girls right over there and then let's go awaaay down into The Coconut Grove on the corner next to Rock 'n' Roll Denny's. Right next to Rock 'n' Roll Denny's. Cassius. You going to. Kill me."

And his cockswain — the lengthy, ashen-white scarecrow with strewn, long black confetti for hair, cheap echoes for eyes, and a crowbar for a smile, pushing and running from behind and then standing on the wheel bar of the chair to coast for a while, just yelling right back, "Whooaa there, young Soda. I'm just standing here on the back along for the ride just like you. Get your hands off them goddamn wheels and quit spinning us so fast or you're going to get us both killed for sure and forever. I have no control. Look at me, for I ride just like you. Quit spinning the

225

goddamn wheels . . . but not before you get us over to our friendly friends there on yonder corner and then down the road to Rock 'n' Roll Denny's."

But in the end their friendship, even courtship if I can state it as such, frightened me. It was fostered with a great speed and it seemed to me that they knew each other just a little too well and entirely too soon. I did, and was allowed to, tag along on these sojourns and journeys up and along the seedy soils of L.A. and its beaches. But I soon grew tired of it, physically and emotionally, never having quite the stamina to absorb and celebrate that which the plundering puppeteer and his merry marionette were able to see, buffer, and glean through their sucking of sugar and sopping of green. And that was how Ross had always intended it. He had Soda. And either I was not allowed to go or was not capable, somehow not worthy, to run the last lap with Ross.

But I really believe that he just loved me too much to let me bear that burden and wear that mantle.

It was immediately after I had been replaced (once again and forever), or perhaps cut loose, that Ross enlisted Soda for his daily visits up the coast to that house in Malibu, where Ross continued his stalking. Soda's condition was in a rapacious decline, due at least in part to the fact that Soda now lived on our roof, where Ross would carry him nightly, to a bed he made for him right above his window, and goad him to even more spectral amounts of the juice that made them both see yellow and finally, for Ross, put a halo on his sacrifice.

It was where Ross would also sleep, on nights when Lizzy was either cast out for what had happened, or on the rare occasion she had sufficient strength and sobriety to ward him off by avoiding his company.

I do not know exactly why he chose Soda. I've even entertained the thought that Ross's unfortunate flair for the internal drama that he loved to play out on the stage wherever he walked, with a voice-over that was scarce and always surreptitiously sublime, necessitated a symbolism that only he was privy to. And it was this poor, little, black retard. A cripple hopped up constantly on absinthe, the pay he received from a dealer on the beach for receiving and then delivering a small but sumptuous amount of crack each week from a regular at St. Luke's.

An abbreviated human, maimed in the mind, and gnarled of the body, being consumed and now even cannibalized by not only himself but also his new best friend.

But Ross needed someone — or at least some thing — to lend him a kind, blind hand and be of one last final use as he confronted the vertigines of his bloody, boiled-over heart.

I guess of course that it could not have been that Ross just loved Soda. Loved his purity. His simplicity. Adored his innocence in this world. Observed a sabotaged mind immured in the cruelest and most unmerciful of dungeons and beheld a spirit kindred, if not even the very mirror of himself.

For all the right reasons, just plain loved him?

Yes, most likely. And no, for that would hurt me too much. And then again, understandably. For I believe I now grasp that love very well.

Someone had written on one of the doors of my favorite wall in Van Gogh's Ear:

In seasons of pestilence some of us will have a secret attraction to the disease, a terrible passing inclination to die of it. And all of us have like wonders hidden in our breasts, only needing circumstance to evoke them.

Most of the people I've known (but now I cannot even count myself) are fortunate enough not to cross paths with this "circumstance." Although they may sit and dawdle and wonder on the rim of the pit, like stunned maudlins enfeebled — and thereby saved — by the cowardice that a blindfold of a commitment to faith and responsibility might bring. Ultimately their fall into depravity is simply a matter of luck (bad or good) meeting preparation, and the arbitrary lack thereof.

I believe now that I can actually pinpoint with precision the moment when Ross discarded his blindfold. Exactly when he reached around and untied it and said, "Fuck this and you and me and all of you that wear this and especially those of you that tied this around my head." But then I cannot. I could. But it would be a lie.

I do not know if he took it off at my mother's funeral. At my father's hanging body. Or at reading about Doug's death.

I do not know if he took it off when he was fourteen and heard for a countless time that crashing of my mother's head against the bedroom wall as she forgave a man and pleaded with him to be just that: a man — this, my father — to stay away from the whores in Mexico where he traveled to preach, and the alcohol everywhere else, and not defile the God he preached of every Sunday to his flock ("that lying wolf-fuck all darned in shepherd's gear," as Ross liked to say) in the churches there and in other cities around the country, and not defile the children he was kind to (only in public), to whom he had given only one thing, his name, and nothing else. But never did she ask him to stop defiling her.

And I do not know if he took it off at my father's funeral, where he shed not even a tear, until we got home and he asked me to play catch with him in the backyard where he cried without shame and threw the ball 'til my hand was bruised beyond feeling, because Father never would.

Or at Doug's private 21-gun salute funeral (that he attended uninvited, because no one else knew of their friendship) in the cemetery next to where Doug taught, where Ross would sometimes go to run when, I think, sometimes he really didn't want God to be dead.

And I do not know if he took that blindfold off that one particularly rare nebula night, the night before our penult Christmas (three days after he met Lizzy) when I could not find him. And when, with every good reason, I searched for him in Mom's boneyard (a night he would never mention although I know goddamn well he never forgot, for after that he looked at his scarry, scarry arms every night of his life) and found him there on his back in typical angel sprawl, untroubled and paralyzed on her ground. His arms spread wide and his wrists spread wider. Ripped ragged with dull broken vodka glass bottle. Blood still veining through new, sweaty snow — slow — trying to hide in the dull, dead grass of winter.

He woke the next morning in his own bed with his forearms swaddled and cinched in my white shorn sheets and butterfly bandages. He was all I had. He was blood. My blood. To lose him then was to kill us both. He woke and requested more drink for his pain, and I gave it to him and never left his side again. 'Til there was Soda.

And I do not know if perhaps he removed it after the phone call from Mad-Hatter Malibu. When he first learned about Lizzy being drugged dizzy and the men that then rode her around in a board game of their own.

The phone call from her. The only girl. But much better than that, the only human he had ever fallen in love with — the rabbit's-kiss kind. The phone call when his face frosted pallid pearl and his hair got blacker and his cheeks went sallow and his breast even sallower, and he shifted right before my eyes into that scared and crowed ghost with the honest black soul and the good sharp mind and a damn good sense of humor — that very same scarecrow I have referred to before — and never changed back.

I cannot even say with much confidence if he even actually ever took the fucking blindfold off at all. Maybe he just pulled it down a little bit so he could peek over the top, kind of like he was cheating, thinking no one else could tell, finally trying to pin the tail right.

Or maybe he just cut holes where the eyes were, making the blindfold into a mask, and me into Tonto. Or perhaps he kept the thing on the whole damn time, challenging himself, even playing the spinning game before trying to pin the tail on the backside of God. I don't know. I'm not quite sure.

I suspect he just kept trying to rip it off, once and for all, many different times. Even after it was long gone and cast off. Just kept raking and clawing at it, like an amputee scratching at an itch on an inveterate, invisible limb, until he was scratching at his own eyes, and blinding himself again.

Whenever it was, one thing was for certain, he could see, or at least thought he could see, the extreme blacks and whites of his innards and the great grey area where they converged. He saw both the dark and the light in truth and the vast potential for nobility, his nobility, in the perversion of both. And he found that he could control them. And so he did. He became the mixoligist of his own shades of black and white. His own experiment. Trying to find the perfect proof.

But first he became his own quarry, his own puppet, perfecting his art long before he let anyone else conscript and tie themselves in.

And then he became like Father, at least initially, at least a little bit, having at least been made in his own image. I like to say that he was a shepherd in wolves' clothing (a very clever trick, I must give him credit there) and felt very much at home in his bastardized, byzantine forest, finding the Little Red Riding Hood in us all: this preacher heart-stealer . . . of his own traveling show.

He simply and finally just removed all his restraints, every single shackle he had languished so dutifully in. And did so in the solitude and silence of his own rack-renter soul and stolen spirit. He sought honesty, and in doing so brought out his own true nature, and all the horror that came with it. If he was my blood, he was also my cross, and I could not carry it much longer, especially with him upon it.

XXIV

*B*ut none of this I would have ever known were it not for four crooning black guys who harmonized to brass-ass perfection and sang the songs of childhood love. They didn't sing their lyrics, they serenaded them.

Their voices were the innocence that only parents can protect and once gone can never be retained. But they brought you as close as you could come, nosed you right up to the very edge of the abyss of puerile paradise lost. Close enough so that if you closed your eyes, the wanderlust nipple of that world-without-care (before hearts became brittle, minds mere niggards of fate — where ignorance was more than bliss — it was just a goddamned way of life) stuck in your mouth as the bars in your windows, doors, and wit became nothing more than the sweet security of Baby's little crib. Mother's first manger. (Whatever went wrong in there?)

Ross had collected most of their stuff on our garage sailing blues expeditions and loved them and knew them and listened to them as much as the blues or anything else, just for different reasons. Our mother loved them too, which is how we first heard them, on her eight-track player which she kept on her Mormon-must wheat grinder in the kitchen. That and gospel Elvis ("How Great Thou Art") on Sundays, whose voice would make my mother weep. Until he died and a book came out about all his drinking and women. And one morning all those tapes were gone, hefted out to the garbage (to the bin of a grocery store, lest it still linger on our property) and not only had Elvis left the building, but he was never mentioned again under its roof.

Our verdant Saturday mornings were filled with their melodies and signified a day of no school, hot cracked-wheat, buttered bread frothy on the air, and Father out of town on business (proselytizing to prostitutes). We'd ready our bikes, eat our bread, sip warm cinnamon milk, feel our mother's arms as she'd hug just a little too long (for a couple of young "men"), and steep our youth in the sunny affects of some other brothers' harmony: The Mills Brothers.

John Jr., Herbert, Harry F., and Donald F. Four Midwestern boys from Ohio who were not only a quartet, but real-life sons of a barber as well. But they came from the swing and the rag and Duke Ellington and Tommy Dorsey and only flew close enough to the burn of the blues to warm their wings and singe a thrill up a Coney-Island carnival spine.

And I'll be goddamned if Soda didn't know every one of their fucking songs as well ("You don't say Cassius you. Don't really. Say now, do you? Them's. Was my momma's most favorites of all as well.") He would sit there on the roof and sing them (god, he too did have a wonderful singing voice — I've seen it before with singers — no scratching and skipping when he sang, his sandtrapped speak turned to loam gold when he crooned; a perfect tenor) to Ross until it drove me crazy and I had to sneak up there myself and hide behind the water tank so I could close my eyes and get as close as I could and ride the voices back home.

I resisted for a while. But eventually I was a regular. Hidden. But still a regular.

And then it just happened. One sane and routine crispy brisk evening in the middle of Fall. I had just climbed the stairs to the upper room of our crack-house in the cosmos, having returned from what had become fairly mechanical dark-time walks along the beach to consider my reconsiderations of Ross and me and settling down to dream on my mat and wooden floor, when the three voices melted and pierced me and the whiff of the hot, cracked-wheat, buttered bread was on my tongue before I could deny or even rationalize its possibility.

A bass and two tenors. It was real. It was perfect. And I wasn't even asleep yet.

Up the lazy river by the old mill run
The lazy lazy river in the noon-day sun
Layin' in the shade of a kind old tree
Throw away your troubles, dream a dream with me

Up the lazy river where the robin's song
Awaits a bright new mornin' as we just roll along
Blue skies up above, everyone's in love
Up the lazy river, how happy we would be
Up the lazy river with me

The roof began to creak a bit as well. Very slowly. Rolling and rolling like it was on some kind of sea. It made a bit of a clatter. I wrenched my neck up and out. Sat down on the sill even. Almost fucking fell and died for it. And then I saw Tablet's head — old Tablet, the lord of our land. Just for a second. Just the back of it right over the lip of the rain gutter. And then I saw it again. It moved sideways. One. Two. And then disappeared again. Then sideways. One. Two. Gone.

And then I saw the front little wheels of Soda's chair. Up. Rise in the air for a moment. They jiggled left. Jaggled right. One. Two. Right in time with the beat. And then gone.

They were trading parts. Tablet had the bass. Would take front center stage. Sing a couple of lines. Do a few steps. And then it was Soda's turn. He had one of the tenors. And someone was pushing him. Dancing him in his chair. Of course it was Ross. But I still heard another voice. Harmonizing perfectly, honey-brushed and Mills Brothers black. No way that was Ross. He could sing, but not like that. He had found another friend.

I went through the window in the kitchen, the only one that had access to the roof, and scooted my incredulous little ass out the window and onto the roof behind the water tank. I crouched behind it with my back to the voices. It was still "Up the Lazy River." I turned around and raised up just enough to rest the top half of my pupils on this most eerie and cheery of sights. It was them. Tablet had an eight-track, just like Mom's, and he had it up there on the roof. But there was no new friend. I was wrong, but yes, again.

It was Ross, and another new language.

"*Throw away your troubles, dream a dream with me.* Now you, Tablet. Take it man, take it. Take it all the way and do that little soft-shoe again you were trying to show me before except this time give it that full fucking turn — not the half one — and take it all the way to *where the robin's song* and then Soda will take the last verse. All right — here we go here we go!"

> *Up the lazy river, how happy we would be*
> *Up the lazy river with me*

Up the lazy river. I was looking at Puck Spin and a couple of Lord Jims — one clambering in and out of a limey bottle of *Evian*, one absentia in absinthe, and one with a corn cob crack-pipe — all of them hidden and dancing in the bush on the banks of a roof-top crackhouse, conspiring away on a euphonious raft of barbershop song and having too much damn fun doing it.

"Yeessuhrree, son. I said Yeessurrreeeeeee! Now listen up here an' give me all yuh ears an' eyes an' Ah goin' to show yuh dis step one mo' time, an' yuh too now Soda, son, yuh skin-flin' muthuhumpuh. Yuh be gettin' up out ob dat chair one day an' better damn well know dis here. It's just a step to de right an' den a jump to de lef an' keep dem ol' hips oiled an' don' forget to click yo' heels on de downbeat . . . yeessuhrree, son, loookeee me, loookeee me go! De ol' Tablet still got it . . . still like dey ain't no mo' tomorrows, why here come a *Shim Sham Shimmy*, den a *Maxie Ford*, den on top ob dat ah put de ol' *Paddle an' Roll*. Gotdamn! . . . *Blue skies up above, every one's in love* . Ross, son. Push dat ole Soda up dar, now."

"Aw, now Tablet. I. I. I can't go do no. Dancing like that you just done." His face squirmed at the thought of it. "It just a too. A too. A too painful."

"Cassius gots yuh dar, son. Cassius what de hell yuh waitin' for! Soda's goin' to be missin' his lines here soon."

236

"Right on it, Tablet. Just needed a little sippy-sip of the greeny-green, you know. I can't hold my bottle in my mouth like you got going there going with that cob o' corn-crack pipe."

"Cassius. I. I. I just can't you know that now."

"Here now, Soda. Put your goddamn bottle down and I'll dance it for you. You just keep to singing."

And so Ross did Tablet's step while Soda sang in the center of another one of Ross's stages, each one of them seeming to get closer to the heavens. Ross held his bottle to his breast like he was slow dancing his last slow dance with his truest love of all. Tablet "Yeeesssuhrrreeed" on his pipe in approval, and smiled and smiled and smiled. And Soda looked up and serenaded, and did justice to yet another starry, starry, yellow-haloed Santa Monica sky that even Vincent himself would have been proud of.

"Up the lazy river, how happy we would be. Up the lazy river with me."

Ross was getting that little slow soft-shoe move down pretty good and started to speed it up. His bottle slipped from his hands and he started to juggle it, lost his footing and fell into Soda's lap. But Soda didn't miss a beat. Could not take his black eyes off the bright night, and just kept on singing. Ross sat up and just stayed on his lap. He winked at Tabby and Tabby winked back.

And then, and I don't know where he got the fucking strength, or I guess I didn't know that he had just had it all along, Soda grabbed the wheels of his chair, tilted it back, and had them both in the air in a wheelchair wheelie of song. And then, very slowly, but still singing away and staring at the sky, he spun his chair around. Him and Ross were spinning. They were in the air.

237

Ross looked down at Soda with a great glassy glimmer of pride in his eyes. And then he looked at Tablet. He raised his bottle, and Tablet raised his pipe.

"Why Cassius, Ah do believe yuh done been raised up dar by yo very own retárd!"

Ross smiled so large that he almost made his crooked mouth go straight. "Lookee here, Tablet. You well-read motherhumpin' son of a bitch. I believe indeed you are right. Right as London rain, for sho'."

Tablet would only make it up there once or twice a week. But Ross and Soda would sit and sing together almost nightly. Sing each other to sleep. And in between songs — sometimes right in the middle and during the melodies themselves — and for the very first time, I heard the sad, sad, story of Lizzy.

Between the likes and loveliness of, "You're Nobody 'Til Somebody Loves You," and after and before the awful charm of "You Never Miss the Water 'Til the Well Runs Dry." It drew me to the roof every night. I even had a pillow hidden underneath the water tank. "I Don't Know Enough About You." "Opus I." "Glow Worm." All of it.

But most of all and without fail I'd hear the story right before, and then sometimes then again right after, "Paper Doll." Hear the tale over and over again, and catch glimpses of Ross's mind and machinations, as he would sing that beautiful, beautiful song:

I'm goin' to buy a paper doll that I can call my own,
A doll that other fellows cannot steal
And then those flirty, flirty guys with their flirty, flirty eyes,
Will have to flirt with dollies that are real

DAVID NASH

When I come home at night she will be waiting,
She'll be the truest doll in all this world.
I'd rather have a paper doll to call my own.
Than have a fickle minded real live girl

XXV

$\mathcal{H}$is rooftop tale. There would be times when he would have Soda tell it with him — and for him — on those days or nights when his mind would still not deny him the purgation and justification it brought him. The analgesic absolution promised as a preface to what he finally began to envision, not as a vision any longer, but as an inevitable reality. The final act before the levity of his conscience and the total absence of guilt ferried him to insanity, and took away finality's meaning. And took away the only meaning he had left:

"And he took her, Soda. The man named Sinboni. The middle-aged, rotunda-waisted, pudgy-handed fuck with Panama hat to hide a voracious toupee and Hawai'i-flower shirt and heavy gold laid in his proud grey protrusion of saggy-titted chest hair. I've seen him. I followed like coyote. Ripped-jean shorts. *Rolex* watch. And sandals made for surfers.

"Plucked her right out of a grocery store there in the middle of Malibu at the most innocent part of the day right in the middle when the day is at its brightest. Just like a ripe piece of edible-fleshed virgin pomegranate, so red and of satiny fine leather, he could have got just two aisles over. Took her for no fault of her own but just because she was tall and beautiful and took her of no fault of her own, but of God's fault.

"Because He made her tall and beautiful and innocent through and through, virgin to the point of weakness. And gave her a bastard father who left her for no good reason except that her mother was a slut. A slut of the worst kind, for she was a slut with good intentions, which made herself all the more the whore."

Soda would then come in, when Ross would pause long enough, and pick up where he left off. "What chance she have. Then, Cassius? She beautiful like Hollywood and the shiny. Pictures in the magazines. And a nice old gettin'-grey man ask her if she in the movies in the nice old. Grocery store when the sun is out. And she say no. And he say can I take your picture. And she say. No again. And he tell her he. Doin' TV shows and movies. He show her his nice car outside. Black. Cherry. Mustang. And she say she have a boyfriend in some old. Rock band coming. Out to the Hollywood. And he say he can help. And he give her a business card. And say call me."

"Yes, yes, Soda. That is how it went. Then that sweet stupid slut who thinks she can fucking do me some kind of goddamn favor calls up that stupid fatty fuck that very same day and says she'd like to talk about it. And lets the shark-finned fuck pick her up right in front of that same green grocery store and drive her to his fucking palace and his lair, hidden away in the Malibu mounds piled behind the ocean because he says he's throwing a party that night and it would be a very nice opportunistic time for her to meet some people in the 'business'. Very helpful people. People who are just sitting around trying to find new talent and that they would love to help her and the party starts at seven and just come dressed casual but don't tell anyone where you're going because it's a secret address and he can't afford to have anyone uninvited up to his house with all these famous people there."

"And. Then. There. She be to go."

"Lamb to the whorehouse."

"Whore to the. Slaughter."

"And the difference is?"

"Where be. The difference?"

"None."

"And she go in but. There ain't but nobody there except for him and two others with the gold. Why, Cassius, all these nice old men are smoking the. Marijuana cigarettes."

"Have one, Soda. I'll bet they probably have a special one just for you."

"Why Cassius, what big long marijuana cigarettes. You got."

"Why Soda, the better to . . . Here, have this one."

"Why don't mind. Be I do."

"Inhale just like the nice old men, now."

"Okey-dokey."

"How you feeling?"

"Just fine, Cassius. These nice old men are even nicer than I. Thought and my rock 'n roll boyfriend he be so. Proud I just feel numb. All over. But it be a good numbing."

"Why look over yonder, Soda. One of the nice old men. The one with the Panama hat and the special surfer sandals. He's got the video camera pointed at you. And look Soda. The other one is taking your pretty little blouse off. And now he's lifting your skirt up."

"Cassius I. See it. But I. Can't move and I don't feel nothing the old man. Is breathing hard right on me."

"And his gold is smacking you right in your pretty, blue, innocent eyes."

"And he be grunting right in my ear. He saying all kind of nasty things all up. In my ear."

"That's right. And now there's another nice man holding the camera. Look, he's getting a close up. 'Excuse me, Mr. Smelling. Are you ready for Soda's close up?' And now the other nice man. No, now both of them have taken all your clothes off. And they're taking turns with the camera, Soda. Not to mention with you too."

"But I. Can't be feeling nothing."

"I wonder why. They sure seem to feel a lot of something and feeling it good."

"You don't be supposing was something. Else there in the long marijuana cigarettes . . . or maybe that a special. Real special cigarette or. Something in that old glass of wine now . . . do you?"

"Of course not. Now, Soda these are the niiice wealthy Malibu movie men. Not the other kind. They are . . . philanthropists if you will (there are so many here in these hills), who run around grocery stores asking tall vestals and beautiful strangers if there is any way they can make them rich and famous because it just makes them feel sooo good inside, and the world such a better place. These aren't bad men. Hmmm."

"What do you see now?"

"Nothing, now. My face is pushed. A too goddamn hard into this here. Lamb-skin couch. They be doing something. There up my backside. But I can't really feel nothing. I can't even. Move my arms so I just be laying here all a jumbled and peaceful-like with my eyes open but I. Can't even talk or feel nothing."

"In fact, you'll feel it real good when he dials the number you left on one of his business cards in your own handwriting before you left, and calls you early the next morning, when you're still waking from your crippling. You dizzylizzy. The rape of my frock. And he asks you if you had a nice time, and you say 'yes' on his recording, before your memory is back, and you realize your vagina is swollen, and you can't take a shit because your ass is scabbed shut. Like your memory. But they will both open up soon enough."

"Oh yes, Cassius. I know I be feeling. That. That's why I be. Calling you in Utah that very next morning I be calling you. For some comfort. Because I be too afraid to tell no one else just too. Afraid. I just keep drinking Mama's wine 'til you get here. Mama's wine be fine. I just call you, Cassius."

"And I'll just come running, Soda. Put you right back together again. You broken little boiled egg. You don't have to worry, Lizzy. I'll fix everything."

And, like I said, sometimes Ross would tell the whole thing, and sometimes Soda would, and sometimes the both together, just like they sang the songs. And sometimes they would end up laughing. And sometimes crying. But I could tell the laughing was for the future, and the crying for the past. Or maybe it was all for the past, at least for Ross.

Maybe this whole thing was just a cycle to him. A ride he couldn't get off of. A ride he was convinced he wasn't supposed to get off of. Like a merry-go-round, with the only option being to mount a different horse. A different painted pony. But always go in the same direction. End up in the same place. These were the ponies that only had one trick. Round and round and round. And getting dizzy never is something for getting used to. It never stops, until you fall off trying to make it.

Or you just let go of the brass ring, release your own self, and tumble for the oblivion. Drunk on the cause. Or maybe drunk off it. What does it matter to the poor bastard who's trying to catch you?

And I saw and heard many other things on the roof seated behind the water tank. In front of the backs of Ross and his bender-itchy trigger finger. With his grotesque green fiend, I mean friend, who was getting greener with every waxing of the moon and who seemed to get taller next to Ross in the night sitting in his chair with wheels.

But I knew it was not Soda who grew taller, but Ross who got smaller, as he shrank and crinkled each night on the roof. His sadness and madness and fear and loathing imploding him and calling him home. Back to the fetal and the curled. Like a timely cancer that swells from the bowels, shrinking him like a not-so-bad grinch every time he told his tale — the final peg upon which he had been able to hang and avoid the elaborate rationalization of his predicament. And when it was removed, when he had finally removed it, nothing stood between him and the chartered results and final solution of his malformed soul.

Now — and he knew it right then, I know he fucking did — it was only a matter of debate within himself of when time would come to claim. And all the colliding and conspiring articles of his faith should smash him to pieces. And then — and only then — would he be free to let go, to tumble, head over heels, and cease his flirtations with this last ludicrous series of events which had hastened him to the final (but only designed and premeditated) debacle of his life.

XXVI

*Y*es, Tablet was there too. He had started to linger after the gambol on the gambrel, after the sessions of song and dance, and finally fell in love with Ross and Soda, just as they had fallen for each other.

I burst in on them one very bright Thanksgiving night. We'd eaten earlier that afternoon in honor of the day. Ross and I had shoplifted a couple of frozen roosters (only birds left the night before that day) and made white bread rooster sandwiches with mayonnaise, ketchup, and salt. Tabby brought the real treat of that day though: several large pitchers of homemade lemonade and a great big mess of black-eyed pea boogaloo with turkey necks and pig jowls (or was it ears?). Of course he didn't tell us what the meat was 'til the next day ("Why A'hm goin' to tell yuh now, boys. It's turkey, sons. Gotdamned good holiday meat. If yuh gonna move dat mouth young Wood, have it be chewin' more, an' axin' less. Gotdamn, yes suh!"), which was alright by me because it was delicious and I would've never eaten it otherwise. "Dis here Ah learned to cook watchin' ma momma an' den got it real gotdamned right durrin' all dem Thanksgivings out at sea in all de different countries shippin' round on every sea an' blue water. Eat up, sons! Yuh ain't never had turkey dis sweeeet a'fore in yuh lifes."

Later we ate some pumpkin pie filling straight from the can and then the three of them went up to the roof while I stayed to wash dishes and then just went to bed.

And there I dreamt of Mom and the Thanksgivings we'd had together. Just the three of us: She, me, and Ross. And how it always made her so happy just to watch us eat (any meal for that matter, on any day of the week — even on the saddest of her days the sight of me and Ross chewing like fools brought beaming smiles to her face). And how she would kiss us each on the forehead right before cutting and then serving great silent slabs of pumpkin and mincemeat pie. She would always serve me first. Every year. And I remember distinctly in that dream observing for the very first time in my life that Ross would never mind this fact, that of me always being served first and usually with the largest portion, as he was also with those very same smiles beaming.

And all of this brought me great warmth in the dream of that night. Even delight and the sudden and unusual ease of a rightful existence in my own skin. I seemed to float outside the tiny tremors of terror that had ever my whole life coursed my veins with the casual bump and flow of my very jingle-jangled heart. And my thoughts, as such always most innocent and original and plain, were each one there uncocooned from their envelopes of shame.

Then, of course, with the din of their dancing and singing from above I awoke in the middle of that night, alone in my room there in Venice. And with the sudden evaporation of that perfect sehnsuchtian vision, I felt the tremors flow again.

And I watched those thoughts fly home to their prisons like butterflies back to their jars and some even to chains staked to the earth. Others also staked floated like kites dead and petrified in the salty wind while still others were yet alive and lifting — trying in vain to fly away. And then there was one I remember quite distinctly beating its wings in a fit of madness while sealed in a perfect globe of glass. All its dust in the air like rainbowed snow.

All of them heaving their breasts and winding down their meanings for never would they fly again. And all of this on a beach as wide as my mind. While the ocean crept on them like a natural born killer, one modest and wicked wave of mutilation at a time, to cleanse its coast and consign all these magnificent mute beauties, this great soundless ever evolving ultraviolet mosaic of me, the mirror reflection of my soul, to the wet death. One unique vein and scale at a time.

And, then, how should I say . . . well, I cried. Like a little baby I cried (and this I do say with a fair amount of shame).

And of course as I always had all my life, since before the days even of remembering, when my soul would tighten and wrench, somehow knowing that all that would ever await me in the world was brokenheartedness and large empty spaces. And also because I could never go to my mother, for that which might drive me to her — the very sounds of her own sorrow and fear, either locked in her room alone because of my father or indeed with him there and at the end of his hand — did simultaneously keep us apart. And so I would search out my brother instead. For he could make it good again. He always made it all right.

And so it was without the least bit of hesitation that I followed the sound of the dance and the song and was out the window, up that ladder and on to the roof in the middle of that very vivid night. And there. There was a scene there that was of double-dyed panic and horror at first sight.

All I could do was stare, stare, and stare. The kind of stare you might only experience once or twice in your life, where you have to remind yourself to blink because your eyes start aching from getting dry. But the scene was true. Too true. That night was real. And the images to this day make the thuds of panic and dread in my head and my breast heave me empty — sometimes until I feel nothing inside but the void of hard, barbed white.

I should first reveal that all that I saw there was accompanied by song (as was all activity and pursuit up on the roof). But this one song specifically I had never heard before. Not the tune nor the words. Ross and Tabby were trading verses as they were wont to do, with dancing and tapping, shadow boxing and Cassius calling, standing up and then sitting down. But now all of this was seemingly in an attempt to use all the swords and knives that happened to be there with them on that night (yes, even nicely, neatly spread out on a giant swath of old U.S. Navy blanket). And yes, use them all as either dancing props or instruments of beat and syncopation to keep time with on the backs of their chairs or on the rims and sides of their big, tall glass pitchers of vodka lemonade and Green Fairy wine.

But that was not their only use. No, no, no. Not at all.

XXVII

For the most unspeakable sight of all, the most luridly macabre vision I beheld that night, one that I had never before seen, nor thought possible even to imagine (for this type of imagination would never be part of what I could ever possess; nor could it possess ever even the smallest part of what does constitute me), and one that should it ever present itself before me again, would instantaneously give me the perfect knowledge (thus conquering the full gullibility of my faith) that I must then at that moment be true to that destiny and finally and once and for all acknowledge and confess that God hath not only already consigned me to hell but that in his great and gloriously omnipotent impatience and wisdom had brought hell so beguilingly early to me. He would not then wait for my proper death. But why rush hell early to me, while alive? Why not simply rush me early to hell, in death?

It occurs to me now that hell must have a more special taste and feeling in mortality (one reserved for only a very special few). A more delighted fury. The prick more piercing to the touch. The tart more sharp to the taste. Its unblushing presence consuming in every sense and dimension. But then to have to sleep with it? Yes, to have to sleep with it. To take the living nightmare with you to the sheets. Where warmth beneath them can be no longer. Most surely there is no nightlight for that; no dream-packing sandmen visit then. And most surely this is not a

251

concern for the dead. For they are already in relief — having no need for sleep.

And all of this under a bastard, bald moon of sightly calm and the most quiet of big brightness. And all of this under stars that on this night did not twinkle and play in small, standard, and very well-mannered vibrato. But instead witlessly spun large like giant pinwheels of homemade paisley linen and orange peels (the kinds with orphaned buttons fastened in the middle), all in the same direction, and all of them turned inward and looking down as if to indicate a certain shared shame and disgust between them and me. All while the moon . . . well, the moon just looked the other way — charitably dispensing its illume, yes, yet electing to remain aloof, staying its ground as it were, as if it were above it all.

As a matter of fact this particular heaven made Ross and Tabby glister all the more that night, adding eclat to their black, and pomp to this most squalid of ceremonial affairs and circumstance.

Dewy red and daubed in blood, that is how they danced and sang that night. This blood welled through them and over them and seemed to come from nowhere. Like sweat dripping and reappearing on a hot and humid midsummer midday, they unmurmuringly dabbed at it with their balled up shirts and many a strewn beach towel in the middle of what was actually a rather cool and just on the cusp of Christmas-like night.

Their arms, their legs, their torsos, yes, even their personal and private portions (as they had both stripped down to their not almost utter nakedness) — indeed, they seemed to bleed right out of their very goddamned pores. And just a bit off to the side of all of this was Soda — sat, asleep, but clean. Not tainted nor stained in the least. And with an empty cup still in his hand.

And I do believe that it was Tabby singing their song when I first arrived that night.

"Ah remember it right Ross, Ah remember it well when dat boat smacked that ice and went home to hell . . .

> *So up jump Shine from de deck below*
> *Says, Cap'n don' you know*
> *Water comin' in your barfroom do'*
> *Say Shine, go back and pack a few mo sacks*
> *'Cause I got fifty-four pumps to keep dis water back . . ."*

"Do it, Tabby. Do it good. Go, man go!" Ross picked up a machete as long as my leg from the blanket spread wide before them and tucked it under his arm like it was some kind of dancing cane. He then thrust it straight out in front of him with both arms, did a couple of Tabby's tappers, tucked it under again, reached for the invisible top hat on his head with his other arm, and then sweeping it down across his body took a long, deep, audience-oriented bow. And then he paused. But just for a beat, before turning his head softly and slowly to me, and winking, as if his perception had been that I had been there with him all along.

And after replacing the machete to the blanket he picked up some kind of three sided, silver, shortened, fire poker-like stick (save its big blue molded handle) and began to wave it over all the blades on the blanket, like a magic wand, as if to cast a spell. He finally let it rest above one of the swords, and keeping the poker in his left hand he picked up this particular sword with his right and with a delirium and frenzy not at all light, brought the two crashing meaningfully and continually together above his head.

"Ah hear yuh sharpenin' up dar, Ross. Cassius boy, yuh done learn to sharpen real fast. An' real good quick. Bastard Cassius, boy. A'hm goin' to tell yuh dat yes, suh!"

"Tabby, this will be the sharpest motherhumper yet. You just wait, old fool. You shan't feel a thing you fucking coy Cassius worldshaker. Closey your eyes, there. And see if you can tell me where! Close them eyes and start a spinning. Arms out, man. Now spin, motherhumper. Start a turning and tell me if I actually touch you or not."

And with that Tabby did close his eyes, put his arms out wide and start to turn real slow. Slow enough to keep his balance, but turn he did, like a great piece of bloody meat, somehow cruciformed on a spigot and stuck straight up in the middle of all those embers in the night. But he didn't miss a beat or pause for a moment when it came to the singing. He did sing and spin.

> *Say yes sir, Rossy, I know dat too*
> *But dis one time yo' work won' do;*
> *So Shine went down, he began to think,*
> *Ah t'ink dis big boat won' sink.*
> *So Shine jumps overboard and begins to swim*
> *So all de people on de boat were lookin' after him!*

And while Tabby sang his verse Ross tiptoed, right in time with the song, right on over to him. All the while smiling as big as the grin without the cat. And just as quiet too. He got over to him swiftly. And I lie to you not when I tell you that he brought that blade down, however slow and careful (for it was easily the biggest and heaviest sword out there — the only one for which Ross had to use both arms in order to pick it up), right across old Tabby's back. But Tabby just kept on singing.

Say now the Captain's daughter came up on the deck.
She had her hands in he'r cock and her tits 'round her neck.
And she say, Now, Shine, oh, Shine, save poor me.
Say, I'll give you more pussy than one Shine can see.
Shine say, Now, you may have good pussy and that might be true,
Say, But women on land got good pussy too.

"You feel it, man? You did not feel nothing. Did you, Tablet. Nothing!"

"Well, dat's 'cause yuh ain't done nuttin', Ross boy. Son, yuh didn't touch nothin! Yuh ain't fooled me dis time."

"Ah, buuuullshit, brother. I gots you good. Lookee here, Cassius. I say lookee here, man! Look at what I gots in my hand."

And with that Ross picked up a still fresh, white towel and passed it across Tabby's back. Tabby turned around and Ross held it before him with pride. "I just wiped off your back, man. And what is it that you do you see here, motherhumper. What's this here, you big fucking motherhead. It's red! This fucking blood is as fresh as fresh can be." Tabby had opened his eyes. He stared at the towel real hard before sharing Ross's grin. And he smiled big, I must say. Proud big.

"Why Ross, yuh little boy Cassius cunt-thumpin' trickey-dickey. Dat's de sharpest lick yuh done got off dis whole

255

gotdamned night. What blade is dat? Was dat de *Chinese Chicken Sickle?*"

"No not even close, Cassius. Not even the right fucking country."

"Give me de gotdamned country."

"Alright then. Vietnamese.

"Heaven's Will?"

"Yeeesiree."

"Gotdamned. Ah know'd it. Ah know'd it fo sho'. An' Ah was savin' dat fo' me! Dat's de one Ah actually had fashioned an' made fo ma-self while Ah was over dar in Vietnam. Gotdamnit. Yuh know'd dat was ma favorite, Ross! *Heaven's Will* was mine alll mine."

"Wooohooo! Well now it's my favorite too."

And then Ross began to dance again. And now *he* began to sing.

> *Tabby, Tabby, you know what she say?*
> *Now, Shine. oh, Shine, if you don't save poor me,*
> *Say, I'll cut it out and throw it to the sea.*
> *Shine say, Before I let that matter pass,*
> *I'll cut my dick off to the crack of my ass;*
> *I'll make my dick into an oar,*
> *And paddle that pussy back to shore.*

"Now me, Tabby. Now you do me!"

"Gotdamned, Ross. Gotdamned. Gotdamned. Gotdamned!"

And with that Tabby scurried back to his chair at the foot of his end of the blanket and in one grand motion sat down, leaned forward, and scooped up a big square of stone (a "whetstone" as

I now know it to be) and with a hand on each end held it flat up against his forehead. He held it there like it had power, studying the rows and columns of machetes, bolos, scythes, sickles, and knives before him. And then looking across and studying Ross. And then looking back down at that stone.

"That stone ain't going to help you Tab. It only works for me. I think we should trade back. I think you were sharpening yet better with the stick, man. That there be a Ross-stone. And don't you try to read it none 'fore it just make you go blind. Ha!"

Ross then just decided to drift distant and cool at the head of his side, just behind his chair, and with the *Chicken Sickle* picked up the beat on his glass and sang with conviction. And thoughtfulness. And intent.

> *Say Shine looked over to his side and got a hell of a surprise,*
> *A forty-foot whale was swimming by his side.*
> *Say, but Shine shook his head and wiggled his tail,*
> *And did the deep-sea shuffle and fucked that whale.*

Tabby set his stone down. He was having trouble. Trouble deciding which one to pick up next. And it must have been then that he saw me standing just a few feet behind Ross.

"Brentwood! Gets yo ass over here young sailor, boy. Come on, now!" He waived furiously at me. And I went over to his side. Not so much in the way of courtesy nor obedience, rather much more so to get away from Ross, who now dripped, strew, and sprayed blood like a hell hound just fresh from a cool down in his river Styx, even as I began to walk away.

257

How Shine swam past a preacher afloating on a board
crying save me nigger Shine in the name of the Lord,
and how the preacher grabbed Shine's arm and broke his stroke,
how Shine with one hand strangled the preacher's throat.

By the time I got to Tabby I was beside myself in an apoplexy of foulness and grief. But I still kept my voice down real low.

"What the fuck is going on here, Tabby. What the fuckfuckfuckfuckity fucking fuck in the name of the gotdamned fuckey here is going on? What in the name of the sweet baby jesus lying beneath the goddamned fucking trash are you guys doing!"

"Wood. Quiet, boy. Can't yuh tell a concentratin' man! Yes, suh." We were both whisper-hissing. Almost like we were trapped in some church. "Why, what do yuh mean what's goin' on here, Wood?"

"Tabby! What do you mean what do I mean how can you not know the meaning of what I mean! Fuck."

"Oh, dis here. Dis game here we be playin'. Yes. Well, nuttin'. We just barely makin' paper cuts. Ah bin just showin' Ross ma collection dese last few weeks from all ma travels in de navy. Ah collected swords, knives, everythin', yes suh. From everywhere Ah did go. Ah'm sure Ah told yuh dat. At least a couple ob time."

"Not even once."

"Ross likes to see them. Likes to know their names and where dey come from. So Ah brought dem out. Brought dem on up here, like he axed. Unpacked it an' den laid it all out. An' den we

258

got to talkin', yuh know, 'bout which one was sharper an' which one was not. An' den Ah sharpened one up for him an' den he sharpened one too. An' den it was which one was sharpest an' who could sharpen de best. An' den, how was we supposed to know dat? How could we test it? So we just did what was elementary an' logical ob course an' den made it into dis here game . . . Ross be callin' de game, *Who Touchey Me Now!* Now gotdamnit, Wood. Help me out here. Dar's extra points if 'n yuh guess de name ob de blade. It's a tie an' Ah gots only one more to go. Which one? Which one? Help me out a little here. Makes yuhself useful. For de love ob de lepers beggin' on Jesus, help me out, son. Ah'm starting not to see too well, yuh know, gotdamned."

"I fucking will not, Tabby."

"Which one?" he whisp-hissed again.

"No!"

"Come on now, son."

"Well how the hell should I know!"

"Keep it down, son. Ross is over dar dancin' an' singin' but yuh know gotdamned well he a mighty concentrating an' listening to what we say. He's as sneaky as dat long, skinny snake in de tall, tall grass, oh Wood don't yuh know it fo' sho'."

"I've never held nothing, nor know'd nothing, more than a goddamned steak knife. And you know that . . . All right, what's that one there in the middle? What's that one? . . . And then maybe we'll go get him."

"Yes!" screamed Ross. He had paused for a moment from his performance and was looking to his left at a spot just a few feet in front of him like a blind man with eyes wide open. "Have Wood help you. You need all the help you can get, Cassius."

"Shut yo' self, Ross. An' keep dem eyes closed! Keep a mind dar to yuh singin' and sippin'. Yes, suh! Best watch out now when ol' Tablet goes to battle."

Tabby looked up at me and squinted real hard.

"Which one yuh be pointin' at? Yuh be pointin' at about four dar at de same time."

"Fuck, man. Tabby. You're bleeding all over the place. Take a towel or put some clothes back on for the love of god."

"Plenty ob time fo' dat after. Now those four in de middle. Dey all be pretty good. Matter fact, Ah been savin' dem fo' last anyway. 'Cepting ma *Heaven's Will* dat Ross already done stole from me. Dese ones here look all old an' real rusty an' Ross hasn't even taken a look at one ob dem to consider it fo' play. Ah been trickin' him good. Now, yuh gots out dar a *Gung Ho American Marine* from the second big war, a nineteen inch *Civil War Bowie Tobacco*, a *Guillotine Marine Filipino Bolo Style* — even has de iron wood handle — an' an *Executioner Sword*, all de way from de Germany."

"Man, I don't know Tabby. I"m a bit out of my element here."

"OK, OK. Go grab all four den. Ross will see dat an' den get all fuck*tee*fied in his head."

I no sooner grabbed them than Ross was cackling away. "I say now. I say now. I say now, I do now say . . . Why is Wood out there grabbing more then just one? Maybe two, three, or four? Now, Tabby what you up to you old Cassius, son boy? How you figure on using more than one. Ha! Who will end up being the world champion of *Who Touchey Me Now!*, Ladies and Gentlemennnns!"

"Keep yo' eyes, shut, Gotdamnit, Ross. Ah know yuh more den prone ob a cheat."

Tabby then turned his back on Ross. He put all four blades down in front of him. And then he had me hold a towel out in front of his back, like a curtain, in front of Ross. Just to make sure he could not see and cheat.

Tabby poured some more oil on the stone. And then suddenly the glint, flicker, and flash of all that riling on the rock. Tabby was sharpening like it was his last day on earth.

"Indeed, indeed the sweet sound of some sickle getting wet and hot. Getting ready to meet me in secret. I likey! I likey, likey, likey. Likey a lot!" Ross continued to chatter while he danced.

Tabby was humped over real good. Huffing and puffing, real shiny and red, with muscles still taut in that weathered and wrinkled skin. He was pissed. Ross had gotten to him. I'd never have guessed the old man could still move in just such a way. But with that I noticed more blood on him too. It began to drip now good and quick. And I worried for him and his life. And hated Ross for the danger he was putting old Tabby in.

"Ah almost got it here, now, Wood. Dis is it. Ross we'll never feel a thing. Ah hopes tuh Gawd Ross be sippin' up a storm. Ah need him good and numb-dumb. Gooood and numb-dumb."

Ross could hear the sharpening too. And he tried to out do it as he howled out and over us to anyone within his reach.

All you good peoples come on down to me.
So de debbil turned over in hell

261

And began to laugh and grin
Say, Yo' took a might long time comin', Shine,
But yo' welcome in!

As I kept the towel up I could not keep my eyes off of Tabby.

"Come on, Tab. I'm sure that's enough. It's sharp enough. Let's go get him. Let's go do him in."

"Yes, yuh right. It's ready. It's ready fo' Ross. Here we come, Ross! Arms out an' start spinnin'. We're comin' over. We're comin to get yuh now, boy. Start yo' spinnin', motherfucker. Yuh best start twirling yo' ass again. Whoooo Touchey Me Now! Gotdamned! Yes, suh!"

And as Tabby began to raise himself up from his chair I dropped the towel, in unison, almost like we'd rehearsed it. And with a couple of arched grins, first most satisfyingly shared just betwixt us two (and neither of us wanting for a just as devilishly and finely cocked brow), we turned as such to share our grins with him.

And I'm sure they must have vanished from our faces in unison as well. And with just the same speed.

He was gone.

There was nothing on the other side. Just his empty chair and the bottles and all the bloody linen. But not him.

He was nowhere to be seen. And, motionless, we stared for a good while at that nothing (although I'm sure it was only a good few seconds — maybe five, perhaps ten). And then we looked at each other, confused and feeling foolish. A sudden sense that the whole night was senseless (for that was the look in our eyes) gripped the both of us, as we tried to read each other not just for answers but for what the questions might be first.

And then I just finally said, in a voice I remember having used only one other time since (my first day in prison, in a manner and expression that would have made my mother most proud — for its politeness, humility, and general aplomb — when asked for a list of future or potential visitors and friends: "I have none . . . "), "Where the fuck is Ross? He was just right here. Where has he gone?"

And it was Tabby who saw him first. I could tell it in the big jumps of his eyes and the sudden toad-drop of his mouth as he looked down and just right behind me. But a word he did not say. At least not before I felt the tiny tug at the bottom of my pant leg. And then the two finger three-time tap tap tap on the back of my naked and blood-dribbled heel.

"He's dar right behind yuh, Brentwood." Tabby kept his arm in pressed tight against his chest, but extended and bobbed his index finger, in a very specific and most helpful way, down at where Ross was tugging on my pants. I shook my leg loose and turned to look at him. He was flat on his belly. He still had one arm extended toward me and with the other tried to push himself back up. Then he just flopped all the way back down again, banging himself square in the nose. It began to bleed as he turned his head to the side before laying it back down again. His eyes never opened.

And then he just kind of started to mumble. "Shake it baby. Salome, you little slut. I love it. I love you. Shake it, shake it, shake it, Salome. Just stay right there in one spot and shake it one more time for me. And then you got me. I'm yours forever. Shake it, shake it, shake it. Sa-lo-me."

And then he just plain old passed out.

"You drunk fuck, Ross. Get up. The sun's coming up. Let's go."

"Dat gotdamn right, Cassius. An' yuh done lost de game as well. Ha-ha! Passin' out is a forfeit fo sho'. Like it is in anythin' else in life. Yes, suh."

XXVIII

And for the next four weeks Ross and Tabby (and of course Soda too) retired to the roof every night. And there they healed. In part I believe now by telling stories and exchanging toasts. And of course with the dancing and singing as well.

But there was one story told more often than the others. The very same one I spoke of before. For I listened to them all. Sometimes hiding behind the water tank on the roof. And on quiet nights just listening as I fell asleep by the window below in my room.

And so Tablet also knew this story well. Ross's tale. His unraveling ball of spider web yarn. And also became a sniggerer and a weeper. Laughing men, all of them, tied to their very own Joshua trees. Making the sounds of the snort and the titter. Sounds often confused for crying. Or tolling peals of pain. Depending on your point of view. Or where you are.

Soon I was hearing about their trips to Malibu. How he broke in to Sinboni's house again and found an extra key and made a copy. Returned the original. And always kept the key in his pocket like a pocket full of gold.

How they would sit outside the house keeping watch, as I once did, while Ross went inside.

But after a while, after he had Sinboni's schedule down, Ross felt safe enough in there by himself to loiter even longer. Not that he was ever worried for his own well-being, but rather the well-being of not being discovered before he could drop his other shoe on me, God, and Lizzy. And the others he loved who were now all in the ground.

And he told them how he would sit in his house. How he would walk around. And lie in his bed. And sit on the lamb-skin couch in the screening room. Where the video camera still stood with a video tape still inside.

How he sat at the Sinboni's bar and drank his drinks. His expensive adult beverages from all the countries in the creation save his own (a brand known as *NASILNIK* became Ross's darling of choice).

And try on his clothes he did too, although most of them were much too wide and short, and swagger through the fun-house posing for the many mirrors. Pretending he was him, and it was it, and he was all of them, and they all of him.

"There are fucking mirrors everywhere. In the halls on the walls behind the tables and in the bars and on the ceiling of every bedroom. In the clocks and on the candles, lamps made of mirror, two-ways in corner quarters made to look like closets, there's even a picture of a mirror hanging over a mirrored fireplace. I tell you boys. I tell you I tell you I tell you. The house is just one big . . . reeling . . . reflection. You might just see yourself forever. And in the dark, and it's always just a wee bit dark, everything is in white silhouette. Like a big old . . . print negative I think is what they call them. Why Soda, you and Tablet would be as white as I am the night. Just wait 'til you're white for a night. Just you wait."

266

And he told them about all the pictures. About all the enchantresses captured by the hunter which hung on the wall in the one big room with the big, big screen.

He sat in all his chairs, and tried all his beds, and sampled all his liquor — until everything fit just right. He wanted to make sure everything was just right. He listened to his answering machine and found that the Sin would be gone a certain weekend, and so he went there and stayed. Took Tablet and Soda and the Mills Brothers too. Two nights, three days, all expenses paid. They even ate up all the food — "just clean up pristine and pretty, the old bloated hairy-armed motherfucker throws so many flings and orders out so much he never takes no notice of what's in the fridge or if the cupboard be bare."

Treated them all there, high up in the Malibu mounds — where every Tablet and all the Sodas are prohibited play. Aren't allowed to even dream it. Gave them both the five stars, the whole nine yards.

But more often than naughty, Ross would just go up there by himself. The lank and lonely clown beneath the clouds liked to go lonesome.

And stare. Stare with a hundred eyes. Go up there and take that one particular video out of the camera. The one labeled "Liz" with a certain date. And lie in the lamb-skin and hold it and stare at it and fondle it and stroke it and put it on top of the VCR and under the big-screen TV and stare at it some more.

Then put it in the VCR (but not turn it on). Then take it out. Then put it in again. Take it out again. In. Out. In. Out. In. Out. And in and.

Outandinandoutandinandinandoutandinandoutandinandoutandout. And then leave it in. And then take it out. And then put it back in the camera. Back in its sheath.

He couldn't watch it. Wouldn't stab himself with it. Turn it on himself. Loose it on himself. He didn't have the guts. He was still too sane. But what to do? What to do! Ross had his wolf by the ears — and could no more hold on to it than he could let it go. Try and try and try as he might. But stare at it he did do. Gape gawk gaze glance glare goggle glow (like the worm turning in his heart) and even grimace flinch growl and sneer, before he teared.

Stuck it in his mind — like a hot branding iron and a cold dull knife. And played it in his mind over and over again until, autolobotomized and selfsodomized, the results were the same and ten times the beastly.

And soon I heard Ross ask Tablet about the tar. And ask about what was inside the pillows. And about the hammer and nails.

"The soup's got to be hot. Must be boiling. The black stuff must be boiling. Boiling to a bubble. Just get me some fresh stuff there, Tablet. I'll cook it right and nice right there in his own goddamned kitchen. On the stove he never uses."

"Yeessiirree now, Cassius. I'll have it all put in an old paint can in the trunk of your car so you be taking it whenever you dandy. But now you know, Cassius son, I can't be knocking up there with you and the Soda. Oooowwweee, I just can't. But Momma give me the devil if I wouldn't love to return the vengeance on, what you call him? — Mr. McRape?"

268

"Mac Ape." Ross flicked the last of Soda's sugar cubes off the roof and into the street and into the spotlight of a street lamp that was busy siphoning the moths right out of the inky, Venice-night air. Sweetness shattered into galaxy; it fed ants in the morning.

"I don't like the word 'rape', Tablet. Besides, I can't let you go. There is no sense in jeopardizing you taking any kind of accountability. Especially with you already being on parole. That just would not make any sense at all and besides me and the old Soda will have this well in our hands. Just put that stuff for me in my trunk by tomorrow, thank you very much, and throw a couple of down pillows you got downstairs in there with it, and, oh yeah, one bottle of special Soda sauce, there should be some left in your ice box . . ."

"Yeessiirree, yuh bet your little green ass dar plenty more ob Soda's juice. Yuh still want dat needle wid all dat?"

"Yes, please. Put a cork on the end and place it under the spare in the trunk with everything else. Yes, please."

Soda stirred in his chair a bit. His whisper was the weakest I had ever heard it. He sucked on his juice without any sugar and turned to look at Ross. Even I could see the yellow in his eyes reflect off of Ross. The yellow that veiled his ache and ate his liver and buoyed his bobbing spirit like a small, broken, floating-toy in a shallow, mean puddle. His first and only ocean of faith — and Ross had shown him where it was.

"This be it Ross. This be it, Cassius. This. Me. And you."

269

XXIX

The night before our last drive up the coast to Malibu was also the night before he spun on the barstool at the very beginning of my story. The night when I caught him, I believe, actually trying to initiate the killing of himself by perhaps amputating his one last limb of love. Securing and ensuring, placating whatever was left of his burdensome conscience and fractured piece of mind — so that his life truly would be devoid of all its injected meaning when it ended, and not be wasted in his death. But rather caught and recaptured in his fall. All of his other tokens had been taken, save one. And so his Rossicide began vicariously, by trying to kill Lizzy. (But where was I in this grand plan? And why do redeemers always have to be so full of murder?)

Ross had finally figured out a full-proof way. To have her gone for good and to forever rid himself of all the love he had for her and the horror that came with it — possibly even avoiding, or granting himself (and others) a reprieve on what only he knew he would be doing the very next night — passing the cup back to her so as not to have it last on his very crooked lips.

And I remember what it sounded like in their room. I again was trying to sleep and trying not to dream and one thing was for goddamn sure, it didn't sound like good old Jim Croce in there sobbing to the operator.

270

If it was anything, I mean if it sounded like anything somehow identifiable, it sounded like Satan had finally struck a Jesus Christ pose. Like he had finally given in to the host in his heart. Binded himself down and bawled like a treacherous little baby for buttermilk, once and for all.

It was the mad-dog screech of a vulture laboring for patsy scraps and a mother's final mule-bray variation in a last-ditch effort to save an only child, all evilly rolled up and dolled into one. Up on the rooftop on top of the friendly crackhouse where we lived on the Venice Beach in California Los Angeles.

I had already gone to bed. The heat wouldn't let me press a pillow on my head to muffle his voice and besides I had heard things similar before and the next day had always proven that everything was always going to be all right and normal.

The walls beneath his perch, a cheaply rigged balcony that he, Tablet, and Soda had anchored to the roof and which jetted out a few feet over the face of house, out past the front of the roof, were banging. Our whole apartment shook. Like I said, my room was directly below and his was the corner-left. From the angle of my window, I could just barely glimpse his legs hanging and dangling from his little plank, as if it were a diving board over the pool of concrete front-yard beneath. Then crawling back up like an acrobat whose feats had gotten too easy sober.

Then I heard Lizzy's voice. She was sitting on his window sill in the room just adjacent to mine. Her normal whimpering. This surprised me as she had always expressed a profound fear of heights when asked to go anywhere near the window or the roof before. I scrambled out of my egg carton, threw some underwear on, and went out the window above the stove in the kitchen at the back of the house to the ladder, and scampered myself up onto the roof while Ross's full attention was still in his words. I had to scamper while the scampering was good. While Ross was still roaring and snarling and unable to hear or feel the rattle of the ladder. Besides, I was too scared to stay underneath.

The first thing I saw didn't really seem to happen. But it did. Ross jumped up and over the two foot guard-rail of his homemade grotto in the sky, his bottle of green stealth in one hand, caught the lower bar of the guard rail with his other, and swung like a simian calmly measuring the distance to the next branch. He looked down at someone or something just a few feet lower, his legs still working with Darwin, and he started talking to where he was looking.

He was hissing at Lizzy. He got back up in his chair on the edge and was sucking on the last half of an unripe fifth and jabbering away in what suddenly seemed like some very civilized conversation. He had his legs crossed like some English professor or banker or something, his left hand flat across his chest and his right hand just petting and smoothing away new hairs on his chinny-thin chin.

"I'm trying, Ross." I still heard love in her voice, in a tone, however, powerless to flee. That was the first time I heard her. She was close to him. Half-naked and beneath him on the sill. Her voice was all hoarse and worn. There was no pleading in it anymore.

"Now, back to our exercise, if you will. Remember, you are to repeat everything that I say, verbatim. Only changing the 'you' to 'I,' and saying it as if you are hearing me say it for the first time, until I change the sentence. Remember, Lizzy, its very repetitious. Tautology For Trollops 101. And if you even for one syllable sound redundant, you must take another sip from your bottle. The key here is repetition without redundancy. Roulette without the ball ever dancing the same dance twice, but always landing on the same number, the wheel never knowing the difference. Your best Argentine tango. Remember also, MOTHER Lizzy, you mustn't move from where you are standing. Or are you sitting now?" He leaned forward and looked down. "Sitting. Very well. Indeed. Ready?"

"Yes."

"*You* are quite the fool for sitting in that window sill."

"*I* am quite the fool for sitting in that window sill."

Ross had been glancing down every few moments while he was talking. I walked to the right far end of the roof and looked down in the same direction. There she was. Still just sitting there. In the window of Ross's room-closet. She had her eyes closed. She was concentrating so hard. She rocked back and forth and gripped her own bottle — whiteknuckled as if it was anchored to the sky and was the last thing she had to hold on to.

Ross took another tug on his bottle and barely sounded the next line out, forcing Lizzy to lean out, straining to hear.

"*You* are a slut."

"*I* am a slut."

"*You* are a slut for sitting."

"*I* am a slut for sitting."

"*You* are a slut and a fool for sitting on that window sill."

She tried to smile. She thought she was doing so well. "*I* am a slut for sitting on that window sill."

"No, no, no! No, no. That will not do. That is not what I said Mother-Lizzy. I said slut *AND* a fool. What do *we* do now?"

She jerked the bottle toward her mouth tilting it as high as she could to make up for the fact the she couldn't raise her head anymore. Her body spasmed. She leaned further and pitched herself nearer the street below.

"Now say it right this time."

"*I* am a slut and a fool for sitting on that window sill."

"Good one Lizzy." Ross applauded, politely. "You are getting better all the time. Let's press on. Ready?"

"Yes."

"Indeed."

"I am ready, Ross."

"*You* know Little Bo Peep?"

"*I* know Little Bo Peep?"

"Yes, *you* know Little Bo Peep."

"Yes, *I* know Little Bo Peep."

"Little Bo Peep."

"Little Bo Peep."

"Why, Little Bo Peep has lost *your* sheep."

"Why, Little Bo Peep has lost *my* sheep."

"Little Bo Peep has lost *your* sheep . . . and does not know where to find *me*."

"Little Bo Peep has lost *my* sheep and does not know where to find *them*."

"Good crimany shit Jesus in the heaven, Lizzy. You fucked it up again. To find *you*. *You*. *You*! Not *them*. The opposite of *me* is *you*, not fucking *them*! Ah, now. But what do we . . ." But before Ross could finish Lizzy was already sucking and that pleased him enough (even as she gagged and coughed and leaked vodka through her nose). "And anyway, besides," he got low in a crouch, right on the edge of the roof, and hiss-whispered to her again, "That would be reasonable? Would it not? It would be reasonable enough to assume that if Little Bo Peep had indeed lost her sheep that she would *NOT* know where to find them. Is that not reasonable?"

"Yes, Ross, it is."

"What is it you wear there around your neck?"

She felt for it to make sure it was still there.

"It is what you gave me. The symbol for us and what we are. I should give it to you. Back to you."

"Why, I don't . . . Yes, yes. Perhaps you should. Give it to me."

"It will make me forever sad but I will if you think I should."

"Well enough, then."

She handed the silver twister of a symbol over to Ross and Ross put it around his own neck then.

He jumped back down and hung off the edge with the ease and grace of a monkey raised in a zoo keeper's tree. His agility was improving with every sip, even as his old "Who-Touchey-Me-Now" scars began to open and slowly bleed. He swung to get as close to her as possible, and steadied himself for a moment on the sill. But he did not touch her.

He whispered in her ear with a request. She leaned out into the air to give him a kiss. But Ross swung away. Lizzy almost fell.

That was the point.

He had been trying to get her to this point all along. And I believe now (even if he did not know it at the time) since we had landed in Venice.

Now about what I did next. Whether I did right or wrong or whether I did it for Lizzy or for him I don't really believe I'll ever really know. I know I didn't do it for me. I already had peace of mind for some reason. (Although, I must admit now, I possess it no more. It went with Ross for some reason, I guess. But why blame reason? Ross took *it* with him. And since then, I really don't know anymore.)

But when he finally got back up to the roof and was teetering there trying to situate himself back in his catcher's crouch, I just walked over as calm as ever.

"Lizzy, shall we try again?"

"Yes, Ross."

I picked up the spinning stool a few feet behind him. He held his stare on Lizzy's window sill.

"Everything will be all right soon, Lizzy. Just keep up with me. Just keep trying to keep up."

"I am trying, Ross. I'm trying really hard."

I raised that heavy, spinning bar stool high above my head. And he just kept talking to her, never abandoning her gaze. "I know you are. You are trying real hard. Don't you think so, Wood? Brentwood, tell me. Wouldn't you agree, that she really is trying?"

He spun while still in his crouch, suddenly facing me right at my feet, looking at the chair and then back at me while still addressing the sill below. "Lizzy, why don't you climb . . ." And

I crashed it upon his head with all the force that I could collar, grabbing him at the same time so that he didn't topple over.

I got lucky. He collapsed and was unconscious immediately. No blood neither. He would wake hours later with a bump on his head and the same ravenous hangover that would drag his quivering and thirsty hands to his bottle again and he would assume he passed out. The bump on his head would be nothing new. He was full of them, both inside and out. At the end of his long bouts, some lasting for more than a couple of days, he always hit the ground head first.

I went back down the stairs and got Lizzy out of the window and carried her down to the anteroom and lay her down next to the tree and window she'd just been decorating. She would remain passed out there for just about a day.

She still looked so beautiful. Even with her hair newly shorn a violent and ratchedy pageboy bob — by her own hand no less and an old, dull pair of Christmas-paper scissors — still all the more beautiful to me.

And I knew she would never remember seeing me, nor having ever been in my arms.

As I made my way back to get Ross and tuck him in his room I passed Tablet going out to the old, yellow Fairmont. I watched him from the window. He put a paint bucket and a pillow into the trunk, along with a few other things I couldn't quite make out.

"What you got there, Tablet?"

"Oh, dar ain't nothin' here at all, son. Ross be helpin' me out a bit. Just riddin' myself ob some clutter. Movin' things around."

XXX

So on that last day — the last day of Ross' laboring under the rented whip of sunken innocence and the spurious spur of memory's guilt — I went up to the roof and just stood there all on my lonesome.

The sun was straight, high, and grew no shadows. I stared down at the street, just watching the people go by, occasionally putting my back to the ocean and eyeing the East. I was just thinking and pondering on the ground in Pleasant Grove. I heard the familiar crunch of the Fairmont door down below. It was Tablet.

I went out to it (Ross and Soda had gone to Van Gogh's for their daily vigil in the balcony) and opened up the trunk to see what all this hammer and nails and tar was about. A paint can, a pillow, red shiny new packing tape, the bottle of Soda's green, and — on top of the spare tire — an empty cork-capped syringe and needle. Then some long planks of wood, nails, and a pair of gloves. I couldn't make a damn thing of any of it, except that Ross maybe had some kind of vandalism in mind with some paint. But I couldn't imagine how a pillow, syringe, and packing tape would contribute at all to the destruction of anyone's house or belongings.

I opened the paint can to see what kind of color Ross had in mind for his next work of art. It was black. But not a black, black.

It was some kind of deep-stew black — bubbly with a blue, copper beam. I put the lid back on. The syringe scared me.

I think I kind of decided then — to do what I did next. I knew better than to ask Ross about any of this. He would have just lied, and my water-heater hideout would be revealed, and I'd be banished from the roof forever.

Ross always put Soda in the front seat of the Fairmont. And in the back he always kept a bunch of blankets beneath the seat for those occasional nights when they'd go down to the beach on the corner in front of St. Luke's, so Soda could make his exchange for his absinthe and then they'd just sleep on the sand and watch the stars get yellow with their new green graft.

I think I sensed something final about this next pilgrimage to the hills (but that's knowing what I know now, now that my memory is able to cheat). It didn't drop on me at the time, but the day before, Ross had taken Soda's bed off the roof and given it to Tablet to use for a new tenant he had moving in downstairs. Besides that, during those prior days heading up to this one they had been visiting every single haberdasher haunt, place, friend, and knick-knack pad and hack niche of Venice and L.A. like an elderly couple walking through their old two-story for one last time. Saying goodbyes and bidding fond farewells to every memory (good and bad) in every room, before they retired and drove somewhere West, knowing they were never coming back.

I knew they were heading to Malibu that night. And I knew I'd be in the back of the car underneath the blankets holding on to Ross's tail for what I didn't know would be the saddest and the cruelest of all the last times.

I went out there that night as soon as it was dark and I hunkered myself down in the back seat. Flat on my back with the blankets all over me. I lay there. I fell asleep twice. I tossed and turned. An hour went by. I dreamed once about playing catch with Ross in the backyard the day he found Father. And then I woke myself up because I didn't like that dream. Never have. And I tried to keep myself awake by humming Mills Brothers melodies and pretending I sang as good as Tablet. But I fell asleep again. The next time I woke up it was because Jack had bounded into the backseat, laid down, and rested his head on mine. I peeked out at him and he greeted me with a lick and nose-to-nose-open-snout pant. But he did not let on to the others that I was there spying on Ross yet again.

The drive up the highway on the coast of the Pacific was the quietest it had probably ever been. The sun had gone down good and it was probably also the quietest drive, period, as far as being in a car with Ross was concerned. Soda didn't say a word. And Ross only said a couple of things. The first was right when we left: "The world will be all straight soon." And in between that neither said a thing to each other. They just sang. Dueted all the way up, "Paper Doll." Traded verses and harmonized on the chorus. I could hear them trading the inexhaustible bottle too, passing it back and forth and slugging it hard on the backs of their throats. Then when we finally got to the house in Malibu, Ross just shut off the Fairmont and sat still for a moment, his voice staring into nothing.

"One last time, Soda. I will sing this one to you one last time, as you have been . . . aside from my brother whose time has not come yet and whose time I shall not rush, and besides he is the blood of my mother and the only one left for snow angel-making beneath her stone on the last sacred place on this God-beached planet that was never *really* forsaken because God left it long before he ever intended to fix it back up again . . . I will sing it to you one last time, Soda, as you have been the only goddamned, soft and still, born and breathing angel. A true angel. *My* bastard beatitude.

"And I promise to you, Soda. I do vow to you to do everything and comply to your last wish and save you the demise and awful bad and slow ruin that this world planted in your blood. That thing you have asked of me here tonight, yes yes, it is not in me to do it save that I know all you request is to stop the suffering — and that I believe I can do. And besides, I have promised it."

And then he sang him a song that I knew, but I didn't know that he knew, nor had I ever heard him in my whole life sing it before (when and how had he been singing it to Soda?). Or even mention it by name. Or even utter the words.

A song that Mom used to sing when she'd nurse her black, bloated eyes, or beat up ribs, while she'd hobble around the house mothering me and Ross. A song that she would only sing to herself, but that I remember finding once in those books that are in those backs of those seats at church. And a song that she saved exclusively for herself, choosing never to sing it to me and Ross. Because, I think now, that somehow the words were just a little too much and too sad.

But Ross did sing it to Soda there in the Fairmont in the dark, in front of the great Sin's munificent castle and comely lair. Sang it in a deep baritone that he rarely used and when he did,

did so in pure gospel-mock of his favorite Elvis. But there was nothing to mock on this night. This night he sang it with a gem-hearted sincerity. He sang with love and patience and great pride — like mothers sing their children off to sleep. Yes, that's what it reminded me of. Maybe Mom was singing to us. Singing to us though she could not bear us to look upon her all punched-up and rotting. Still singing us off to sleep anyway. But I know that there, even if he was singing it to Soda, Ross was singing for himself.

A poor wayfaring Man of grief
Hath often crossed me on my way,
Who sued so humbly for relief
That I could never answer nay.
I had not pow'r to ask his name,
Where-to he went, or whence he came;
Yet there was something in his eye
That won my love; I knew not why.

In prison I saw him next, condemned
To meet a traitor's doom at morn.
The tide of lying tongues I stemmed,
And honored him 'mid shame and scorn.
My friendship's utmost zeal to try,
He asked if I for him would die.
The flesh was weak; my blood ran chill,
But my free spirit cried, I will!

Ross then reached into the glove compartment and pulled out a fresh never-before-worn pair of California Angels batting gloves. Shoplifted of course and Official Major League certified, I do recollect and believe. He put them batting gloves on just like he had a thousand times before, though they did seem a bit small (and American League gloves at that, with that goddamned unhallowed designated hitter rule — why could they not have been the Dodgers of Los Angeles; the gloves then more befitting on more than one level). Staring up and away into some nothing testing the velcro and crimping the leather in between each finger just like he was getting back in the box.

"You make sure now Soda, my friend. You touch as many things as often as can in there. Especially *any* and *every* mother-in-the-corn-field-fuckin' thing I do. *Especially* that Sinboni."

"I gots it Ross I gots it all real good."

"Now let us get the up fuck out of here. And then let's all go home."

And then Ross ripped out of the car like he was going in for a gig. He came over, got Soda, tossed him in his chair all ginger-like, wheeled him around to the back of the car as quick as one could with a shopping cart full of eggs, unloaded the trunk into his lap, checked his pocket for a pocket full of gold, and then they went up the windy path of yellow and wealth.

And as I peeked up over the car-door edge I saw the moon glimmer for a moment on Soda's hospital-metal, emergency room chair. And as they disappeared behind one of those rare Japanese Bonsai trees that was up toward the walk, I even saw — and no, I am not goddamn lying about this one — I even saw Ross, both hands still on Soda's polished pushcart, jump in the air and click his heels, once to the right, then another to the left.

Just like some other scarecrow me and him had seen in a movie on TV a couple of times when Mom had let us stay up late.

I can now only imagine what tune he might have been singing then, and what he was after at the end of that path.

I laid myself back down in the car and played with the pretension that all was well and that Ross and Soda were just headed up there for their usual bit of fun in the fun-house — that Ross was just a too bit giddy to do anything all that awful and terrific. But my lie to myself didn't last long and I could feel the plumb in my throat sinking down into my gut and then I knew with all surety and despair that this indeed was a different night.

I sat up and waited and waited and paced through my mind and raced to be kind to my thoughts and my druthers and with every car that slowly milled the hill in front of the house and illuminated and ran my shadow across the Fairmont roof above my head — but never addressed the driveway — I knew what he was waiting for.

And so I went in.

XXXI

*N*o, I didn't go in. I wanted to. I sure as like hell wanted to but when I politely knocked on the door all the lights went out and then I tried to politely turn the goddamn knob, and nothing. It was locked tight. So I not so politely started banging and requesting kind of rather loudly that he let me in but the house just got darker, and the louder I appealed the quieter it got.

The big oak door that I had been banging about was set back roughly six feet or so in the middle of the house between two great, glass rooms. Two rooms that were nothing but goblets of pane. Some kind of glass, or windows I guess they'd be, squared off in chessboard blocks bordered with gold. The porch light was on above my head and with how dark it was inside, it was like standing in between a couple of walls of mirrors. They were angled just slightly though, not quite perfectly parallel to each other, which, depending on how I stood, gave me all kinds of different angles and access to reflections of myself I had never before seen — or even knew existed.

I found myself turning around like a silly, slow, toy top trying to find some spot, viewpoint, or feature (not ever really having considered prior to that most unusual moment to consider such a thing: that there were parts of me with whom even the most common, nameless stranger was more familiar with than I) to get a real good look at and see if it met up with whatever expectation I'm sure I had, although I'm not really sure I had ever

285

thought of it before. Especially in terms of the ampleness of my head (or was it the thickness?), I had never thought to look at it from the back and all. And being such a big guy, I suddenly wondered if I had ever grown into it, as it was a topic much attended to around the dinner table with Mom and Father — well, mostly Father. For Mom I just always tried to stand up straight (and I was looking in the mirror for that as well).

I was trying real hard to do all of that in that one most inappropriate, ephemeral moment. Staring real hard to get a good glimpse of these unseen parts of me. Just studying real hard. Almost had my nose right into the glass. I even had to back up a couple of inches as it was getting all foggy from my breath. My breath. All foggy from my hot breath and I was trying to wipe it off with the sleeve of my shirt, making a fist with the sleeve of my shirt clenched inside my fist and rubbing the circular motions on the glass, but it wasn't coming off. There was hot breath there but it wasn't rubbing off.

'Til I finally rubbed the window so hard that the glass went bright and the inside of the room full bloom — bursting and then imploding into luxurious slivers and jagged *Fabergé* egg and flakes like the inside of one of those shake-em-up Christmas worlds we used to have by the side of Mom's bed. And right there in my face, even eye to eye and tooth to tooth, was Ross.

He was there for less time than even I know how to measure, for most of him I only saw on the downside dull of the brilliance (and even that, now that I think about it, was probably just some exiled imprint, hasty and white hot, left branded on my brain). It was that kind of light that lingers behind — coursing through the air like the aftermist flare of the family-camera flash bulb, or the trail of Fourth of July sparklers carving circles out of dark.

His image was somehow even with mine, and although our sudden gaze did certainly connect, his eyes would not see mine. Instead, they swallowed me. They just drank me all the way down.

And they were the slain, stuffed animal eyes of taxidermic birds in captured, ruined flight. Bleak and bigger than brown, all made of dirt and usurped. Maybe a little bit of life left in a reflection of me.

And then they were gone.

No, the breath would not rub away. It was on the other side.

I didn't even know I was in motion 'til I bounced off the wall behind me and ricocheted back down the path I had come. I was pissed and in a huff and my heart hurt real bad and I just stayed in unbroken motion 'til I got back down to the car.

He didn't care anymore.

Not even enough to get mad or scream and curse me for trespassing his world that night. All he had left was pure and simple indifference. The anesthesia of apathy, all ridden of care and concern. My brother was gone from me.

It crushed me.

I had a mind to take that Fairmont and point it right back to Venice and then right back to the beehive state and right back to Mom and her stone and leave him there stranded on the seashore and in old Sin's house and may the authorities and the devil and all the world that he had so carefully trampled upon just have their way with him. May God damn him. But I could not.

Oh, yes. I would go home. That I had my mind right to do. Go home to Mom and work it out with her and start all over and start on my own — fresh scars and all. But I would not strand him. I suppose, had I had his heart, I surely would have had the will and not just the wish. But a bastard-dragging heart like his would never have dwelled well in me. My mind was too weak to suffer it.

But no, I would not strand him and leave him with no way home.

Besides, I didn't have the keys.

So I would walk. In two hours or so I figured I could walk it back to Venice. And in the meantime figure out my way back across the desert and into Pleasant Grove.

In fact, I had just crossed the street and was making my final descent out of those hills when the car came trolling down the street. That kind of car with the fancy, flying cougar on the hood (I recognized it from when Ross used to let me help follow him around Los Angeles). It slowed down a bit as it passed the Fairmont and I believe it even slowed down a bit to have a blink at me, and then it just went ahead and pulled in the driveway.

It was Sinboni.

And then after that I believe, all of us, yes — me, Soda, Sinboni, and even Ross, well maybe not Ross so much (at least not yet) — we just all got behind the mule and held on for dear, sweet-eternal life.

The Sin went straight away in and no sooner did he shut the door behind him than did the lights glow bright again with another yuletide seasonal swirl before it all went dull again just as hurried.

But there must have still been some light there inside, because I could see shadows. At first they were faint but every few moments they became a little darker and they shimmied and shook when they moved and even when they moved not.

I walked slowly back up to the house. By the time I got to the path though, I found myself in a dead, blind sprint. I found the door again and pressed my face against the same glass where just a few minutes before I was trying to find myself. Soda was there inside all by himself now. He was wheeling himself around all slow and methodical. He had a candle in his right hand, and was pushing himself with his left. I banged and kicked on the fat glass.

"Goddamn you, Soda! You let me in, now. It's Brentwood and you had better come on over here and open this door. Jesus Christ in the heaven, you open this door!"

He looked over his shoulder once, even pausing and squinting his eyes like he might be looking for something lost. When he saw who it was his eyes got big as thunderstones and his face all twisty with pang. He leaned forward from his crippled little perch on the earth and his mouth gaped wide and his sinewed little see-through neck flexed ugly in a most strained and toiled screech. But I didn't hear anything. And it wasn't because the glass was too thick neither. No. Because I could hear the Mills Brothers just fine. They were singing in there just fine as could be (probably louder than they ever cared to be or ever had before). Loud enough that I could feel them through the glass. And then Soda suddenly got all sad. His face gave up like he just realized maybe he hadn't seen nothing at all, or seen something he had seen a thousand times before, and he just turned back around and went back to lighting a couple more candles. He was lighting one in each corner of the room.

And then again maybe he did not see me. The porch light had been turned off and I was probably just standing there clamoring away behind a reflection of him. No, now that I think about it, perhaps he never had a chance to see me at all.

But he did see Sin — who was lying on the floor all rolling around and trying to raise himself up, bleeding about his head, brand new red packing tape across the mouth of his muted mewl and eyes so horror-hemmed and dumbfounded-struck that he looked like what I thought one of them slaughterhouse veal calves might look like right after it's been clubbed in the head, right before it's strung up like a tire-swing to bleed dry.

Yes, Soda must have seen Sin, for he had to wheel over one of his legs to get to the middle of the room to light his last candle (that made five in all). Sinboni didn't seem to notice him.

And then there was Ross. He walked in from some room in the back, dressed in that gold hyena robe, ruby satin slippers, and twirling some kind of cane or fire poker in his right hand. He pulled the drawstring on the white, lacy table-cloth shades in front of my window until they were flush to the ground. Yes, right there again (and so disrespectfully so) in front of my own fucking face (so, indeed, I was visible, at least to him!), and then receded all at once into a four-parted shadow of himself as he gathered on Sinboni in the center of the room.

I ran around to the window wall of the room in the front of the house, but shades had been drawn there as well. And then to the other last, third side — and it was the same: all curtains for me. And like a frantic, dull, and-forever-bailing dog — who

290

forever and in a frenzy circles the pool (loyal to the long death but still too afraid of a little dip) of a drowning master whose only concern is for a frolic and a wallow in his favorite noon-day sun — I ran from window to window to window.

I was left with nothing but the shadows and my reflection, and a veil just barely in between.

And the shadows were such that they reached everywhere and beyond — no matter where I went and from which window I stopped to view. Heads, legs, and arms flickered long and endlessly, breaking apart and then coming back together again. They sprung forth from beneath the floor until they reached and penetrated the ceiling. They danced and skipped across the room and sometimes there were only two, and other times too many to count. The only still object was Soda's empty chair.

But then not empty at all. For as a man was cordially led and then invited to sit, it did begin to spin. (Perhaps the whole room . . . no, no, it was only the chair!) It whirled while two figures kept tight and hovered above. Their arms working like mad surgeons, or perhaps barbers (I could not tell), as it spun like a red-ribboned staff — spiraling for terra firma in candy cane red and white — until the gilt knob, the very brass basin with the notch in it to fit the throat, fell off. It crashed, but only for a moment did it ruin my silence.

And as the ribbons disappeared and the bloodletting began, the spinning slowed down. Then stopped. Beneath the silence I even thought I heard Mom's most angelic quartet.

It was all so very silent that I do remember even marveling in moments at the disparity between movement and sound. A silent movie puppet show — at times the long black strings were even exposed, dangling down from some mad Gepetto way too high in the night.

Really though, it was not quiet at all. Just very reverential.

It was, of course, the Brothers Mills. Because that's when it all made sense. With their *Paper Doll.* Then it all came together.

All got slowed down and syncopated and choreographed and controlled. It was when words were made to match motion. When language lost all discretion.

I slowed down too and made my way finally to the front door and went nose to the glass again, succumbing ultimately to my role as benighted passerby.

I'm goin' to buy a paper doll that I can call my own . . .

It was rented. It was a juke joint before jukes were known and then the whole motherfucking place was rent. They were phantoms. One was in a chariot and the other whirled a rod and still another tried to soft-shoe along (but kept falling down) and it was the happiest most merry shadow dance that there ever was with hugging and kissing and cackling and pissing and yelling and whispering and sure as God there must have been some weeping. I felt all giddy inside and started to sing along.

A doll that other fellows cannot steal . . .

I felt I had earned the right to be inside there, though. What had everyone else been able to so deliciously do (even Lizzy included, as for a moment there I swear her shadow soared above them all, and I never did even see her strings) to earn the right to have so much fun. To all come together as one. It was my blood, not theirs, that had led them all there. Ross was my blood!

And then those flirty, flirty guys with their flirty, flirty eyes . . .

But still ignored I was. Still on the circumference I sat. And the only fun that I could have was with whatever was leaking out. All the jubilation was trickling away.

"Paper Doll" was being played over and over and over again, but the only one left standing was Ross. The only one left moving was him. What must have been stiff, slumped Soda was exhausted and crumpled in his chair. And then I thought Ross and Sin were still dancing along, still hugging to belong, but then the body dropped like dew. Rattled right into my window where I was spectating and singing and living all so vicariously again. His head, face up, separated the curtains at my feet.

Will have to flirt with dollies that are real . . .

"You fat, raping-ass fuck . . . *will have to flirt with dollies that are real!*" sang the fabled Ross. I heard him that time. I heard him because he wasn't really singing. Rather, screaming. And he wasn't a far-away shadow anymore, because he was standing over Sin's head, right there in front of me, and was tearing down the curtain. Then he brought down the very most end of one of those metal golf clubs (a sand wedge I believe it must have rightly been) right underneath Sinboni's left ear and in two smart strokes made it flop right off. Like a slice of fleecy cheese. Blood spurted up all the way even 'til I was looking at it eye to eye, and that old golf

293

club stayed stuck somewhere there right above his jaw until Ross had to plant his foot on Sin's forehead and pry it out like a shovel from recent rained-on, hard earth.

Ross then took the necklace from his neck he had retrieved from his Lizzy and in one deft movement he picked the ear up from the floor, produced a nail from a front golden hyena pocket, carefully pierced the ear right through its center and strung it along the silver string with the other chiral symbol as a pair.

And then he wore it again.

Oh, my breathtaking Ross. Beautiful, broken, inelegant Ross.

> *When I come home at night she will be waiting,*
> *She'll be the truest doll in all this world.*
> *I'd rather have a paper doll to call my own.*
> *Than have a fickle minded real live girl . . .*

XXXII

$\mathcal{I}$ tore out to the car full of doom and dread, or at least trying to stay a couple of paces in front of them. Ross had gone to the front door and unlocked it, and as I stumbled and sprinted out to the Fairmont yet again, I had just assumed that he was right behind me. But he was not. So I waited. I dug nails into the wheel and waited for a long, long while.

But he did not come. So after a minute or two, as soon I was suddenly sure that time had stopped, that the daft slowness of eternity had finally set in, and I could no longer bear the beat between the "tick," the waiting for the "tock," yes, maybe it was even less than that minute or two — I chased my shadow back into that place once again.

Ross sat at the bar. The very same where he had most probably offered Sinboni his last sup. And it occurs to me now, a bar from where Lizzy herself had once been seated and for all intents and purposes, was served and drank her last cup as well.

He had rested the body of Sinboni, full-length and on its back, straight across the bar. Ross sat on a barstool and leaned directly over his head.

He had placed Soda back upright in his wheelchair, and wheeled him right up alongside himself. The right side, actually. Soda had his bottle of green back in the bones of his right hand. He clutched it, or so it seemed. Ross had his arm around his

295

shoulder. He held Soda's head so it rested on his shoulder, and then lay his own head down on top of it.

Ross's shoulders bounced. They bounced until he had to inhale, even gasp and then drag his breath back in very slowly, long and deep, and then they would hop once again, causing both of their heads to follow.

If you took everything else away, they looked like a couple of jolly-japered lovers — trading jokes at a bar and sniding about the times. But I knew Soda to be dead, and Sinboni even deader.

I circled around the front of Ross, trying to avert my eyes from the body on the bar — checkerboard bloody, nails strewn about on both sides, left eye dolloped like a scoop of freezed-up, honey-dew melon on the same ear-ridden side of his head, and tarred and charred and feathered about the groin (I guess I didn't avert very too well).

His arms and legs lay neat and straight, reaching hard in opposite directions, one on top of the other, all fingers and toes pointing straight out in a most unnatural way. Like cliff divers do to disappear in water and only make it gurgle.

Ross was still clutching the hammer tight in his left hand, and I never did bother for a closer look at Sin's hands and feet.

And then there was Soda. His head (now less Ross' shoulder) was cocked and hanging so far back that he finally did look dead, like a perished, dried, red-to-rancid rose snapped high on the stem. Snapped by a needle, and a syringe still harboring a little bit of green and now blue blood, that I then saw fletched and dangling flat on the side of his neck — poor guy was so skinny there wasn't even nothing left there to hang by.

Ross had just skipped everything again and gone straight to dumb witless animal. And I was there to retrieve him. Just collar him up and take him back home. As his brother I had to get him home. I had to force charity upon myself.

He was crying.

Like a little baby, he cried. The nascent baby baby-cry it was. He cried the big flow stream of wet and writhing red face with eyes sewn shut and heart attack wind knocked out breath trauma that a little baby does when it gets popped. Or dropped. By a fairly tall person. On accident of course. Or forehanded by a drunken father. He had the same face contortion of Sin at my feet, just a few minutes earlier that evening.

He just cried like a fucking baby.

I felt bad. The sad kind. I started to cry even myself. Just kind of sniffling away really, nothing like him. Which was a good thing. Because when Ross saw that, well, it just kind of busted him back out of sitting at a bar and sobbing while hanging on to a couple of dead people (dead by him no less). Then he told me to stop crying.

"Goddamnit, stop crying, you big baby." He wiped his tears on the shoulder of his blood-stained, gold and purple hyena robe. He even wiped a few on the top of Soda's black dead head. "We need to get out of here."

Yes, we just left the other two right where they were. We would not bury the dead. Ross had found it entertaining enough to consider and conclude all the other six acts of mercy while in Venice. All of them leading up to this one. But no, I suppose number seven would have been too much. He'd had too much — too much drunk on his own kenosis.

297

XXXIII

*B*ut you know what? We did not leave them both there. We didn't leave anyone there at all.

We'd made it about half way out to the car when Ross suddenly slowed. He took a few measured steps and then without completely stopping and all in one swift motion he spun and headed back inside meeting instantly his speed of only several steps ago.

He took Soda's head in his hands from behind and there kissed him lightly on the center of his still shiny, glistening crown before reverently wheeling him clear to the side and finally a little bit out of harm's way.

"Take him, Wood. Gently. Sit him in the back of the car. Close to the window. Jack will get in his lap and keep him still so you lay his head, gently, on the window. Then get your ass back here. I don't know if I can do this alone."

Out to the car.

Back to the bar.

It was then that I noticed Sinboni had been nailed to a board. More precisely, the surfboard that had previously hung on the wall above the mirror of the bar.

Ross grabbed the board just at the base of Sin's feet and spun him off the bar and to the floor in a most violent way with great soul grunting and spitting and gnashing of teeth.

And then there from the floor Ross hefted up his Sinbone. Surfboard and all. It was long and tall. He set it upon his back wrapping his hands around the Sin's neck on wood and then he just started dragging him through the goddamn guy's own home bumping and knocking him and the board hither and thither and crashing into furniture everywhere.

I offered a hand.

"No. He's mine," he hissed under his charge.

His wounds from the Thanksgiving game bled with this exertion. Like sweat. Perhaps cooling him, even.

But the strength he had always known was now no longer.

Through and out the great, oak front door, on a board and on Ross's back, Sinboni just would not fit. Not the way Ross wanted him to. Not with him on his back. The doorway was just too small. He tried bending but just fell to his knees. And so on his knees he stayed. And on his knees he went. Backing up and then shuffling them through the broken glass of the ceiling mirror that had come crashing down and puffing and huffing and cursing the burden on his back all the while.

I got behind him. I got right in line. On my knees as well. Ross accepted my help by not nodding me away and so together, over all the glassy shards and through that hole and hatch of Ross's last hive of a hell on earth, we kneed our way through — lockstepping it like prisoners primeval — brothers in alms, knees getting damp and dark and all chewed crude in the blood new and the blood old. In the stains there before and thereafter. First the juice of Ross and then mine mixed and sealed on top. Until out we were. Jettisoned and free. And I let him take Sin the rest of the way out to the car alone.

299

Yes, and there we both burst back out into the night. And oh, boy. What a big, beautifully precious night it verily, verily was. It was Christmas Eve, you know. Precious and precocious: Christmas Eves; as they are and always should be. We age. They never. That's the sorrowful spectral of that particularly non-negotiable night. Supernaturally wrapping us up, bows and all. Pretty as pictures past. And leaving us always just at the foot of our private memories and wishes future for more of what we can then only hope to divest from God's aching acre of immemorially inaccurate imaginations and dreams.

But they are sweet, nevertheless. And for this reason we do so ourselves enlist so heartily and always with a glow in this season.

And so it was that on this solar, mean Christmas day he heaved the man Sinboni — nailed down good and tight to (if my recollection still serves me well) a nine-foot, bright red, classic *Tunnel Fin* surfboard — probably manufactured right there in Mal-ee-boo — to the top of his yellow Fairmont car. And then tied the whole Santa Claus conjunction to the roof. Tied it down real good. Real nice. Like a package (he might have even left a bow). Head out over our windshield and feet straight up at the stern

He looked up at the sky and then down at Boni's Tunnel Finned head. It coughed a bit.

It was not dead; but bled. And dripped drops that streamed and centered the windshield of our car.

Ross looked up at the sky again. "Brentwood," he said, a bit balefully but mostly just painfully plain, "Brentwood my brother, would you mind taking the wheel and driving me home? And please use the wipers on that fucking blood."

XXXIV

*A*nd so I drove us home. Ross laid himself down in the back putting his head in Soda's lap while Jack moved to the other door. It was real silent there for the first minute or two save the wheezing of muzzled tears. Jack had trouble with this. So he moved straight above Ross and stood right there upon him and licked his face quiet and still and gathered him up until Ross was right behind me. Sitting just like Soda (save the dog-dried eyes wide open) with head leaned on the glass of the door. And then Jack jumped over and took the last empty seat — passenger side, right next to me. The four of us each proper on each of the windows.

Yes, the Ford Fairmont really was meant to be a family car.

Now, if my memory serves me well (and I believe it has, at least up to this point of my little story) it was one of the most handsomely angelic Christmas eves the world had ever presented to me and one of the more pacific nights that Malibu had ever had to offer us. As we headed down and out of the hills and toward the trembling blue sea-stars that grazed on the water and out on to the highway that not only bordered the ocean but slithered us back home, the sky seemed to open up even more than usual. A gaping space of helical blue with stars not quite falling but sure as hell dangling and as big and happy as the snowflakes that can only fall in your very own backyard.

We were fortunate and only had to stop at one light all the way home. The one right where you make a left at the ocean and head south down Pacific Coast Highway. And there suddenly appeared (for I did not see how or from where they arrived — and nor would I later see just exactly how they were able to disappear) what looked to be like even Christmas eve deer. Two of them. Bold and bridled and leading a handsome but oh, so lonely man out on some kind of predawn lope about their land. Crossing the street there right in front of us at the intersection. Their halos even the colors of Christmas as they shaped from red to green with the changing of the light — their canter crisp while puffs of smoke plumed from heads turning smartly one side to the other — but of course I knew them to be even more than that.

For yes it was Christmas but no these were not deer. They were the wellborn, liquid, and chamber chested beauties known as Greyhound. Out simply on their early morning measure of this part of their fields and grounds. For a moment the three of them locked eyes with Jack and there seemed to be between them a mutual huff, hum-grunt, and nod.

Strange, I thought.

And then for a moment they locked eyes with Ross and they had a mutually known matter of factly kind of huffing-hum nod as well. They even looked at me; but now the man smiled (as if quite pleased). And then just as such the three of them were gone into the margins of the night.

The night hummed. Constant and loud, I felt it on my skin, like waves of grand, gigantic butterfly wings beating about me and droning like machines. But it was a quiet loudness, enough to make you raise your voice, but still spread out agape and unseen, enough to cover you in sleep. It was the noise of protection. Like old air-conditioners that stoop loose and leak in bedroom windows. And trains when you live nice and close to the tracks. Close enough to reach out your window and touch them. I found it comforting.

I drove slow, like we were invisible. Like low-profile, bashful ghosts — and our path was parted. All the other cars seemed to know, and drove even slower than us, letting us make our way. The world became gentle. It turned so suddenly considerate and benign just when we really did need it to be. When we needed to be safe more than at any other moment of our lives.

When we got to the pier in Santa Monica, right before we entered into Venice, where the Ferris wheel stood still, sleeping and dreaming of the day, Ross finally spoke.

"Brentwood, some things I cannot do alone."

"I'll drive the whole way home, Ross. Don't worry about it. I got it the whole way. I will get us there."

"You get me home. You'll help me on the roof. Yes? Tablet will help carry what's on top. You get Soda. Just put him on your back, gently of course, and then place him in the chair upstairs by the tree. But after. After you'll help me on the roof there, yes?"

"Sure, I'll get you to the roof. Whatever you want and then I'm going to bed. This has kind of been a long, tiring night for me and I would just as soon not talk about it . . . maybe tomorrow we head back to Utah . . . we haven't been to see Mom in a while. Snow will soon fall. I believe we need to leave here, Ross."

"Yes, you need to get back. You will get back. So will I. I am asking you to help me on the roof. I cannot . . . alone."

"I said I'll help you up the stairs and to the roof. And then I need sleep and tomorrow we leave."

I parked the Fairmont in the back of the house, just in case anyone saw us in Malibu or worse even tried to follow us home. Ross got out of the car on his own. He had composed himself. He jogged on into the house before I was even halfway out of the car. "Just wait for me on the roof, Brentwood." He spoke without turning his head. "Don't let me down. Just don't let me down."

A helicopter circled twice overhead, shining its big, old, Hollywood spotlight on the street in front of our place. They were always buzzing about overhead in Venice. I fantasized about it having followed us all the way from Malibu. Like we had tripped some silent alarm system back at Sinboni's and they had been following us the whole time. But then I shook it off, not letting any kind of unnecessary paranoia get to me — just trying to be as cool as Ross would have me. "Paranoia's for people already bracing to lose, already assembling to die, there Brentwood. You got something to be scared about, it's either because of a lack of preparation or because you wanted to get got and face down some bastard-fear anyway. No reason to be collecting and hoarding all the perishables of life, unless you plan on leaving them before they leave you. And now just who does that? Either way, none of them is any cause for paranoia." That's what he'd say, growing up (especially after Father finally used the belt on himself), every time I thought he was doing something wrong or was about to get in trouble (I never could quite put together the part about perishables, though). But he never did get in any sort of trouble. Or at least it didn't seem so to me.

Besides, I knew Ross wouldn't have planned that bloody yardsale over at Sin's (as awful and evil as it was) without being aware of some kind of alarm and how to negotiate it. He was the smartest and most savvy human I ever knew. Streets and books. Nothing was never left undone and something undone was never for nothing. Except for maybe. Me.

Then came Ross jogging back out from the backdoor of the house. Tablet followed only a two-step behind — probably the only man in history to soft-shoe his way up to a murder scene.

They descended upon the Fairmont in a harmony of silence. Not a word did either speak as they untied the surfboard, Sin and all, neither of them crossing the other as they circled more than a couple of times myself and the car and then suddenly they were done and gone. Jogging again the both together, Ross taking the front end, Tablet the back, with the surfboard high above their heads and Jack happily just below in a scamper back and forth trading nips at both sets of rambling feet.

I followed soon behind with Soda on my back. I had put his arms around my neck and crossed his hands firmly on my chest. He was lighter even than he looked. And his face was quite cold on my neck. I felt sad as I remembered our very first meeting that one night just a few months ago on his bench. And my first time drunk when I woke him. And he was warm then. And his rattled-bones laugh and how he sent me retreating back to sleep the night in a sandy shower right on the beach.

There was no chair next to the Christmas tree so I found one and placed it next to one of the windows facing the street. I leaned him there and he sat just fine. Just like he had the whole way home. I saw the cord to the tree right behind him then. On the floor. I don't know why but I plugged it in. But of course because I thought Soda would like it. Like those lights on and blinking in the window. Just like St. Luke's.

Jack trotted in from somewhere and curled up at Soda's feet. He was old and tired easily and liked the blankets there at the bottom of the tree which out of habit we had put there just like Mom always did so Santa had a soft place for the presents. Then he saw Lizzy on the couch, still asleep, and moved to be with her laying himself just beneath her head.

I went back down to the car to shut all the doors but soon found myself inside instead. In the back I sat. But that's not true because I know my head was hard-banging on the steering wheel instead.

I wanted to drive right into the ocean.

Right off the Santa Monica pier.

If I could just get around that old Ferris wheel.

Or straight through the sands of Venice Beach.

Either way, right into the ocean.

On one of those waves of mutilation.

A moonlight drive right into the ocean suddenly felt so free.

I know I could have done it too.

It only took a minute or less for the floor where we lived to brighten and bustle. Lights went on and off in this room and that. Ross's window flew open. But then he was gone. He was in anteroom next. I then spotted him with the surfboard right back in his. I saw him next in the kitchen. And then anteroom. And then right away right back in his.

Up and down he bounced several times in the window until suddenly he was gone. Just disappeared. And then in quick sequence all the lights just went out. One, two, three. Maybe it was him (maybe it was me). All dark. Save the Christmas glow of the anteroom. Green, red, and white. Where the tree was. In the room that connected them to all the others.

I was still in the car when I saw Tablet come calmly out the backdoor just a shuffling and a tappin'. He came over to my side of the car and stopped (but not that dancing, in fact he swung his arms even a little more).

"Lookey out, now, boy Cassius. Dat lef' jab yes, suh, man! Ah'm real fast. See dis, now, son. Ah'm so fast dat las' night ah turned off de light an' was in bed 'fore de room was dark! Yes, suh, son, boy Cassius!"

And then he turned on his heels just like he had on the roof and was out and down that back alley made to hide the garbage trucks on trash day.

"Ol' Abraham Lincoln unda' dat flo' gots to love dat Ross gots to love him mo'." (And I ain't never seen nor heard from Tabby since.)

It was then that I began to ignore the helicopter. While still sitting there in the car. Even when it came back. And the other which joined it, I ignored that one too. And I pretended not to hear the sirens that seemed to be coming from just down the street.

XXXV

$\mathcal{F}$inally I did hightail my very unparanoid and assembling-not-to-die little ass up out of the car, through the yard and into the house. My destination was my room and onto my egg carton mattress on the floor (forgetting all about helping Ross on the roof) and underneath my one white sheet and with all my might try to throw myself into a dream or a nightmare or something un- or at least sub-conscious. Anything that would let me consider that whole night in the safe world of sleep. In the distance of dreams or even behind the mask of nightmare, I truly had no druthers. As horrific as it could have been in either place, even ten times the worse, at least in a dearth of fact and cobbled warm beneath a sheet, I had the chance to tame it all.

But as I came up the stairs and entered that anteroom I saw him there placed right in front of our tree. The Sin yet lived. Still. And now sat straight up in a chair. Complementing that other side of the tree just opposite dear dead Soda. He sat still and with a face so communicatively screwed and distorted, it was as if he were much wishing to share with me a thought. But could not. In fact, he could not utter a word and at the time I did not know why for all I could do was observe the fact that his face seemed dyed lacy white, but then would suddenly go green indigo mad. And then right before me it changed color again. Stretching horrible red, round, and puckering. Much like an ape's incontinently empty and contorted ass.

I could hear Ross in his room. He seemed as calm as Tablet had been just not even a few moments ago. "I'm sorry," he said flatly. "But I know your sort. Your ilk. Your kind. What's undone in you is undone through and through you. It's coursed through you over time and become you. It has not just touched you. It *is* you. We have this in common, friend. And for men like us there cannot be shown that for which you have just requested. I believe you called it . . . *mercy*."

Ross had tied him to a chair. And as he sat his groin was a nacreous dark menstrual mass that yet grew through the towel plugged there between his legs. And then out came Ross from the doorway dark. He bore his favorite sword in both hands and in the same time it takes to swat a spider in the corner window sill — and while yet still wearing those goddamned designated hitter *California Angels* gloves — he stepped his left foot in the direction of where the Sinboni sat and did his head directly lop off.

One big, college baseball swing brought two thick licorice red ropes rising swiftly to life. Two others, with the same intent but sans the same energy and ambition, struggled from the same stump. They all four arced left while his head rolled right and then rested right at my very own goddamned feet. "Sorry," said Ross to me. "I'll get that."

And before picking it up (grabbing it by the hair no less, which I guess is where one would most conveniently grab such a thing), and resting there as it did, for seemingly no other reason than to absorb my most reckless and unmindful gaze — absorbing it I did even with Sinboni's eyes still communicating and cockling and still yet streaming tears — I did notice that betwixt the lips, having been stuffed a good mouth's measure inside, peeked the man's own black-feathered cock and crumpled balls.

I looked up at Ross. He looked at me. "Ross," I finally said, "I think maybe you might be finally crossing the line here."

And then yet again I just scrammed for my room and bed.

And therein was where I saw him next. Just as I told you at the beginning of this not-so-tall tale. As I lay there still. Some two or so minutes later. That was when Ross dropped down. Wrapped in a suit of lights. Green, red, and white. He hung down outside my window and started tapping and rapping like some big, black Christmas eve eldritch of a bird.

At first I ignored. Gave him the ol' cold shoulder. I turned my stereo up loud as could be. Blaring his favorite Christmas carols, as a matter of fact (why the Mills Brothers, of course, crooning Christmas classics). But he knocked and motioned me again. And like I said before, so he beckoned me up there and so up there I did go.

In other versions of this account I have reported that we spoke quietly, calmly, and I have given the impression that we most likely had a conversation commensurate to most of those had when the crowning moments of one's life and demise seem so impendently at hand. But that cannot be, it occurs to me now (and to be honest with you I have no idea what "most" of those fucking conversations sound like or have the least, if anything at all, in common).

But if there is one thing that I am sure of — it is that sound. The crack. The sound of the cracking of the shell of one's world. It cracks not like an egg, however. But like bone. It breaks and gapes and it's open and then all the musky marrow flows out like wine from an amontillado cask.

Quickly gravity was suspended and horrible carnivals of rude chaos gushed forth from a hell above and then another below and there was not darkness or quiet anywhere.

And the pendulum of time stood its ground between another tick and a tock (it was all so horribly hickory-dickory) as great swirls of propeller made us both straddle the ground beneath our feet and light shone us bright and blinded us intermittently until we were both like flashing black aerials to the other.

Black uniforms below bellowed suggestion and high recommendation over loudspeakers stuttering through the rhythm of the hummingbird carriages and satellites of mean love that hung over us like static in the sky. And still other men in costume searched (I guess, as I never saw them until it was long gone over) in short-term vain for the window to the roof while they crashed through doors and hooted and barked orders into rooms of life and death beneath the ground beneath our feet.

Everything else is true, just as I stated before.

Amidst, and in the middling of all this Ross did sing and dance and twirl and play the spinning game in his chair up there on the roof. His favorite blade in one hand and the little baby Jesus in the other. I saw him mouth the words to his favorite Mills Brothers song. Oblivious to everything around him, yet observing it all.

Ross calmly did his soft-shoe routine, shadowboxed like Cassius in the spotlight of the helicopter, paced a thoughtful, lonely swagger as if in the wings of the stage once again, and licked his thumbs and bathed in the blood splattered about his face and body.

And he glowed. He had taken the lights from our tree and wrapped himself right up. Right there up on the roof. With the help of at least one very long extension cord.

About the crown of his head he twinkled green and white. Around his neck, with Sin's ear and the twisting silvery strip (*sad infinitum*), a virtual wreath of red that blinked not at all. And enlaced around each arm: all the mingled colors together.

And beneath the yellow robe he glowed the warmth of dull, midnight, holiday fire.

He got up on the wall and stood and he faced me and he did speak and I did hear him above the roar of everything. I swear I did.

"I *smote* that cock, Wood. I fuck smote it good."

"We have trouble here, Ross. I think we're in trouble."

"You really believe in God, Brentwood?"

"Not here, Ross. Not now."

"Do you believe? Are you a believer?"

"Yes. Why should I not?"

"Brentwood, do you really believe in some hidden man up in the sky who has a list of things he doesn't want you to do because he loves you so much that if you do any of them he's going to kick you in the balls for the rest of eternity? A fiery hell of ball-kicking is what you got to look forward to if you cross good ol' God. Did you know that hell didn't even exist until Jesus? It's nowhere in the history of religion. Not even in the Hebrew book. Not even in the fucking old testament. Good ol' Jesus meek and mild. He's the one who gave us hell. That a boy, Jesus! Where would our heaven be without you to provide for us a hell? And I do mean kick you in the balls . . ."

"There are no balls in heaven."

"Who says you're going to any goddamned heaven?"

"I thought you didn't believe in heaven."

"Don't be a smart ass, Brentwood."

"I'm not. Goddamn. You said yourself that it's entirely illogical that there could be a heaven because that would mean . . ."

"Watch your language, man. You know Mom hates it when you swear. Take the lord's name in vain . . . don't you disrespect her. Besides, there isn't any logic to the things of the spirit and of God. If there were . . . now *that* would be illogical."

"You're not making any sense whatever. You better take another tug on that bottle."

"Another tug on Jesus?" Ross gladly obliged me. "Anyway, as I was saying . . . loved you so much that he sent his ill-begotten son down here to die, get fucking nailed to a cross, which may I remind you has got to be one of the more painful and torturous things one man can do to another, just to atone for all the sins of the world. Who said he had to sacrifice his son? Who does God have to answer to? Sacrifice him to whom? For whom? Zeus of the Greeks? Quetzalcoatl of the Aztecs? Sinatra of the Ratpack? Willy Wonka of the factory of chocolate? Hazel, King of the Rabbitry? Or some other mytholigized en vogue fiery serpent of some other millennium? Just who is demanding all of this snuff-blood sacrifice? He could have just as easily said 'All right, Jesus, you're done, now come back up here, I'm not going to throw you on no damn cross.' He didn't have to do that. He's God. Who's going to fuck with him if he decides to make a last minute change? All this hocus-biblical-pocus with clapping trees and dividing seas, fucking donkeys are talking in the bible like it's goddamn Dr's. Doolittle and Seuss. But ohhh no, Brentwood. That's all symbolic, the *REST* of it is real."

"Ross, don't go."

"If you can question it, Wood, if it's at all questionable or suspicious, why then it's symbolism. I mean all the so-called actual events and facts of the scriptures. But Jesus is real. Rib from Adam: symbolic. Jesus raises the dead: real. . ."

"Don't you leave me, Ross."

"God is a dead man who won't wake up, Brentwood." He cupped his huge hands and shouted at the sky, "HEY, WAKE UP, DEAD MAN!" He heaved and waved his arms at the helicopters above, as they were blocking his way, "Move out of my way motherfuckers. I'm trying to wake him up. WAKE UP! . . . DEAD MAN! GET THE FUCK UP, MAN!"

He waited, staring hushed and frozen with both his sword and plastic Jesus pointed at the sky. But only for a moment. And then he dropped his gaze to his feet and threw his weapons to the ground and left the heavens with one last, blind, sardonic flick of his wrist. "Can't even resurrect his own fucking self. Doesn't want to. Know why? Because he ain't even around anymore. Because he left. He's GONE! He created this mess and went on to make another. There was never any plan to sit around and take care of any of this. The same way you and I build castles on the beach and leave them for the tide. People fucking, because they're horny. Then having kids because they're told to multiply and replenish the earth and besides it will make them as parents real goddamn happy. Bullshit. That through fucking each other, through that brutal act of love they'll somehow be blessed. Blessed with their multiplications. Well look at fucking you and me, Wood. The two of us. We're someone's blessing, Brentwood. Fuck yes, we are."

Ross took the necklace with the ear and the silver strip and tossed it gently at my feet. "Please make sure Lizzy gets that." And then he continued, "The byproducts of a couple of good fucks without any thought of reproductive repercussions. That's what God did. Just like we do. That's the way we were created. It's just one of them good old-fashioned vicious cycle clichés. 'And God said, Let us make man in our image, after our likeness . . .', fucking Genesis 1:26. I love how man created a God that would create a man in *His* own image. That's fucking great! Brilliant! Idiots. Great for the man. Not so great for God. If you ask me.

"That, my dear young Wood, makes sense. Nothing else. Construction, destruction. Impossible any other way . . . I knew all those years of memorizing scriptures in church would come in handy one day. Ahh, what the fuck am I saying. I don't believe in the horseshit anyway."

He was still drawing on the scriptures. Right out of his head, and right to the end. Like he always used to, regardless of the topic or context of a conversation. And then always saying afterwards, like he was talking to himself for reassurance, "I knew memorizing scriptures in church would come in handy one day . . ." And then suddenly snapping out of it, "Ahh, what the fuck am I saying. I don't believe in the horseshit anyway."

And then Ross just finally said it. "I cannot. Alone I cannot. Help me now, Brentwood. Here. I want to see Mom again."

He then pointed behind me and I looked. Heroes from the West (badges, guns, black boots, hats and all) had made it to the top and crouched and edged slowly and held their guns like they do on movie screens and yelled that we all fall down . . . all fall down . . . there are no more bridges . . . just all fall down.

"You're full of shit, Ross."

"Wood, don't let me down."

But I knew Ross would not leave of his own accord. And so I ran to him. Yes, I ran to him. I threw my arms around him. I held him for as long as I could.

The pendulum above us began to swing again. Time sped up, then got normal again. "I'm full, Wood. I'm full of it. I'm full of the world. I'm full of shit. You are right." Then he dropped his bloody, gold, laughing robe and let it fall to the ground, like a repentance gown, about his feet.

He was naked. Save his suit of Christmas.

He looked at me and then he looked back down. He leaned a little out and then came back to rest again.

In his eyes I could see what he wanted. To go. But as I continued to look I began to see even deeper. So deep that I was able to look right down into his heart, and once there witness his flesh, blood and bone suddenly rotting, ruining, and eating its own self until there was nothing at all left save his spirit.

And then there it was, just as I had always suspected. A glistening, grinding hole of great, black endless love. And me right there in the center. I could see my own reflection. And I saw that it was even stronger than him. I could not believe it. Such was its strength it pulled him back toward me.

And as he gave up and began to step down from his ledge. Down to me. Dropping his arms in defeat while at the same time opening them to me, I pushed him.

I pushed him as hard as I fucking could just as the hinge of time had caught back up with the hanging of the world and our trap set for the next day's sun . . . And he went down. And I stood above. And he hung.

Ross had securely wrapped part of the Christmas tree cord around the base of the water tank. It strained and pulled tight; seeming even to want to snap there for a second or two. But in the end it held just fine. I was very happy to hear later that his neck was abruptly and cleanly snapped. There was no suffering. Not in that moment of exit at least.

And that's how I hung Ross off the front of our last house. He swung back and crashed through the anteroom window shattering some of the glass on the dark uniformed boys below (luckily they had already removed Lizzy). They covered their eyes from the shower and when they looked back up there was Ross. Naked. Swinging still just a bit. Slow and calm. And still all aglow and blinking there in the window that faced the street. A window which from a distance was just as cheerfully lucent and full of yuletide and alive as any of the others on that street that night on Christmas eve. And now that it was busted open was full too of the Mills Brothers booming, "Blue Christmas" (yes, I swear it's true).

I remember having the oddest presence of mind to try and view the whole scene from the sky. From maybe where Ross suddenly now was. And to be looking down into that house through a window as he might have just been doing in that very moment with all of us inside motionless and pacified like good little snow globe statues in a perfect little miniaturized West-evening redness wintry wonderland.

At rest.

Like a snow globe. It was Christmas.

Could you shake it, Ross?

Would you shake it, Ross?

Shake us all just one more time?

But there was no snow for Ross on that last day.

They eventually got him down. Untethered him. Undoing him for the last time at about the same time that I was being done up for my first time (but not my last time, by the way).

I gave my brother the greatest gift a brother can.

For I did not save him. But I did set him free.

Ross never cared much for being saved to begin with.

And so I finally understood.

He had allowed me to finally understand how I might love him, and Mom and Father as well, the only way they could ever be loved. A way that they could never love each other. And though I do it chained and convicted, confessing and humbly full of all of the guilt associated with my crime, I am yet free of all the weight that the innocence of the world would have imposed upon me, of all of its perishables it surely would have had me bear, of all the dignity and refinement it would have tried to have me choke down, and all . . . well, it doesn't really make sense to put it into words.

Language, it seems, just isn't big and beautiful enough.
No more waiting for snow, Ross.
No more waiting for snow.

photo credit: Ivan Nikolov

DAVID NASH was born in Utah and grew up living in California, Indiana, the Philippines, New York, Taiwan, Arizona, and Argentina. He earned his master's degree in fiction from the Arizona State University M.F.A. program and now lives and works in New York City.